Bedding Down

Bedding Down

Kristina Wright
Gwen Masters
Alison Tyler
Marilyn Jaye Lewis
Isabelle Gray
Sophie Mouette
Shanna Germain

Edited by

Rachel Kramer Bussel

red

AVON

An Imprint of HarperCollinsPublishers

HarperCollins books may be purchased for educational, business, or sales promotional use. For information please write: Special Markets Department, HarperCollins Publishers, 10 East 53rd Street, New York, NY 10022.

FIRST EDITION

Designed by Elizabeth M. Glover

Library of Congress Cataloging-in-Publication Data

Bedding down : a collection of winter erotica / edited by Rachel Kramer Bussel.—
   1st ed.
      p.cm.
   ISBN 978-0-06-156063-7
1. Erotic stories, American. 2. Winter—Fiction. I. Bussel, Rachel Kramer.
   PS648.E7B427   2008
   813'.01083538—dc22   2008029504

08 09 10 11 12   OV/RRD   10 9 8 7 6 5 4 3 2 1

Contents

Contents

Introduction: The Perfect Chill

As I write this, the weather in New York has just started to turn chilly, bringing those first crisp breezes, the first hint that winter will soon be here. While summertime is known as the season when flesh is bared, the truth is that winter is probably when we need companionship the most, someone to cuddle up with beneath the sheets, or in front of a roaring fireplace. Someone to keep us so much warmer than any heating device ever could.

The seven novellas presented here offer up stories in which passions rise in winter, where the flurries of snowflakes provide not just something pretty to look at but an excuse to drop everything and get naked, sometimes actually in the snow. These characters boldly stare down winter, daring it to derail their lusty plans—and sometimes winter rises to the challenge.

In Kristina Wright's "One Night in Winter," a woman confronts a man she thought she'd left far in her past, only to have him get under her skin in the exact same way he used to do. As she tries to elude him, she only finds herself more and more attracted to him, the inclement weather conniving to keep them together. Gwen Masters brings us a loner hero who's deliberately secluded himself in the woods, without phone or television or anything resembling human companionship. But when he finds a woman trapped in the woods, he takes her in for a stay that's far longer, and more intrusive, than he intended. California girl Alison Tyler puts a spin on the very meaning of winter with her heroine's resolutely anti-winter boyfriend; no matter how sexy of a snow bunny she makes herself, he just can't quite warm her up in the right ways. The lengths she goes to to woo him are seductive and surprising. In Marilyn Jaye Lewis's "Baby, It's Cold Outside," a couple almost break up over a breakdown. They're forced to discover that their passionate memories of lusty outdoor sex spur not only their arousal, but their love for each other, as they try to rekindle their romance. Another couple trying to revive their former glory is seen in Isabelle Gray's "Northern Exposure," as the pressures of marriage weigh heavily on them. The "Hidden Treasure" in Sophie Mouette's story turns out to be much naughtier than the criminals seeking it expect, and provides the inhabitants of a historic museum the chance to repeat the hottest parts of history. Rounding out this collection, Shanna Germain gives us something delicious and delightful to curl up with in "Sweet Season."

What they all have in common is the search for someone to make these men and women forget about the chill in the air, forget about the potential dangers and discomforts of winter, and simply revel in the thrill of having someone nearby to ward off the cold. Someone whose kiss is enough to ignite a fire deep within, who can make magic happen with a touch of their lips or a sensual caress. Winter here is both a state of mind and a time to bed down, to remember what you loved about a person the first time, and fight to hold onto that sensation. It's a time when we may bundle ourselves in layers, but are just waiting for the right person to come along and peel them off. It's as sexy as sprinkling snow over a lover's naked body, as huddling close into his jacket, of breathing deep and letting go, and having a special man there to savor it with. I hope *Bedding Down* will keep you warm this winter.

Rachel Kramer Bussel
New York City
2008

One Night in Winter

by Kristina Wright

Chapter 1

Winter came early to Minerva, Virginia. Even the oldest residents couldn't remember snow falling before Christmas, but on Thanksgiving night the mercury dropped. By the time the last turkey platter had been washed and piece of pumpkin pie consumed, the snow had begun to fall. It was an anomaly, one of those nonevents that have everyone buzzing for a day or two because there really isn't anything else to talk about. Then Susannah Greer blew back into town on Thanksgiving night and gave everyone a different topic to discuss over their morning coffee. If the editor of the *Minerva Daily News* hadn't been so preoccupied with announcing "Winter Comes Early!" on Friday morning, he might have run a headline saying, "The Home Wrecker is Back! Hide Your Men!"

Of course, no man would have her dressed as she was, looking like an ice princess in a white bridesmaid's dress. Susannah smiled wryly as she studied her image in the full-length mirror at the Bridal Boutique. The dress was lovely, emphasizing the dark red tones of her long hair and making her brown eyes look dramatic, but it was just so darn . . . white. The other brides-maids got to wear black dresses, but the maid of honor—her—looked like the bride runner-up.

"In the event the bride is unable to fulfill her duties," she muttered under her breath.

"I can't believe you're here," screeched the bride-to-be as she burst into the dressing room and wrapped Susannah in a bear hug. "I thought I'd have to send Brad out there to drag you home."

Susannah felt a moment's guilt. "Out there" was Seattle, about as far away from Minerva as she could get without leaving the country. She hadn't been back to Minerva in four years. Liz had visited her twice, but not once had Susannah made the trip back to her hometown. Unlike Liz, who was six years younger and whose memories weren't as tinged with bitterness, she couldn't move on with her life as long as she was mired in her past.

"Hey, sis," Liz said, meeting her gaze in the mirror. "I'll be an old married lady like you by tomorrow."

At the reference to her marriage, Susannah instinctively looked at her ring finger. The weight of her diamond and platinum wedding rings was nearly unbearable, and she tried to distract her sister to avoid the topic.

"So, everything ready to go? Bridesmaids organized? Grooms-men clean and sober?"

"Brad and Derrick are picking up the other groomsmen from the airport tonight and Brad's sisters have already had their last dress fitting," Liz said.

At the mention of Derrick, Susannah flinched. She hadn't

seen Derrick Frost in four years. If she never saw him again for the rest of her life, it would be too soon. Unfortunately, her luck simply didn't run that way.

"How is the dick—I mean, Derrick? He must be working on his fourth wife by now, right?"

Liz sighed. "As far as I know he's only been married once. I don't even think he has a date for the wedding."

Susannah tried to ignore the little jump in her pulse rate. "The better to bed the female wedding guests. Not that being married would stop him."

"He's the best man, Suzie Q," Liz said. "Please try to get along."

Susannah bit back her retort that the only thing he was "best" at was giving a woman an orgasm and breaking her heart at the same time. Once upon a time, she had been hopelessly infatuated with Derrick Frost, the star quarterback of Minerva High School. She'd been a lowly sophomore when he was a senior, but by then they had developed a strange and special friendship based on a shared love of horror flicks—and the fact that they lived next door to each other.

In the span of one year, her mother had abandoned her and Liz and Derrick had gone off to college before she ever got up the nerve to tell him how she felt about him. They spent time together during the summers, but it was never the same between them once she was living across town with her grandparents and trying to be a mother to her sister. By the time Derrick returned to Minerva to settle down—with both a Juris Doctor and a new bride—Susannah had been on her way to graphic design school in Seattle.

Derrick had arrived back in Minerva in June and she had

been gone by August, but one hot night in July their paths had crossed at the only dive bar in town. Susannah had been celebrating her birthday with girlfriends, and Derrick had looked awfully sad sitting by himself at the bar. By the end of the night, they were at her apartment, having earth-shattering sex.

For a few weeks, they'd had a tumultuous, wild, secret affair. When she asked him about his marriage, he only said it had been a mistake and he wasn't ready to settle down. It had been enough for her. She had never felt so alive as she did during those few weeks with Derrick, but the feeling came at a very steep price. Derrick's wife had found out and told everyone. Derrick wouldn't answer her calls and then time had run out and she had to leave for Seattle. His silence, more than the rude comments of people she'd once considered friends, had destroyed her belief in "happily ever after." Not that she deserved a fairy-tale ending, she told herself bitterly. She had seen what infidelity did to her parents' marriage and then managed to break every rule she believed in anyway.

She looked at her sister, so wide-eyed and hopeful that marriage would provide the stability their dysfunctional childhood never had. She ruffled Liz's auburn hair the way she had a thousand times during those difficult years after their father had run off with his mistress and their mother had left Minerva to follow her newly divorced boyfriend to New York. Susannah couldn't fault Liz for trying to find her own happiness, she just didn't believe in the possibility for herself.

"I'll do whatever you need me to do," she told her sister.

"It'll be all right. You'll see."

Nothing would be all right until she was out of Minerva and back in Seattle, but Susannah nodded anyway. "Of course it will."

"Good. Now we'd better get changed. The florist is supposed to be delivering the flowers to the inn by five," Liz said. "You should see them; they're all white, of course, with greenery and ebony ribbons."

Still talking, Liz floated out of the dressing room on a cloud of satin and hope. Susannah shook her head, but she couldn't help but smile. She'd never been like Liz, so head-over-heels in love with the idea of love. Of course, she'd had a little help in coming to terms with reality. Having their father abandon the family for his mistress, then seeing her mother become "the other woman" in a scandalous relationship that made her abandon her daughters, had taught Susannah a few things about love and marriage. She cursed under her breath as she tried to free herself from the satin ties that laced up the back of the dress.

"Liz?" she called. "I need help."

The dressing room door squeaked behind her just when she thought she'd have to sleep in the damned gown.

"Help me get undressed, will you?" Her arms were twisted behind her in a futile attempt to free herself from the knots she'd made attempting to untie the laces. "I need to get out of this dress *now*."

"My pleasure," said a deep and achingly familiar voice.

Susannah turned slowly, catching a glimpse of his profile in the three-way mirror, and her first thought was that he hadn't changed a bit. That thought fled when she faced the real deal.

He looked older. More . . . masculine. His shoulders looked

broader and his jaw seemed harder, but it was more than physical; there was a seriousness in his expression that contradicted the memory she had of a happy-go-lucky player with nothing on his mind but sex and booze.

"Maybe you didn't notice, but this is the women's dressing area," she said, managing to keep her voice even. "The men's tuxedo shop is on the other side of the store."

His lips turned up in a faint smile, as if it took too much effort to turn on the charm. "I thought it was the bride who was supposed to wear white."

"Not my idea, believe me." Turning her back on him, she returned to her task of untying the laces.

"I could help you with that."

There was no hint of a come-on in his words and she felt a twinge of disappointment mixed in with relief. The sooner she got out of the dress, the sooner she could get away from him. "Thank you."

He worked the knots loose, but he wasn't gentle about it. She heard a startling rip and was suddenly able to breathe. The relief at being free of the offending garment was countered with dismay.

"Did you have to be so rough?"

"There was a time," he said, his fingers running up the length of her spine and making her shiver, "when you liked it rough."

As if her body was detached from her brain, she found herself leaning into his touch. She knew she should pull away, demand he get out and make sure he didn't touch her for the rest of the weekend, but . . . she couldn't. Part of it was because she hadn't been touched like this—slowly, sensually—in longer than she cared to remember. The other part was simple: as much as she loathed him, she had never been able to forget Derrick.

"You not only liked it rough, you begged for it," he murmured in her ear as he caught her long hair in his hand and gave it a firm tug. "Remember?"

She closed her eyes and gasped at the sensation that ran along her scalp and made her weak in the knees. "There are some things I'd rather forget," she said, hearing the catch in her own voice.

"Not me," he said. "I remember pulling your hair like this while I fucked you, so deep inside you I thought I'd died and gone to heaven and I didn't give a damn."

She couldn't help herself—she whimpered and moved back against him. His erection was impossible to ignore through the thin material of her dress. She pressed her ass against him, feeling him hard and hot through the layers of clothing.

He groaned and tugged her hair hard. "A month with you wasn't damn near enough."

His words were like a splash of cold water in her face. She took a deep breath, reminded herself of why she was here, and pulled away, ignoring the sting in her scalp when he didn't release her hair immediately. She met her gaze in the mirror and, galvanized, turned to face him—and her past.

"Things have changed, Derrick."

He arched one cocky eyebrow. "Really?"

She raised her left hand, hating herself while also feeling relieved. "I'm the married one this time. I take my vows seriously."

He laughed in disbelief. "I have a hard time believing that with the way you whimpered and rubbed against me just now."

Despite a flush of embarrassment, she remained firm. "Believe it."

He was staring past her, at her reflection in the mirror. "You'd be more convincing if your dress wasn't unlaced down to your very sexy ass."

She fumbled behind her, attempting to hold the fabric together, which only served to make the bodice of her dress slip. "Would you please get out of here?"

He opened his mouth as if to speak, then shook his head. "Whatever you say, Susannah. Just one thing—"

"What?"

He dipped a finger into her cleavage, setting her skin on fire and causing her to gasp. With a tug of the silky fabric, he pulled her up against him until his erection was pressed at the juncture of her thighs. He stroked the swell of her breasts, rocking his pelvis against her, fucking her through their clothes. He moved his hands lower until his fingers grazed her hard nipples, leaving a trail of heat everywhere he touched her.

She pushed her breasts toward him, nearly out of her mind with desire and oblivious to the fact that her dress had fallen to her waist. Her eyes fluttered closed so she wouldn't have to gaze at his hungry expression that she knew mirrored her own. Her nipples ached to be pinched and tugged, but he wouldn't give her the satisfaction she craved; he touched her gently, teasingly.

Her barely controlled arousal flared again and her pulse raced, despite her good intentions. She moaned, and the sound echoed off the mirrored walls of the dressing room. She wrapped her fingers around his wrist and held him to her breast, silently pleading for more.

"There's still some unfinished business between us," he whispered in her ear as he finally gave her what she needed and tugged one nipple insistently. "That rock on your finger isn't a shield. I'll respect your marital status only as long as you do."

He was gone before she could open her eyes, which was probably for the best. Her pulse pounded in her ears and she was slick and wet with desire. If she had been able to utter any response at all, it would have been a plea for him to put her out of her misery and fuck her senseless.

"Too late," she muttered to herself. "I'm already out of my mind."

Chapter 2

Since the lease had run out on Liz's apartment, she was staying with Brad's parents until after the wedding. Which meant Susannah was, too. Holding to the old-fashioned tradition hadn't surprised Susannah. Liz seemed to believe that if she followed the rules, she would be happy. Thankfully, the groomsmen would be staying at Brad's house. Susannah was still throbbing hours after Derrick touched her and she didn't think it was a good idea to be alone with him again.

"It's only for two days," Liz said later that evening when Susannah tried to make a joke of her concern about getting through the weekend without causing a scandal. "Surely you can get along for two days."

She didn't tell Liz the truth—she wanted far more than to "get along" with Derrick and it was the nights she was thinking about, not the days. Instead, she smiled at her earnest younger sister and ignored the ache between her thighs. All her good intentions of keeping her distance and getting out of town as fast as possible had fled when she'd felt the proof of his arousal. He still wanted her—as much as she still wanted him. She tried to tell herself it was only physical, only sex, but it wasn't a comforting thought.

"Of course we can," she said. "Your wedding will be perfect and if that jerk does anything to ruin it, I'll smack him silly."

Liz glanced up from the wide, white ribbon she was making into elaborate bows for the reception tables. "I'm not worried about him."

"You think I'm going to do something to ruin your wedding?"

Liz worried her bottom lip between her teeth. "No, of course not. I'm just worried that, you know, you haven't dealt with your emotions where he's concerned."

Susannah shook her head, hurt and anger bubbling inside her. "Come on, Liz, you know me. He caught me off guard, that's all."

She hadn't told her sister all that had transpired in the dressing room, but Liz had heard enough. Susannah cursed her lack of control and vowed to make Liz's wedding day the best it could be.

"What's next on the agenda?"

They were squirreled away in Mr. Montgomery's study for some privacy, a fire roaring in the massive brick fireplace to ward off the cold in the big Colonial house. Brad's parents had gone to bed an hour ago, but his sisters Kelly and Dana were watching chick flicks in the living room. Susannah suspected Liz didn't really get along with Brad's family as well as she pretended, but not having a family of her own made her try that much harder. Brad and Derrick had gone to pick up the two other groomsmen and were planning to stop by on the way to Brad's house. Susannah planned to make herself scarce when they did. The farther she stayed away from Derrick, the better.

Liz paused for a moment, as if she might say something else, before taking off on a tangent about the flowers and caterer. Susannah let out a breath she didn't realize she'd been holding. Liz was all the family she had and she wouldn't do anything to jeopardize her sister's happiness. Derrick Frost wasn't worth it.

"Susannah, you haven't heard a word I said."

She shook herself out of her thoughts. "Sorry, just jet-lagged. What did you say?"

Liz gestured out the window, where snow swirled across the broad expanse of lawn. "I said, do you think it's good luck or bad luck that it's still snowing?"

"Rain is good luck, so why not snow?"

Liz shook her head. "It wasn't good luck for the florist. I can't believe the flowers won't be delivered until tomorrow afternoon. I'm going to be a wreck by Sunday morning."

"I think it's fabulous that Mother Nature decided to coordinate her decor with your wedding dress," Susannah said.

"And yours."

Susannah wrinkled her nose. "I'm still not sure I should be seen in white around here. The locals are likely to tar and feather me."

"Don't be silly." Liz looped ribbon around her fingers and pulled it through, making an enormous white bow. "That's all in the past."

"Is it?"

The sound of the front door opening interrupted whatever Liz might have said. Her face immediately brightened and Susannah felt a twinge of envy so strong it made her heart ache. What must that feel like, she wondered? The ring on her finger hadn't guaranteed that feeling for her.

"Can we take a break?" Liz asked, looking anxiously toward the closed study door. "I need to talk to Brad and I want to say hello to Marcus and Elliot."

Susannah waved her away. "Don't worry about me. I'm not feeling very social right now anyway. Go be with your man and his friends. I'll make bows until sunrise or the ribbon runs out, whichever comes first."

Liz gave her a fierce hug. "You are the best sister in the world. Thanks for being here." There were tears in her eyes when she pulled away. "I'm sorry your husband couldn't make it."

Your husband. Liz had never met Thomas. Susannah hadn't even told her sister she'd gotten married until after the fact. They had married six months after her arrival in Seattle and both times Liz had visited, he'd managed to be out of town. It was a slight that she wasn't sure Liz would ever get over—or that Susannah would ever forgive herself for.

"Liz, I need to tell you—"

There was a rap at the study door and Brad popped his head in. "Hi, honey, I'm home."

Susannah felt like she was witnessing something intimate in the look the two exchanged. She wanted to caution her sister not to hope for too much, but it made her heart hurt to see how in love they were. Not because she begrudged her sister anything, but because she wanted that feeling so desperately for herself.

She had everything else—the education, the job, the friends—why was true love, *passionate* love, so elusive?

"We'll talk later," Liz murmured against Susannah's cheek as she gave her another hug. "Love you."

"Love you, too," Susannah said as Liz left the room with her fiancé.

After the study door closed, Susannah held her left hand up to the light and stared at the rings that sat on her finger like a grim reminder of her failure. She had married Thomas impulsively and it had been a decision she'd regretted almost as soon as they said their vows in the dingy little room at the courthouse. She was twenty-five years old at the time and tired of feeling alone in the world. Wearing Thomas's ring and taking his last name hadn't made her feel less alone or more like she had a family of her own. She had dropped his last name, Schaeffer, almost immediately after they were married, citing awkward alliteration as her reason. But reverting to Greer had only made her feel lonelier. That last name represented the family she didn't have—the father who had run out on them and the mother who had left her to take care of her younger sister when what she needed was someone to take care of *her*.

"Admiring your good fortune?"

For the second time that day, Derrick managed to surprise her. She dropped her hand to her lap. "Shouldn't you be somewhere else, doing something else?"

Instead of taking the hint, he came into the study and closed the door. "Nope."

She sighed. "Derrick, I really don't think it's a good idea for us to be alone together."

He smiled, and there was nothing but pure masculine pride in his expression. "Can't resist me, can you?"

She shook her head in exasperation. "Sometimes I don't know whether to smack you—"

"Or kiss me?" He sat next to her on the couch, which was big enough to accommodate four people but suddenly felt very cozy.

"I was going to say laugh at you."

"I like kiss better," he said, holding up a length of satin ribbon. "Is this some kind of kinky wedding night getup?"

Susannah snatched the ribbon from him. "Don't be ridiculous. It's ribbon to make bows for the reception tables."

"Easy, Susannah, I was only kidding," he said softly. "I've been to a few weddings."

"Including your own," she shot back.

He cocked his head. "True. But mine was over before it even started."

"Because of me," she said, unable to look away from his steady, solemn gaze that was so unlike the Derrick she once knew—or thought she knew. She stared into the light blue eyes that had once mesmerized her and felt herself slipping into the past.

He covered her hands with his and it was a gesture of comfort, not seduction. "Because of *me*," he said. "Because I wasn't ready to get married and was looking for a convenient excuse to get out."

Bitterness, cold and hard as the diamond on her finger, rose up to choke her. "And I was convenient, wasn't I? Some would say I was practically *easy*."

"You were . . . ," he trailed off. Some emotion she couldn't identify clouded his expression. "You were . . ." he started again.

Not wanting to hear him say she had been nothing more than a meaningless affair designed to convince his young new bride of his philandering ways, she leaned forward and pressed a kiss to his lips. His lips were warm and soft and familiar. After a moment, she deepened the kiss, urging him to open his mouth and sighing when he did. Despite all the touching and fondling in the dressing room that afternoon, they had not kissed. It wasn't until this very moment that she realized how much she had missed it. She slipped her tongue into his mouth as his arms wrapped around her. The only sound in the room was the crackle of the fire as they shifted closer together.

Part of her mind—the tiny, rational part that was drowned by her emotions—knew she was playing with fire of a different kind. Knew it, and didn't care. His hands spanned her waist as he shifted her onto his lap, stroking her back slowly. She leaned over him and teased his mouth with the tip of her tongue. He rewarded her with a moan when she licked his bottom lip. When she bit down gently, he gripped her hips and thrust against her. He was hard and wanting—wanting her. She felt a rush of power that had been denied her that afternoon in the bridal shop when he'd caught her by surprise and left her breathless with desire.

He pulled away after a long moment and stared at her with heavy-lidded eyes. "What are you up to, Susannah?"

She shifted on his lap and gasped at the pressure of his rigid cock against her crotch. "I wanted to kiss you," she said, her voice breathy with emotion. "You talk too much."

He searched her face for something, as if unsure whether to take her at face value. "That's all?"

"What more do you want?"

"I want," he said, cupping the back of her head and bringing her down to meet him for another kiss, "all of you."

Something shifted between them and their kissing became intense and sexual. She rocked on his lap, stroking herself against the rigid length of his erection. Her yoga pants and panties were thin and it wasn't long before they were soaked through from her arousal. She didn't care; she kept moving against him, lost in her desire.

He slid his hands down her back and over her bottom, cupping her ass as he guided her against him. She was on top, but he took control, rocking her back and forth on his crotch as his mouth devoured her hungrily. The dull ache between her thighs becoming an insistent, throbbing need. Her pussy was swollen and sensitive, as wet as he was hard. The thought of him sliding inside her, filling her, made her whimper and rub against him harder. She no longer cared about the past or what he thought of her; she only cared about satisfying that long-denied need.

He fisted his hands in her hair, pulling her away from his mouth and trailing hot kisses down the arch of her neck. She gasped as he licked the hollow of her throat, the sensation so intense and erotic she could feel it between her legs. He was driving her out of her mind with lust and she writhed and whimpered on his lap like a wild thing.

"You're so hot," he murmured against her throat. "What do you want, Susannah?"

She couldn't form a coherent sentence. Breathing hard, she

gripped his shoulders and ground her pelvis against his erection, needing the feeling of his hardness against her. Needing to satisfy the unrelenting ache he'd started that afternoon in the dressing room.

"C'mon, baby," he coaxed. "Let go. Come for me."

She had been so ready, so needy, that all it took was his few words of encouragement and she felt everything inside her turn to liquid heat. She bit down on his shoulder to keep from crying out as she came, her body rigid against him as he thrust against her, pushing her higher. They rode out her orgasm together until the powerful sensations subsided and he cradled her to his chest.

"Damn, woman, you could raise the dead."

She laughed softly against his chest, feeling his pulse begin to slow. "Thanks, I think."

He reached for her hand, which was still gripping his shoulder. "Do me a favor next time?"

"Mmm?" she murmured, her eyes fluttering closed.

"Take the ring off. I think I've got a two-carat-sized crater in my shoulder."

She jerked upright, pulling her hand from his grasp. The ring had twisted on her finger and snagged the fabric of his shirt. "Sorry," she whispered. "It won't happen again."

His slow, feral grin reminded her that his lust hadn't been satisfied from their little couch romp. "No problem," he said, misunderstanding her apology. "Just take it off, along with the rest of your clothes."

"I can't do that," she said, climbing off his lap. Her yoga pants clung to her, the fabric a damp reminder of how out of control she'd been with him. "It won't happen again, Derrick."

He didn't look surprised or angry, but she couldn't really be sure because everything was a blur as she fled the room. She heard Liz call to her from the kitchen, but she ignored her and ran up the stairs to the room they were sharing. She'd only wanted to prove to herself that she was something more than an excuse, more than an affair. What she'd proven was that Derrick hadn't changed a bit—and she was no better than him.

Chapter 3

"I hate to ask, but could you go out to the inn and be there when the florist arrives?" Liz asked her the next morning. "I would go, but the roads are supposed to get treacherous and I'm afraid I won't make it back tonight."

Susannah knew what Liz was thinking. "So, if I go and the weather gets worse, I'll have to spend the night—and stay away from Derrick."

"That's not the entire reason—" Liz said, and blushed. "Who would have thought it would snow like this in November?"

Susannah let her change the subject and poured them both another cup of coffee from the carafe on the kitchen table. What she didn't say was that she was relieved by the opportunity to get away from Derrick. "It'll be fine, Lizzie. I'll go to the inn, get the place decked out for tomorrow, and spend the night there, hidden away like the batty old aunt."

"Susannah! That is not what I'm trying to do and you know it."

She did know it, but Derrick was making her crazy. She needed to get away from him and if he didn't see the wisdom in that, she did. She had stayed in bed as long as she could that morning, listening as everyone filed out of the house on the way to various activities. When she came downstairs and found Liz still slaving over the bows she was supposed to have finished, she felt like the worst sister in the world.

"Sorry. I'm just cranky."

Liz smiled. "I bet I know why. I bet it has something to do with what was going on in the study last night."

"Don't go there," Susannah warned. "Nothing went on in the study."

Nothing except the most intense orgasm she'd experienced in . . . She couldn't even remember the last time she'd come like that. She kept telling herself it hadn't been sex, but the way they'd kissed and rubbed against each other couldn't be described as anything but pure, raw sex. The horrifying reality was she wanted more. She wanted naked skin and the feel of Derrick sliding into her wet—

"Daydreaming?"

Susannah shook her head. "No. Absolutely not. I can't even believe you'd joke about it, under the circumstances."

Liz's smile faded. "You mean, because you're married?"

Susannah felt a twinge of guilt. "Yeah."

"Well, dear sister, let me tell you what I know—"

The back door opened and Brad's mother came in with bags of groceries. "Good morning, girls," Mrs. Montgomery said.

"I'm surprised you're still here. That storm is getting worse."

Liz worried her bottom lip between her teeth. "That's what I'm afraid of. We have people arriving all day and I don't know if they're all going to make it in this weather."

"They'll make it," Susannah said. "It's Virginia. How much could it snow in November?"

"Right," Liz said. "So, you'll go to the inn and work on the flowers and get people settled. I'll go pick up my dress and yours and finish these stupid bows."

"I have an idea," Susannah said. "Why don't you come to the inn after you take care of everything? We'll have a girls' night and you can keep your batty old aunt company."

Liz laughed and Mrs. Montgomery looked confused. "Excuse me? Aunt? I didn't think you girls had any family attending the wedding."

Susannah was still smiling when she sailed out the front door with Liz's car keys in hand. There was two inches of snow on the ground and the heavy, low-hanging clouds promised more of the same. She shivered from the chill, but even the lack of a proper coat couldn't dim her good spirits. Her smile faded the minute she saw Derrick's car pull up in front of the house. He got out and walked toward her, looking heartbreakingly sexy in a gray wool coat over a crisp white shirt and black trousers.

"I've been thinking about you all night," he said, his words falling as softly as the snow.

"I'm sure," she said, brushing past him. "Have a good day."

He caught her by the arm and pulled her around to face him. "What's with you?"

She stared at him as if he'd lost his mind. "What's with *me*? Do you remember last night?"

His thumb rubbed her forearm and, even through her blouse and leather jacket, she shivered at the familiarity of his touch.

"Of course I remember. Why do you think I'm smiling?" he asked, his voice low and seductive. "Judging by the smile on your face a minute ago, you remember, too."

"I wasn't smiling about that," she said, though part of her wondered if he was right. Were those few stolen moments with Derrick what had put her in such a good mood? She wanted to believe it was because she was getting away from him for the rest of the day, but she wasn't so sure.

"I'm sure," he said mockingly, as he released her. "Where are you off to in such a hurry?"

"The inn. Liz needs me to hold down the fort there while she takes care of things here," she said, the normalcy of their conversation feeling surreal. "What about you?"

She could have kicked herself for asking, especially when he smiled that all-too-familiar feral grin.

"Why? Want company?"

"Hell, no," she said. "I'd rather be alone."

He shrugged. "Have it your way. I guess I'll hang out here and make ribbon bows with your sister."

"Aren't you helpful?" Susannah couldn't keep the snide tone out of her voice. It was jealousy, she realized with a jolt—pure, raw jealousy that Liz would get to spend time with Derrick while she was alone at the inn.

"Not really," he said, turning on his heel. "The crinkle of the ribbon will remind me of last night on the couch." Susannah stared after him until the front door closed behind him. Despite the cold, she felt warm in a place she had thought had long since frozen over. Her heart.

* * *

Six hours and several frustrating conversations later, Susannah
decided being the batty old aunt was overrated and becoming
a wedding planner was definitely not a viable career option for
her. The florist had arrived with the wrong flowers, followed by
several out-of-town guests who seemed to think Susannah was
their personal tour guide. She tried to explain she hadn't lived in
Minerva in several years and no, she did not know the best place
to get coffee or quiche or the latest best seller. Thankfully, the
innkeepers were there to take the pressure off her and leave her
to sort out the floral mess while she figured out a way to tell Liz
that her white roses were peach and the greenery she'd ordered
had turned brown.

The worst part was that the snow was coming down harder,
and by five o'clock, there was a good four inches on the road
with no sign of it stopping. The picturesque setting the country inn had presented for a late fall wedding now seemed ominous and reminiscent of a Stephen King novel. Minerva had
one snowplow, and it was unlikely it would make it out to
the two-lane road that led to the Calloway Inn. Liz had chosen the inn for the reception because the public rooms were
large enough to accommodate a wedding reception and the
Methodist church where she and Brad were getting married
was less than a quarter-mile away. Of course, in order to get
married and have a wedding reception, there had to be a bride
and groom and wedding guests and Susannah was starting
to think it was going to be her and Brad's extended family
celebrating alone.

She was staring out the picture window at the steadily falling
snow when her cell phone rang.

"Hey, big sister," Liz said brightly when she answered. "The flowers get there okay?"

Susannah thought of the beautiful sprays of flowers that were now tucked away in the inn's refrigerator. Flowers that weren't exactly the right color and surrounded by brown leaves. She could fix the greenery, but she was hoping Liz would overlook the mistake with the roses. "They're here and awaiting your approval. When are you getting here?"

There was silence on the line and Susannah thought she'd lost signal. "Liz?"

"I'm here," Liz said. "Listen, don't be mad, okay?"

Susannah could feel a headache beginning directly behind her right eye. Nothing good ever came out of Liz saying, "Don't be mad, okay?" It was a phrase dating back twenty years when a three-year-old Liz had cut the hair off Susannah's favorite doll, thinking it would grow back.

"What, Lizard?"

Liz made an indignant sound. "Don't sound like that. It's not that bad. It's just that I won't be out there tonight."

"Oh, that's fine," Susannah said. Though she'd promised Liz a girls' night, the wedding was going to take every ounce of energy she had and she was leaving on a red-eye for Seattle as soon as the reception was over. "It's cozy here. Just me and Brad's little old aunties and the neighborhood ax murderer taking advantage of stranded, snowbound women."

Liz laughed. "Okay, now I feel guilty. But there's one other thing . . ."

Susannah didn't need Liz to tell her what the "one other thing" was because she could see Derrick's black BMW pulling up the long, snow-covered drive.

"Liz," she said, putting as much ominous threat into that one syllable as she could muster. "What's going on?"

"He'll explain," Liz said quickly. "Bye."

Susannah was still staring at the blank screen on her cell phone when the front door opened and Derrick came in, a dusting of snow on his shoulders and in his dark, tousled hair. He carried a box filled with white lace bows.

"Let me guess," she said dryly. "You volunteered to deliver the bows."

Derrick didn't crack a smile. "I had absolutely no desire to come out in this mess, but Liz asked me and I couldn't very well say no."

Disappointment, sharp and painful, lodged behind her breastbone. "Okay, fine. Give them to me."

He held onto the box as she reached for it. "I can help you, Susannah."

Whatever response she might have thrown back at him died on her lips when she saw his expression. She kept trying to force him into the mold that her memory clung to, but he just wouldn't fit.

She gave him a grudging smile. "Fine. I need to decorate the tables in the great room and cut some greenery before it gets dark."

He arched an eyebrow. "Greenery?"

She explained about the mishap with the florist and glanced past him. It had gotten late. "I guess I'll go do that now."

He put the box on the floor in the foyer and opened the door. "I'll go with you."

"It's okay," she said. "I'll be fine."

"Susannah," he said, and it was almost a warning. "I'm *going* to help you."

She shrugged and carefully made her way down the long drive with Derrick trailing behind her. She veered off onto the snow-covered lawn, kitchen shears in hand, and began trimming branches from the evergreen shrubs that lined the drive. Silently, she handed them to Derrick, who bundled them together. They worked quickly as darkness fell until Derrick finally stopped her.

"I think we have enough," he said from behind a wall of green foliage.

She laughed. "Sorry, I got carried away. I hope the Calloways won't notice."

He held out an elbow for her to hang onto as they picked their way over the slick, uneven ground and back to the inn. "Don't worry. By the time they notice, you'll be long gone."

Something about the way he said it made her pause. She looked up at him in the near darkness, seeing the snow glinting on his hair and eyelashes, and her heart ached. "There's no reason to stay," she said.

"Isn't there?"

She shivered, unable to respond. Afraid to speak, to hope.

"C'mon," he said, giving her a little nudge with his elbow. "It's cold out here. This weather is crazy."

She looked up at the overcast evening sky and laughed as the snow continued to fall. "It's winter, Derrick. It shouldn't be, but it is." She laughed, feeling something cold and tight loosen inside her. "It makes me think anything is possible."

He followed her into the inn and back to the kitchen, where Mrs. Calloway had left a pot of coffee brewing for them. Derrick hung up their coats and put their wet shoes by the back door while Susannah deposited the greenery in the refrigerator along with the rest of the flowers. The tables could wait until the morning. What she was feeling—and the look in Derrick's eyes as he leaned against the counter watching her—wouldn't wait for anything.

"Want some coffee?"

He shook his head. "I could go for something a little stronger."

She pulled a bottle of champagne out of the refrigerator. "I'm afraid this is as strong as we've got."

"I guess it'll have to do," he said, his gaze unwavering.

She blushed, though she didn't know why, and turned her back on him to look for champagne glasses. With a trembling hand, she poured the champagne and handed him a glass. She cocked her head to the side, eyeing him speculatively.

"What should we toast?"

He clinked his glass to hers. "To possibilities."

"To possibilities," she said, with a nod.

The champagne was sweet and cold. She shivered, still chilled from being outdoors, and met Derrick's steady, uncompromising gaze as she licked her bottom lip. Anticipation hung heavy in the air like the scent of evergreens.

They drank their champagne silently, facing each other like they might dance—or duel—at any moment. She refilled their glasses a second time, her hand brushing his wrist as she poured. He was warm, so warm. She put the bottle on the counter a little harder than she intended and the sound jolted her.

"Nervous?" he asked. She shook her head. "Why would I be?"

"Because you know it's time to deal with this thing between us."

She laughed, but it sounded high-pitched and shrill. "This 'thing' is just sexual tension. If we slept together, it would fade away."

"Is that what you really think?" He put his empty glass on the counter and stared at her. "One night with me and that look in your eyes would be gone?"

His confrontational tone made her feel rebellious. She nodded. "Absolutely."

"Fine, then," he said, taking the glass from her hand and putting it next to his. "Let's test your theory."

"I'm married."

"My body doesn't care about marital status, does yours?"

She shook her head, her pulse jumping as he wrapped his fingers around her wrist and pulled her toward the stairs. Still, she hesitated. "That's it? One night?"

He looked down at her, his eyes reflecting her image. "One night, Susannah," he said. "You can go back to Seattle tomorrow and forget all about me."

One night. All night. It would be enough. It had to be.

Chapter 4

"No more games," he said, once the bedroom door closed behind them.

"No more games," she agreed, as she helped him strip off his shirt. She'd had enough games. What she wanted was passion, passion with Derrick. All the passion she remembered and more. Enough passion to get her home to Seattle without feeling any pain.

"I'm glad we agree," he said, amusement lacing his voice. "I thought I might have to remind you how amazing it can be between us."

She looked up into his eyes, trying to keep her gaze from reflecting her real emotions. "I had good intentions of turning you down," she said lightly.

"The road to hell is paved with good intentions, babe," he said, slipping his fingers under the waistband of her pants and into her panties. "Let me show you the way."

She gasped as his fingers found her clitoris, plump and wet beneath his touch. "I've always had a pretty good sense of direction. Maybe I should take the lead."

He pulled his hands free and shrugged. "Anything you want."

His words thrilled her. *Anything she wanted.* She wanted it all. She wanted all of him, but if she had to settle for one night, she would make it one neither of them would ever forget.

He stretched out on the bed in all his masculine glory. His body was so familiar, and yet so new. It was exciting, having him here like this, a chance to reclaim the past. After all the teasing and flirting and near seductions, he was hers for one night.

She lay next to him and stroked a hand down his chest, broader than she remembered, more muscular. She trailed her fingers down to his tapered waist and dipped a pinkie into his navel, deliberately keeping her eyes on his chest and ignoring the insistent bulge that strained the fabric of his pants. He caught his breath and she felt a rush of feminine power. She taunted him, running her fingertips just under the waistband of his trousers, before moving back up his chest and resting a hand over his heart. His pulse was racing.

"Don't get too excited," she said, her voice deep and throaty like the seductress she wanted to be. "I plan on taking a very long time with you."

He caught her wrist in his hand and her wedding ring glinted in the lamplight. "Take as long as you want, just don't leave me wanting."

Her own pulse jumped at his touch, but the ring was a painful reminder of why this was a one-night stand. She jerked upright, feeling a decided cooling of her passion. He grabbed her around the waist, preventing her escape.

"What is it, Susannah?" he murmured against her hair. "Is it the ring?"

A variety of emotions flooded her senses. Anger, at him for making her feel this way when she knew nothing could come of it. Shame, for condemning him for behavior she was more than willing to indulge in herself. Hurt, because she hadn't been worth more than a brief affair four years ago when he was married and wasn't worth more than that now. Beneath all of those emotions was arousal and desire. Her need to have him—if only for tonight—was stronger than her need for closure on the past.

"Nothing's wrong," she said, forcing her voice to remain even and not betray the internal battle she was fighting with herself. "My head is just spinning from the champagne."

He sat up and brushed her hair from her face. "You had two glasses of champagne. I'm a lightweight."

"You're a liar."

Anger flared again, as hot and demanding as her desire, but she didn't want to pick a fight. She wanted to roll around naked with him until the sun came up. "You know you want me," she said. "You can have me."

"Not yet," he said. He took her left hand in his and slowly worked the rings from her finger. He dropped them on the bed-side table where they settled with a solid metal thud. "*Now* you're mine."

"It's that easy for you, isn't it?"

He tangled his fingers in her hair and tilted her face up to him. His kiss was hot, wet, and demanding, intimate in a way that left no doubt in her mind that he wanted her. She kissed him back, wanting to put the reality of the situation out of her mind and forget that he didn't care if she was married, didn't care about anything but fucking her.

Finally, when she was whimpering low in her throat, he pulled away. His eyes were shards of blue glass, sparkling with amusement and desire.

"Yeah, it's that easy," he said, confirming her worst fears. "Especially since you're not married."

Whatever she'd expected, it hadn't been that. She gaped at him in stunned silence. Finally, she said, "What?" because it was all she could manage.

He laughed as he pulled her down on the bed until they were a tangle of warm limbs and rumpled sheets. "You're not married. You haven't been married to Thomas Schaeffer for over a year."

"How did—how long—when—" It was as if her mind couldn't accept that he knew her secret. The fact that she was wet and aching for him didn't help. A moment ago, she hadn't wanted to think about anything except feeling Derrick inside of her. Now it seemed important, *very* important, that she know what was going on.

He chuckled as he kissed her forehead and if she hadn't been so damned confused, she might have been angry at the borderline condescension behind his laughter and that tender kiss. Unfortunately, her brain refused to engage and all she could do was babble fragments of questions.

He stroked her bottom lip with his thumb. "Liz thought if she invited your husband to the wedding personally, he might come with you."

Susannah didn't think she could be more surprised, but that bombshell proved her wrong. "Liz knows?"

"Of course. She wanted to surprise you, so she tracked him down at work," he went on. "When she found out you were divorced, she told Brad and—when I asked about you—he told me."

Susannah's mind raced. "Why didn't Thomas say anything to me? We're still friendly."

"I'm guessing it's because he didn't know why she was calling," Derrick said. "From what I gather, he said something along the lines of being surprised to hear from his ex-wife's sister and she found a way to get off the phone fast."

"She didn't say anything." There was no hiding the feeling of betrayal now. Liz had known her secret and hadn't said a word. "Why?"

"I think she was afraid you wouldn't come to the wedding."

"Why on earth would she think that?" She twisted in his arms so she could see his face. "Why?"

He closed his eyes and sighed. "Because of me."

She wanted to deny it, to say that nothing would have kept her from her own sister's wedding, but she couldn't. She didn't know. She just didn't know.

"I should have just told her."

"Yes, you should have." He leaned down and kissed her neck. "Even if you didn't think you'd be able to keep your hands off me."

"You wish."

"It's the truth for both of us." He moved lower, kissing her collarbone. "But if you'd been married, I would have respected that. We're not your parents, Susannah."

Despite the shock, her desire for him hadn't faded and his intimate kisses only fueled the flames. She ran her fingers through his thick hair, feeling wetness gathering between her thighs. Her body ached for him, for a feeling only he could give her. He pushed her blouse off her shoulder and slid her bra straps down, kissing the swell of her breasts. She moaned, not caring if the Calloways and every one of Brad's extended family heard her.

Derrick pulled the cups of her bra down and took one hard pink nipple between his lips. She gasped as he tugged and sucked until it was wet and aching before moving to the other one. She reached under her to unfasten her bra, managing to shrug out of her blouse and bra while he sucked and nibbled his way down her breasts to her stomach. The sound of him unzipping her pants made her tremble with barely controlled lust. He got her pants and panties off and then sat back to look at her.

She opened her eyes, watching him watch her. She felt wild and shameless as she spread her legs for his heated gaze. "I'm so wet," she whispered. "You do that to me, Derrick. You make me so wet."

As if to test the truth of her words for himself, he ran his thumb from her slippery opening up to the hard nub of her clit. She moaned and arched her back as he rubbed her, aching for release.

"Open your eyes," he said gruffly. "Watch me get you off." Her eyes went wide, meeting his steady gaze before moving lower to watch his hand move between her thighs. He slid a finger inside her while he kept his thumb on her clit, stroking her inside and out.

"Watch me," he said, again. "I want to see your eyes when you come."

Orgasm washed over her and she bit her bottom lip to keep from screaming, but she never looked away from his face. She came on his fingers, came hard and long as he stroked her wet, wet pussy. He stared at her face, not between her legs, watching her come for him as he coaxed the sensations from her body.

Finally, when she couldn't take anymore, she clenched her thighs around his wrist to still him. "Enough," she gasped. "Please."

He laughed, stripping off his pants before she even had time to catch her breath. "It'll never be enough for us," he said. "Haven't you figured that out yet?"

She didn't have a chance to respond because he was stretching out over her, his cock nudging her sensitive clit. Gasping, she opened for him, wrapping her arms and legs around his muscular body. He slid inside her, filling her, and groaned when her pussy rippled around him.

"If you keep doing that, I'll be finished before we even start," he said through gritted teeth.

She clenched around him again and laughed. "I can't help it."

"I want this to last a long time." He pulled back a bit, then thrust inside her again. "I've wanted you like this for so long."

She whimpered. "Fuck me, Derrick. I need you to fuck me hard."

He reached under her and gripped her ass, pulling her down on his cock. Then he began to fuck her just the way she wanted, hard and deep, until she was digging her fingernails into his back and gasping his name. As if her body couldn't get enough of him, another orgasm swept over her. While she was still trembling from the aftershocks, he rolled them over on the big bed so that she straddled him.

She began moving on him the way she had the night before on the couch, but this time there were no clothes to get in the way. He was buried inside her so deep it bordered on pain—but a good pain, a sweet and intense sensation that made her long for more.

She sat up and braced her hands on his chest as she swiveled her hips. He groaned and thrust into her, making her gasp. She rose up, letting him almost slide out of her, before taking his full length inside her again. She kept rotating her hips as she slowly slid up and down on him, teasing him with her body the way he had teased her with his mouth and hands.

"Oh, hell, baby," he said. "You feel so damned good."

She moved on him so slowly she could feel every inch of his cock sliding into her. "So do you," she whispered as she rode him. "I want you inside me all night."

He groaned again, gripping her hips as he tried to guide her movements. "You're driving me out of my mind."

She threw back her head and laughed. "Good."

He twisted her hair around his hand and gave it a tug. "Enjoying this, are you?" he practically growled.

By way of an answer, she tilted her pelvis back and rocked on him. She was so tight around him, filled by him, and she gasped as he moved inside her. She quickened her pace, stroking him with her pussy until he thrust up into her. He gripped her hair in one fist and guided her with his other hand on her hip. They settled into their rhythm, slow and steady, until even their breathing was in sync. She looked down into his eyes and saw the moment when orgasm overtook him and he lost control. She had never felt so desired in her entire life.

She kept riding him, stroking him, coaxing every sensation from him that he had given her. So was so focused on pleasuring him she didn't notice how close she was to orgasm herself until his thumb found her clit and she exploded around him in a gush of wetness. Gasping and grinding on him until she couldn't stand the intensity of sensations coursing through her body, she collapsed on his warm, damp chest.

"Oh my god," she gasped, still in the aftermath of her climax. "Oh my."

He laughed, a deep rumbling sound that made him twitch inside her and sent ripples from her thighs to her scalp. "You have a way with words—and with your body."

She breathed him in, absorbing every second of the experience so she could recall it later and relive it when he was thousands of miles away and had forgotten. She wouldn't forget. Not ever. "Susannah? Are you crying?"

She started to deny it, but he cupped her damp cheek and sighed. "What did I do?"

Sniffling, she shook her head. "Nothing. Not a thing. It was . . . incredible."

"And that makes you cry?"

She swallowed hard and asked the question that weighed on her heart. "Tonight is incredible, but . . . what about tomorrow?"

He tilted her chin up so that he could meet her tearful gaze. "Tomorrow we'll get your sister married off to Brad."

"And then?" She didn't know why she was pushing him. He had promised her one night and they still had so much time left, but now that her body was satisfied, at least temporarily, her heart demanded the same satisfaction.

"This 'thing' between us is more than sex," he said. "You know that."

She nodded, even though it wasn't a question.

"Now that we're both free, I don't think it will wait another four years to be satisfied." He ran his thumb over her bottom lip, swollen from his kisses. "Do you?"

She nipped his thumb and smiled. "No."

"I know it won't," he said. "I won't let it. I've let you go twice without telling you how I felt. I don't intend to do it again."

"I leave for Seattle tomorrow," she reminded him.

"We'll make this work."

He sounded so determined, she knew it was true. "I hope so."

He leaned down and kissed her. "We will. And I have all night to convince you."

Susannah tucked her head against his shoulder and looked out the window that faced the woods behind the inn. The snow had finally stopped and the moon shown brightly in the midnight sky.

Winter had come early to Minerva and worked its magic— her heart believed anything was possible now.

 KRISTINA WRIGHT is an award-winning author who loves writing stories that are emotionally compelling and sexually charged. Her erotic fiction has appeared in over fifty print anthologies, including *Best Women's Erotica*, *The Mammoth Book of Best New Erotica*, and *Dirty Girls: Erotica for Women*. She also received the Golden Heart Award for Romantic Suspense from Romance Writers of America for her first novel *Dangerous Curves*. She holds a BA in English, an MA in humanities, and is completing a certificate in women's studies while entertaining the idea of pursuing a PhD. For more information about Kristina's writing and academic interests, visit her website www.kristinawright.com.

Six Weeks on
Sunrise Mountain, Colorado

by Gwen Masters

The weathered old porch creaked as Fletcher rocked back and forth in the chair. The moon slowly came up over Sunrise Mountain, casting its silver light over the cedar and pine. Snow had started to fall hours ago, the kind of snow that turned to ice as soon as it touched anything on the ground. The trees were leaning with the pressure on their branches. The road was impassable already and would remain that way for weeks.

Fletcher was completely unconcerned with time and content to be snowed in. He went on rocking and listening to the snow settling on the old tin roof above him. Every now and then he spotted an owl, rising on white wings, gliding soundlessly over the treetops. The moonlight turned the owl's eyes into bright prisms of light for an instant before it disappeared into the leaves again.

The shape of a small animal at the end of his long gravel driveway caught his eye. Fletcher calmly reached for the shotgun propped up against the porch railing, running his hand over the smooth barrel, ready to use the weapon if necessary. Eventually the animal left the shadows and walked through a shaft of moonlight, showing Fletcher the distinctive markings on its face—a raccoon. The little fellow waddled its way up the rocky road that surrounded the cabin and occasionally stopped to sniff the air, barely bothering to glance at the now-familiar man up on the porch. Fletcher relaxed and let his hand fall from the barrel of the gun.

Up on Sunrise Mountain, all kinds of animals might come hunting at his doorstep, but it was very doubtful any of them would be human, and that suited Fletcher just fine. He had jumped into the rat race at a fresh-faced twenty-two, straight from college to a high-pressure job in Silicon Valley. By thirty-two, the dot-com boom had slammed with the force of a nuclear bomb, and he was a millionaire many times over. By the time he was thirty-five, he was so burned out he didn't give a damn if he had a dollar to his name, as long as he had some peace of mind. There was no one he trusted.

It hadn't taken long for him to realize that the worst predators were of his own kind.

Fletcher looked back up at the moon. It danced into the snow clouds, turning the world darker. His ears made up for what his eyes could no longer see in the dim light. Leaves rustled with the breeze. Tiny animals scurried around the sides of the cabin, bolder now that they were under the cover of night. A mountain lion howled, and though the sound echoed with menace through the wide valley between the hills, Fletcher's confident ear knew the big boy was miles away.

The raccoon was still making its way up the drive. Fletcher

had taken a liking to his furry neighbor and kept back a bit of dinner now and again, then set it around the porch for the raccoon to find. Fletcher liked to watch the pretty creature in the moonlight. It was the only company he had up here in the middle of nowhere.

He watched as the raccoon stopped in midstride and looked toward the top of the ravine. Fletcher slowly stopped rocking and listened closely to the sounds he understood just as well as his own language—the slight tapping of one tree limb against another, the abrupt silence of a larger animal when it caught the scent of a human on the air, the unholy scream of a hawk as it dove for prey. The raccoon listened, too, its tiny head cocked to better hear the sounds on the air.

Fletcher heard it then, the sound that was so out of place—a scuffling, bumbling sound, unlike any of the sleek animals so accustomed to wandering through the woods at night.

He rose slowly to his feet, staring at the place from where he was certain the sound had come. The raccoon was down on all fours again, sniffing cautiously, still as a stone. The sound came again, but the coon wasn't making a move to investigate, and Fletcher knew that wasn't a good sign. That raccoon was a smart animal. He knew better than to attack anything bigger than he was.

Fletcher thumbed the safety on the rifle and lifted it to his shoulder.

He had seen more than a few bear and the occasional mountain lion, but something told him it was neither of those things. Surely the smaller animals would have run hard for the other side of the mountain if big game had wandered into his clearing.

Fletcher quietly walked down the steps and trained his rifle on the spot the raccoon seemed so interested in.

The animal turned its black-masked face up to him, and now Fletcher was puzzled. Why didn't the raccoon try to run? Why was it just sitting there? The expression of pure confusion on its face was almost human.

"Oh God," Fletcher said.

Just as Fletcher realized what that sound was, he heard another one: the unmistakable report of a branch breaking, a body tumbling, and a very human scream. The raccoon raced across the yard, away from the sound, finally scared out of its little mind. There was a terrible *thud*, and another scream, cut short on an exhaled breath.

That tore Fletcher out of his astonishment. He broke into a run.

He found the woman at the foot of the ravine. Even in the moonlight, she looked pale as a ghost. Blood covered her forehead and a bruise was already flowering under her right eye. Fletcher fought his way through the brush, dropping his gun along the way—from the looks of her, she wouldn't be a threat. When he reached her, she was shivering hard from a combination of cold and shock. She looked up at him with frightened eyes.

"I'm not going to hurt you," he said, ripping at the branches around her.

"F-f-f-fell," she stuttered, her teeth chattering.

Snow had begun to fall again, and he watched as it caught in her hair.

"I have to get you out of here," he said. "You're going to freeze to death unless we get you to the house right now."

Her teeth were chattering. Controlling her body seemed to take a massive effort.

"H-h-house . . ."

"In the house. That's right. What's your name?"

A tear ran down her face. It froze on her skin before it could reach her bruised jaw. "Jan—Janine."

"Janine?"

She nodded with the slightest motion of her head.

"Okay, Janine. Can you stand up?"

All her movements were slow, as though she were underwater. Fletcher thought it might have been shock, or worse, a head injury from the fall she took. She balled her hands up into fists and stood up, obviously with more than a little pain. She was shaking hard. His own teeth were chattering from the cold. Once a cold front rolled in, it came with a vengeance. The temperature had dropped a good thirty degrees since the sun went down.

"Can you walk?"

She stepped carefully, as if her legs might give way at any moment. The moonlight was just enough to help them make their way up the lane without stumbling. Fletcher carefully navigated the porch steps, moved around the rocking chair, and pushed open the door. Once they were inside, he led her to the bed in the corner, where he admonished her to sit and not move.

Fletcher quickly strode to the fireplace and added more wood, then more kindling for good measure. The fire flared and crackled. In its mellow orange light, Fletcher turned and looked at the woman. She needed a hospital. He had never felt so inadequate.

"Tell me where you're hurt," he said. "Tell me what I can do for you?"

It felt odd to talk to another person again. He was accustomed to not speaking for days, his silences punctuated only by his talk to the raccoon, but the sound soothed him now, made him less afraid.

"I'm so cold." She was still shivering, despite the warmth of the fire.

"Your clothes are all wet." He knelt to the floor and pulled off her boots, his mind racing. "You've got to get them off."

Fletcher helped Janine sit up. When she struggled out of her jacket, he saw the shirt she wore underneath it was thin, almost a summer shirt. She also wore a thick black belt, with metal rings and tabs and—

"You're a climber?"

She was still pale but her voice was a little stronger. "Yes."

He helped her pull off her socks. "Do you need help doing this?"

She shook her head, already working at the buttons of her jeans. Fletcher turned his back as she undressed. Having a naked woman in his cabin should have had the natural effect on him, but it wasn't sensual at all. In fact, sex was the last thing on his mind. The only thing he could think about was what damage was under her skin, what bruises were there that he couldn't see, and what he would do if she was *really* hurt. How could he get her off the mountain?

When he looked back at her, she was lying under the quilt, her eyes closed, still as a stone.

"Janine?"

He touched her face. She didn't flinch. He fought the surge of panic as he gently shook her and got no response. Her breath was so shallow he had to press his hand against her mouth to feel it. He sank to the floor beside the bed, his hands shaking, his head spinning.

"Don't you die on me, you hear? Don't you do that."

Janine, unconscious and oblivious to the world, didn't move. Fletcher stared at her for a while, then went back outside one more time, to retrieve the gun he had left in the brush. The road glistened in the moonlight, a million sparkles glinting from the layer of snow and ice, and the beautiful yet deadly blanket was still coming down. They weren't going anywhere.

She slept all night and most of the next day.

Outside the snow had stopped, but not before dropping a good three feet over the land around the cabin. Most of it was encrusted with ice. The trees were heavy with it. Every now and then a branch would fall or a tree would explode with frozen sap, the sound as loud and sudden as a gunshot.

There was no way to get off the mountain. Snowshoes were useless, and he couldn't carry her while wearing them, regardless. He might be able to use the sled, but the closest hiking station was a ten-mile trek through bear country. Even if they survived the elements, the big animals could sense a helpless human for miles around. Maybe he could make it there and call for a chopper, but in this kind of weather, the cavalry didn't come out unless there was absolutely no choice. Fletcher had worked so many possibilities through in his head, and they all ended up with failure.

When she woke up in the midafternoon, Fletcher was there beside her, holding a bowl of warm water and a few rags. Her face was bruised and her hands were still shaky, but she had more strength than she'd had the night before.

"Where do you hurt?" he asked. "What can I do for you?"

She took a wet rag and held it to her face, dabbing at the cut on her hairline. One eye was swollen, but the other was clear, observant. "My name is Janine."

"My name is Fletcher."

She nodded and looked around the room. Her sharp gaze took in everything, but she was still moving a bit too slowly. Was it safe to give her medicine? Would it help her or harm her? All he had was aspirin, and he knew aspirin thinned the blood.

"I have aspirin," he said, and let her make the decision.

"Yes. Please."

He opened the cabinet in the far corner. The cabin was two rooms—a bathroom was hidden away in one corner, but the rest of the house was wide open. He could feel her eyes on him as he moved around it, stoking the fire even higher, searching under the old porcelain sink for the emergency first-aid kit that he was certain had been left under there at some point. He finally found it behind the gun oil and the can of cooking lard. When he turned back to her, there was an amused smile on her face.

"What's so funny?"

She nodded toward the mess that was the kitchen. "Men are the same," she said, her words a little slurred. "Whether in New York City or at the top of a mountain."

"What were you doing at the top of my mountain anyway?"

Fletcher opened the bottle of aspirin and held it out to her. As she sat up, the quilt fell down, giving him a quick view of her breasts before she pulled the fabric up again. A blush rose to his cheeks and he looked out the window. The raccoon was sitting on the porch, looking back in the window at him.

"I was looking for new places to shoot," she said.

"To shoot?"

"I'm a photographer."

Fletcher stiffened. "You were on private property."

"I know that now." She dabbed again at the cut on her fore-head and winced. "I apologize."

"What kind of things do you photograph?"

The silence was long. Fletcher refused to look back at her. The raccoon waddled a few steps closer to the window, and Fletcher went to the kitchen to get some leftovers. When he opened the door, the coon didn't flinch or move away. It was probably time to name the old boy, because it appeared they were stuck with each other.

Fletcher held out the pan and the raccoon came forward to sniff at it. Fletcher set it on the porch and watched as the black-masked creature carefully selected a piece of flapjack, rolled it neatly with his tiny paws, and stuck it down in the snow.

"I could use some dry clothes." She was standing in the door-way, looking over his shoulder at the raccoon, the porch, and the vast white blanket beyond.

"You can wear some of mine. They are too big for you, but better than that quilt."

He listened as she shuffled toward the closet, then he dropped down into the rocking chair. The chill of the snow immediately seeped through his jeans, but he hardly noticed. He stared at the white world outside his porch as the raccoon chattered away.

A photographer, of all things. Fletcher was willing to put

money down on the reasons she was here. The fall was just a mishap, but she hadn't lost her way. She had been trying to find good cover.

He was glad she was okay, but he hoped her equipment had been smashed all to hell.

After a few long minutes, she came out onto the porch. She was wearing an old shirt of his that fell to her knees. She had on a pair of long underwear underneath that, and a pair of his thick socks. They came halfway up her shins. Fletcher fought the urge to smile—she looked like a little girl playing dress-up in her father's closet.

She limped over to the railing. They looked at each other.

"You know who I am," he said.

"Yes."

"You're paparazzo?"

"It pays the bills."

"I'll bet it does."

Janine wrapped her arms around her middle and kept silent. In the afternoon light, the bruises were very clear. Just looking at her made him hurt. He wanted to apologize for being so rude to her, but on the other hand, he was angry as hell. He wanted her off his mountain.

"I came out here to be away from the rest of the world," he said.

"I can see that. Nobody in their right mind would live so far off the grid."

"Thanks."

She shifted her weight to the other foot and winced as she did it. "Look, it's a job, okay? Some of us have to work."

He rocked and said nothing.

"Everyone wants to know what is going on with you," she said.

Fletcher glared at her. "You're grasping at straws for explanations."

"Do you know what a stir you made when you disappeared?"

"Tabloids don't make it out this far."

"The most influential man in Silicon Valley just drops it all and chooses to live so far away from technology, nobody can reach him anymore? Only Bill Gates would have caused more uproar."

"How is Bill anyway?"

She shot him a glare. "Nobody knows why you ran."

"It's none of your business."

"Once you're a celebrity, it's *everybody's* business, Fletcher."

"I'm not a celebrity. I'm a computer geek."

"You became a celebrity when you started dating actresses."

The chair slammed against the wall when Fletcher stood up. He rose to his full height, towering over her by more than a foot. He put as much venom into his voice as he could manage. It wasn't hard to do—the slightest mention of Amanda could still cut him, even after all this time, and fury was better than sadness.

"Get off my mountain," he growled.

Janine actually cowered a bit, which satisfied him and made him sad all at the same time. She looked at the chair as it settled back down into its usual place. "I would, Fletcher. But I can't."

Fletcher stared at her, the words to blast her forming in the back of his mind, his hands trembling, his eyes watering with anger. In the end he stepped away from her, yanked his coat from a hook just inside the door, and stalked down the porch steps. He strapped on his snowshoes and started walking. It took effort to move across the snow, and he focused on the strength of his legs and the pumping of his heart until he erased all thoughts, save one.

Why can't they just leave me alone?

By the time he came back to the cabin, the anger was mostly gone. He was worn out, physically and emotionally. The fight might come back to him another day, but for now, he was just resigned to dealing with this woman who had crashed into his life.

Fletcher had done a lot of thinking while he walked through the wilderness. If Janine was going to be here for as long as he thought she might be, he would have to be civil. Making enemies with her was the last thing either of them needed. He was accustomed to his solitude and far preferred that to the company of anyone, but if she was going to be here anyway, Fletcher had to admit it would be nice to have someone to talk to.

Besides that, there were more practical matters to think about. She had tracked him down. He wasn't foolish enough to think she would be the only one. If she could do it, so could someone else—his secret would soon be out, whether he liked it or not.

Smoke rose in thick plumes from the chimney. Inside, the cabin was toasty warm. The fire was roaring in the fireplace, and it was roaring in the cast-iron stove, too. He found Janine standing over it, stirring something in a pan, her face flushed from the heat.

"I've never used a wood cookstove before," she said by way of greeting.

Fletcher removed his coat. "Don't burn yourself."

"I'm being careful."

Fletcher pulled a chair out from underneath the small kitchen table and sat down. "How are you feeling?"

"I'm hurting." She looked over at him and shrugged. Her face looked worse than it had before he left, as if the bruises had finally made themselves clear.

"There's aspirin. I'm sorry there isn't more."

"Aspirin is good." She watched the pan for a moment. "Thank you for helping me."

"You're welcome."

She looked at him with wide eyes, surprised at his genial attitude.

"Janine, there are some things you need to know."

She looked at him, wooden spatula in hand, and waited.

"First, I'm sorry I blew up a while ago."

Janine waved his apology away. "You were entirely justified."

"Second, I want you to know why my privacy means so much to me."

She flipped something in the pan. It smelled like pork chops— she must have found the smokehouse out back. Fletcher's stomach rumbled, and Janine smiled at him. Her smile made her very pretty, despite the bruises.

"You don't have to tell me," she said.

"Are you going to print this?"

Janine laughed. "I'm a photographer, not a reporter."

"I had two choices," Fletcher said. "I could declare everything lost and jump from a rooftop, or I could disappear and try to start over."

Janine tapped the spatula against the pan. "I'm listening."

"It wasn't what everyone thought. The rumors were wild but none of them were true."

"The biggest rumor was that you were jilted by a woman," she said.

"Wouldn't being jilted by a man make the bigger story?"

Janine whirled around and looked at him with wide eyes. Fletcher let out a long, hearty laugh and shook his head. "I know what you're thinking, but it's not true."

Janine blushed and turned back to the stove. "Not a woman. Not a man, then. What was it?"

"I couldn't handle it anymore. Life became nothing but pressure, money, and ridiculous expectation. I got into computer engineering because it was my passion. I got out of it because it was suffocating me."

"You disappeared right before the indictments."

Fletcher closed his eyes, remembering the day he learned how much his employees were embezzling. He remembered the Feds sticking that paperwork under his nose, showing him how much he didn't know: the forged signatures, the bank accounts hacked, the expertise of his own company and his own protégés being used against him.

"I didn't give them up, if that's what you're wondering. I found out about it all a few days before the rest of the world did."

He watched as she put the pork chops on a chipped platter. She sprinkled a bit of flour in the skillet, waited a moment, then poured in a cup of water, stirring the whole time. Fletcher watched her as she cooked. Now that he could look at her and not think of hospital emergency rooms, he realized what a pretty woman she was. Her body was long and lean, with the firm calves and shoulders of a seasoned athlete. Her brunette hair was somehow wound around an old, battered pencil—the result was a messy bun at the back of her head, wisps trailing over her shoulders. He studied the fine lines of her neck. There was a bruise right underneath her ear, but he noticed instead the strong line of her jaw, and the surprised way she smiled when she turned and caught him looking.

"I'm a mess," she said, holding her hands up in apology.

"You're lovely," he said, the words popping out before he had a chance to think about them. He felt the blush travel quickly up his cheeks, heating his face. He busied himself with unlacing his boots, hoping she hadn't seen his embarrassment, so much like a little boy instead of a grown man. Where the hell had that come from?

"Thank you," she said. The surprise made her voice light, almost playful.

Fletcher shrugged and started on the other boot.

She set food on the table, a simple dinner of pork chops, gravy, and fried potatoes. She poured ice-cold water from a pitcher and sat down in the other chair, smiled at Fletcher, and picked up her fork.

"Eat," she said.

Fletcher looked at the food, and his stomach rumbled again. It was the first meal he hadn't cooked for himself in almost a year. The last time was at Amanda's house, and when they were done they had forsaken the wineglasses to pour the red liquid all over each other—

"Fletcher?"

Janine's voice brought him crashing back to the present. He picked up his fork and took a bite of the potatoes. They were much better than his, cooked with some of the spices in his cupboard that he never had any idea how to use.

"This is good," he said.

"How do you manage when the snow comes in?" she asked. "You've got all kinds of staples in the kitchen right now, but I can imagine you go through them before the snow lets up."

Fletcher took a bite of the pork and closed his eyes. Maybe it wasn't much different than the way he cooked it, but the fact that it was cooked by someone else made it taste heavenly.

"I have a gun," he answered.

"You shoot your own dinner?"

"There aren't any other options."

She nodded and picked at the food on her plate. For the first time since he had walked through the door, he remembered the fear of the night before. "Are you hurting? Inside?"

Janine seemed to know exactly what he meant. "I think I have a bruised rib. But I don't think there's any bleeding going on in there. I don't really know how to tell, but my breathing is okay, and I don't feel any pain that I can't explain." She shook her head slowly. "Does that make sense?"

"Yeah, it does."

"I think I have a concussion."

"I know you do," he agreed. "You're moving like you're underwater. Sometimes your words are slurred, but I know you didn't get into the moonshine. I checked," he teased.

"Moonshine might be better than aspirin," she said, grinning back at him.

"You scared me last night, when you fell asleep. I couldn't wake you up. I remember reading somewhere that a person with a concussion shouldn't be allowed to go to sleep."

She took a bite of potatoes. "I think I'm going to be okay."

"You were incredibly lucky," he said, shaking his head. "It could have been so much worse."

"You were there," she said, as if that explained everything.

"Nobody knows where you are, do they?" he asked.

"My editor has an idea, but no one knew my actual whereabouts, no. I wasn't sure what to tell them. I wasn't sure where you were, but I knew you were up here somewhere."

"How did you find me?"

Janine pushed the potatoes around on her plate. "Your holdings were listed in the indictments. I got the records through the Freedom of Information Act, and there was only one holding that hadn't been explored, mostly because it was listed as private hunting land. There was no structure listed on the property. But then I got to thinking . . . prime hunting land on a mountain in the middle of Colorado? That's big-time hunting. That's the kind of hunting that can take a man away for weeks on end. A man could backpack his way in, but he would have to be a very skilled outdoorsman to manage living in a tent for weeks. A cabin, however . . . something off the grid, so that it isn't registered with any agency anywhere . . . hidden away in a valley on the top of that mountain. Who would notice?"

"A computer geek living in the wilderness," Fletcher mused with a smile. "What a concept."

"It's the perfect cover."

"A computer geek who had a banker for a father—a father who couldn't bait a hook, much less fire a shotgun."

"But your great-uncle was a fisherman by trade, and you spent childhood summers with him in the Keys."

Fletcher raised an eyebrow. "You lied to me. You said you were a photographer."

"You lied to me, too. You said you knew nothing of the indictments."

They stared at each other over the pork chops and potatoes. Fletcher took a drink of water and studied the young woman across the table from him, one who had turned out to be more of an adversary than he had first thought. She was dangerous, no matter how beautiful she was.

It was going to be a very long winter.

Another cold front came in a week later, and this one brought an ice storm with it. All the animals on the mountain stayed in their hollows and dens, keeping warm as best they could. The silence was almost as maddening as the cold.

Fletcher kept a fire roaring in the stove, but the chill of the snow crept in regardless. He ventured outside only to get fresh snow for water—the usual supply had frozen in the barrels, and no amount of stoking the fire would thaw it out. There was a thermometer on the outside wall of the cabin, but Fletcher was afraid to look at it.

Janine stayed wrapped in layers of clothing. The bruises were fading now, but somehow they looked even worse—instead of black and purple, they were now all shades of green and yellow. She joked that she looked like one of those alien life-forms on the late-night documentary channels.

"I miss television," she sighed.

"What's television?"

She threw a rolled-up pair of socks at him and laughed.

In the few days she had been on his mountain, Fletcher had learned quite a bit about Janine. Once the woman started talking, she didn't want to stop, and that was just fine with him. It felt good to hear a voice other than his own. She brought stories of the outside world, and though Fletcher maintained that he was perfectly happy on his mountain, it was nice to hear tales of the world that was spinning along just fine without him.

"Don't you have friends who worry?" she asked one night, as they sat before the crackling fire.

"I don't think so. I didn't have time for friends."

"What did you do for fun?"

Fletcher shrugged. "I worked. That's all I did."

"There had to be more to your life than that. You were seen everywhere with Amanda Whitmore. You don't date a famous actress if your whole life is spent behind a computer screen."

"You asked what I did for *fun*, Janine."

In the firelight her bruises looked like shadows, and he saw what she would look like when they were gone. Her jaw was sharp, almost too sharp, but the softness of her eyes made up for it. When she smiled, her whole face was transformed, and she went from pretty to beautiful.

"I don't understand," she said slowly.

"It was fun until we became such a spectacle. Do you know what it's like to be followed everywhere? To be constantly aware of what you're doing and how you look, because you never know where a camera is lurking?"

Janine tossed a thin stick of kindling on the fire. They both watched as it flared, turned to ash and disappeared. She picked up the poker and moved the logs around, sending up embers.

"I have no idea," she admitted.

Fletcher stretched his legs out in front of the fire. "It destroyed me and Amanda. It became more about what the public thought about us than what we thought about each other."

"You really loved her, didn't you?"

Fletcher didn't look at Janine. Instead he studied the fire, watched as the flames changed colors, and thought about Amanda. Where was she now? What was she doing? Who was she with? A woman like her wouldn't be alone for long.

"I did love her," he said. "But love doesn't conquer everything."

Janine stood up and walked to the kitchen. Fletcher was left alone with the fire and his thoughts, like he had been so many long nights before, and suddenly he wondered if it was what he still wanted. What would it be like when the snow melted and the ice disappeared? Janine would leave his mountain, and there might be a story or two about him, but eventually he would be written off as an eccentric and mostly forgotten. That didn't bother him much. What bothered him was the return of the silence. It had been comforting when it was all he had known on the mountain—when the cabin's walls had never heard a voice other than his own—but now that illusion had been shattered.

She came back with two mugs of thick, rich coffee. He sipped it while he listened to her settle down beside him again. She had a quietness that took time getting used to, a way of moving that made him slow down and pay attention. He watched her delicate wrists as she took a sip from the mug.

"Is there anyone who misses you?" he asked.

Janine shook her head. "Not really. My folks died a few years back—cancer, both of them, within six months of each other. No siblings, no kids. My work is my baby. My friends are used to me going on assignment for weeks at a time, so they won't be alarmed just yet."

That wasn't what Fletcher meant, but he couldn't bring himself to ask the question he really wanted to ask: Was there a *man* who missed her? Was there someone special back home?

"Do you miss New York?"

"Manhattan. My offices are within shouting distance of my apartment. Sometimes I think the two are interchangeable."

"I know exactly what you mean."

Janine nodded. "Do you ever miss your work?"

"I miss the fun of it. When I was in college, I would spend days on end just figuring out code. Numbers are fun to me, like blocks to a baby. It holds my attention like little else can."

"What else holds your attention?"

Despite his admonitions to himself to be the perfect gentlemen, Fletcher glanced at Janine's long legs. Her rakish grin said he was caught in the act. He leaned closer to the fire to hide the blush on his face, but now that he had been caught, it was easy to steal another glance.

"The wilderness holds my attention," he said. "Trying to fight Heisenberg."

"Huh?"

"The Heisenberg uncertainty principle. It's a little nugget of quantum physics. It states that simply by observing the world, you influence it. I like trying to influence the world as little as possible."

Janine stared at him as if he had grown two heads.

"What?"

"I'm starting to see the geek inside."

Fletcher laughed. Logs dropped in the fire, sending up a hiss and a shower of embers. They looked at each other in the fire-light until one of them either had to look away, or do something they both might regret.

Fletcher was the one who looked away first.

"Hey," she said.

"What?"

She reached over and took his hand. Her palm was smooth as silk and warm, almost hot, with the steam from the mug of cof-fee. He looked down at their joined hands. As he watched, she laced her fingers between his, their palms pressing hard against each other. His thumb brushed her wrist, and he could feel the heartbeat.

"I'm sorry about you and Amanda," she said. "I don't know what it was like to go through the constant hounding you had to endure, but I do know what it is like to lose someone you love, over circumstances you can't control. I know how it hurts, and I'm sorry it happened to you."

Fletcher nodded, not daring to look up at her. He was afraid of what kind of openness he would see in her eyes, and scared of what would happen if he did. He tried to remind himself that she was a reporter, one of those who had been instrumental in following him and Amanda to get the story for the front page, but he found it difficult to put Janine in that category.

"Thank you," he said, the simplest thing he could think of to say, the only thing that wouldn't spark more conversation. He felt her gaze on him, as obvious as the flickering light from the fireplace. When she sensed nothing more would come, she sighed and looked back at the fire.

But neither of them pulled their hands away.

In the light of day, things seemed a lot less complicated on the romance front, but maybe more complicated in other areas. Fletcher realized this when Janine's litany of frustrated sighs turned into curses. She was tired of being snowed in, angry at the cookstove for something he couldn't guess, and mad as hell at the world.

"Shit!"

The wooden spoon flew across the room. It bounced against the wall of the cabin and landed on the rug in front of the hearth.

Fletcher looked up from the shirt in his hands. He was stitching with a needle and stout thread, mending a tear he had gotten while carrying in an armload of wood. He pulled the needle through and watched as Janine stormed about the kitchen. They had checked off days on the old, faded calendar. Yesterday marked two weeks of being snowed in.

It was the longest two weeks of Fletcher's life, for so many reasons.

"What's wrong with you?"

She whirled to glare at him. In the time since she had fallen from the ravine into his valley, the bruises had healed nicely. She now had only a small spot of darkness at her hairline. The rest of her face was pristine, unlined, and young.

"I'm trapped, that's what's wrong with me. I am *suffocating* in this cabin on this mountain. The whole world is out there but it might as well be another planet. What I wouldn't give to have a working cell phone. Just for five minutes!"

"There's a satellite phone down at the hiking station. I think it works."

"Where's that?"

He carefully made another stitch. They were small, evenly spaced, the work of someone with a lot of patience and an understanding of making things solid. "About ten miles out."

"Then let's go."

"But no vehicle can make it in to us, even if the phone does work," he pointed out.

"What about helicopters?" she asked. "They carry lost hikers out all the time."

"You're not lost, are you?"

That won him another glare.

"We can go to the satellite phone anyway, if you want to try the hike," he said. "You can call out if you want to tell someone where you are, and that you're okay, but nobody will come get us unless it's an absolute emergency."

"This feels like one."

"It's not. We're safe here."

She sank down on the chair and watched Fletcher's hands. Her face was etched with a frown.

"I'm not good company?" Fletcher teased.

Her eyes rose to his. She had a straight-on gaze, the kind of look that made him very conscious of the fact that she wasn't just seeing him, she was probably seeing right through him. She pinned him with that look, made it impossible to turn away.

"On the contrary," she murmured.

They stared at each other for the space of several heartbeats. It was suddenly hard to breathe in the little cabin. He didn't move as she stood up, watched him for a few moments longer, then turned back to the cookstove. The sudden absence of her gaze made him aware of how furiously he was blushing.

Fletcher very deliberately went back to the stitching, but he couldn't stop smiling.

"What the hell is that?" Janine hissed.

Fletcher sat up from his bed on the floor. Janine was already up and standing at the front door. When another *thump* came, she carefully pulled back the curtain and looked out the window.

"It's a bear."

He tossed the covers back and stood up in his long underwear and flannel shirt. He padded across the floor and looked over Janine's shoulder. "A big one, too."

The bear stood on its hind legs on the porch, looking up at the rafters, silhouetted by moonlight. It was very thin after hibernating for months, and now that the slightest bit of warmth was flowing down the mountain, it was not only awake, but ravenous.

The water barrel made a deep *thud* when she knocked it from the corner of the porch with a powerful paw. She sniffed at the door, certain there was something behind it, but not sure what. Fletcher was concerned that she had come so close, especially when there was smoke coming from the chimney and the smell of humans all around.

His boots were right by the door, and he pushed his feet into them. He pulled his gun from behind the door and checked the chamber. Janine put her hand on the barrel and pushed it down toward the floor.

"You can't shoot her! What if she has babies?"

"She probably does."

Fletcher stood at the window and watched. Janine looked like she was ready to kill him instead of the bear, and he wasn't surprised. She hadn't seen one of them close-up, hadn't seen what one could do, especially when it was desperate or sick. Fletcher was pretty sure this bear might be both.

"It's not normal for a bear to be checking out the cabin like this," he said softly. "They are usually more scared of us than we are of them. She's desperate for food or she's sick, which means we are in trouble if she decides to come through that door."

Janine looked at him with wild eyes. "She can't."

As if on cue, the bear leaned against the door. The hinges squealed in protest. The bear stood there for a moment, then walked away down the porch, turning around when she got to the steps, still looking things over. Fletcher put two extra shells in his pocket, just in case. Janine watched but said nothing. He put his hand to his lips, admonishing her to stay quiet, as the bear slammed against the door again, this time hard enough to rattle the pans over the stove.

Silence came after that, but soon they could hear her snuffling breath as she explored the doorway with her nose. Fletcher knew they were in trouble. There was no reason any sane bear would make a point of going after humans, and he *knew* she could smell them. She knew they were there.

The bear roared. The sound rattled through the valleys, bounced from the mountaintop, and made her intentions entirely clear.

He raised the gun and took aim at the door. Janine stood beside him for a moment, but at the next blow from the big animal she moved toward the far side of the cabin, where she could see at an angle through the windowpane.

Fletcher kept the gun trained on the door, even as his mind raced. The responsibility of keeping Janine safe was foremost in his mind. What would she do if the bear got past him? He had a loaded rifle but that wasn't a guarantee. Fletcher had learned to never underestimate the power of a wild animal with a hungry stomach.

Then another sound came from high on the mountain, one that made the bear pause and turn to stare. Fletcher held his breath, hoping he was wrong. He stood his ground and listened as the roar came closer. The bear leaped from the porch, running and bellowing.

Outside, a tree cracked, snapped clear through by the pressure.

Fletcher dropped the gun and grabbed Janine, pushed her to the far corner of the cabin, toward the back door. The whole building began to shake.

Please be coming from the east, he thought. *That's the only chance we've got.*

"What's happening?" Janine screamed into his ear.

His explanation was lost in the unearthly roar. The sound was impossible, filling everything, erasing thought and stealing breath. He wrapped his arms around Janine and hunkered down against the door as the whole cabin creaked. Pans and tins fell from shelves, their noise a mere whisper against the sound from outside. Constant *thuds* came from all sides of the cabin. Snow sifted down through the chimney and the fire went out, leaving them in darkness. Janine clung to him, her breath hard and fast against his neck as he held on tight.

Just as quickly as it had begun, it was over. The pounding stopped. The cabin creaked once more, then seemed to shudder on its foundation as it settled against the weight of the snow.

"Avalanche," Fletcher said into Janine's ear. "That was snow from the top of the mountain."

Fletcher pressed his forehead against her shoulder and took a deep breath. She had no idea how close to death they had come. He was certain the snow was at least to the roofline, if not covering the cabin. The darkness was absolute, and that scared Fletcher more than anything else.

"Stay here," he said. "Don't go anywhere. I can't find you if you do."

He moved away from her. Janine's hands trailed along his arms as he left, and he squeezed one of her hands, telling her silently to trust him. He carefully walked through the cabin, occasionally kicking a pan or a sack of something that had fallen from its nail on the wall. He found the door and opened it, only to be greeted with a wall of snow. He couldn't see it, but he could feel the coldness of it. It cascaded in over his boots. He started to dig with his hands, praying he would find a pocket of air. There was no telling how much snow was out there, and how much of it was sitting right on top of them.

Janine's voice came from right beside his shoulder and scared him half to death. "What about the bear?"

"The snow carried her away. She won't come back."

"How can I help?"

"Start on the back door. Grab a rag, anything to protect your hands."

Janine moved away from him, silent as a mouse. He kept digging, more snow coming in on him, forcing him to step on top of it every few minutes. He was working up a sweat, which meant he was using more oxygen, which might be something they couldn't afford. He picked up the pace, though his shoulders burned and his hands had lost all feeling.

Suddenly Janine shouted from the back of the cabin. "Here!"

Fletcher abandoned his efforts and stumbled toward her voice. Janine grabbed his arm as soon as he was close, and then he realized he could see a sliver of light. She pushed him toward the opening and he took in a deep breath of air, so cold it burned his lungs, so welcome it made his eyes sting.

"Thank God," he said.

Together they dug at the tiny hole, making it bigger with every handful of snow. Finally a huge chunk broke away, and the air rushed in.

Fletcher couldn't feel his hands. He squeezed them into fists. "We've got to clear the chimney. We have to get the fire going again."

"Not yet. Your hands are frozen solid."

She took his hands in hers. Fletcher could hardly feel the warmth of them, and he wondered if that was because she was cold, too, or because he was really that numb. The narrow beam of light through the snow was just enough to see her face. She stared at him with wild, worried eyes as she pulled him closer, pulled his hands up underneath her sweater, and held them against her warm, flat belly. She slid her hands up underneath his chin, giving herself the warmth she needed, too.

Long moments passed as they both struggled to catch their

breath. Suddenly the numbness of his hands turned into a burn-ing, stinging pain—the warmth of Janine's body was working, and the circulation was coming back, blood fighting its way through with tiny pinpricks of pain. He clenched his teeth against it, even as Janine pulled his head down to her shoulder, keeping him close.

"We're going to be all right," she said, her voice entirely calm, as if nothing like an avalanche had happened here. "We're going to be just fine. Stay still, let your hands get warm. We'll start the fire as soon as you can feel again."

Whether she meant it or not, Fletcher read a double meaning in her words. He turned his head and nestled deeper into her shoulder, breathing in the scent of smoke and lye soap and clean clothes, and more than that, the unique smell of a soft, warm woman.

Janine touched his face. Her fingers were warmer now but still colder than they should have been, and the sudden touch made him aware of just how hot his face was, of how hard he had worked to dig a path through the snow. He lifted his head and looked into her eyes.

"Fletcher."

The fear brought on by the bear, the avalanche, the long nights of sleeping alone on the floor while she lay only a few feet away—it all finally came down to one moment, when she said his name in a way she hadn't before. All his careful caution disappeared.

Fletcher wrapped his arms around her.

The touch of her lips heated him all the way through. Weeks of pent-up desire, frustration, and helplessness unleashed when she wrapped her arms around his shoulders and let out a moan of permission. He was aware of her body pressed against his, her breasts rising with each breath, her hands taking fistfuls of his shirt and holding on hard.

"The bed," she murmured. "The quilts. We have to stay warm."

The world of white snow forgotten, Fletcher led her through the darkness to the bed.

It had been a long time since he had been with a woman. He knew all the tricks to make a woman arch and sigh, but it had been so long since he had done any of it, he was afraid he would be too fast to please her. He told her as much, while his hands shook as he undressed her. With every article of clothing that disappeared, they pulled another quilt up, until they were in their own little cocoon of warmth.

He paused when the final piece of clothing was kicked away, and buried his face in her shoulder again, suddenly shy. "I'm not sure . . ."

"You'll do fine," she murmured into his hair. He bent his head to kiss her collarbone. The bruises on her body were long gone, but he touched her gently, as if they were still there. What he couldn't see with his eyes, he traced with his fingers. Janine threw her head back and granted him as much access as he pleased, and Fletcher marveled at that undeniable show of trust. Her body was hot, as if a fire had been lit from within. Her chest rose under his palm as he felt his way, his fingers bumping against one hard nipple before he bent to take it into his mouth.

The moan that ripped from her was enough to make all his

fears vanish. He pulled her closer, working her with his tongue. He slipped his fingertips over the line of her ribs, counting them with a tender touch. When he fought the urge to rush and slide his hand between her thighs, she made the decision for him by grabbing his hand and placing it right over the heat at her center.

"Don't wait," she hissed. "I've been waiting for weeks."

The slow seduction he had planned turned into a raging fire. She arched under him, pulling at his shoulders, the blankets pushed down, the cold air rushing in. Her fingers slipped down his body and he sucked in a breath at the sweet, sudden touch of her soft hand.

"I want to taste you."

Her boldness was shocking and welcome all at once. He laced his fingers through her hair as her mouth sank down on him, tasting him, sucking him in to the hilt. Her breath came hard against his hip as she moaned around him, the sound sending a shiver of desire through him, making him harder than he had ever thought possible. He was quickly crossing the point of no return.

"You have to stop," he said, and she deliberately moved faster, refusing to let him go. He warned her again, and this time she reached up with one hand to press her fingers against his mouth, hushing him while she did whatever she damn well pleased.

He cupped her head in his hands, closed his eyes to the darkness, and let himself go with a long, low groan.

Before he had a chance to catch his breath, she was lying next to him, her body pressed hard against his. She pulled the quilts up higher, covering them again from the cold. "Now that we got that out of the way," she teased, "it's my turn."

He took his time. He started with her ear, with that sweet spot he had contemplated over many long nights in front of the fireplace, the curve where shadows liked to dance. He made her shiver, then worked his way down, kissing the places he wanted most to taste—the inside of her elbow, the bend of her knee, the sweet hollow of her hip. By the time he spread her legs and inhaled her scent, she was fighting for breath.

He touched her deep and shallow, hard and soft, until she arched up to him and offered more. At the first touch of his tongue, she went perfectly still. He soothed her legs with his hands as she rode on the pleasure, her hips rising and falling with his tongue. When he finally sucked her clit into his mouth and slid two fingers into her with one deft thrust, she came with a scream.

He loved that moment, when she lay stunned underneath him and babbled incoherent words that meant he had done all the right things. He moved over her and she welcomed him with open thighs and eager hands. When he pushed into her, she took in a deep breath.

"You're so hot," he murmured in surprise, and she was—hotter than anything he had ever felt. Every stroke sent the flames inside her higher, until they engulfed him, consumed him, and made him call out her name as he erupted with a force that almost knocked him unconscious.

When it was over and he opened his eyes, he was stunned to see a bit of light coming through the hole in the snow, the evidence that the world hadn't really stopped turning, after all.

Then Janine laughed, threw her arms around him and pulled him down to her once more. "Giddyup, cowboy," she laughed. "The ride is just getting good."

Fletcher laughed with her, then set about showing her just how much better the ride could get.

"We've got to stop," he panted. Sunlight was now pouring through the hole in the snow—they had been playing under the quilts for hours. He could hear the constant drip of snow melting down the chimney, and the unmistakable sound of water rushing down the hill from the cabin. When spring came to the mountain, it didn't waste any time. "We've got to dig out around the doors and get up to the roof."

"Later," she murmured against his lips.

"We can still freeze to death."

Janine sighed. "How long will it take to dig out?"

"Half the day, if we're lucky." The last thing he wanted to do was dig out. He wanted to stay right there in bed and explore every inch of her. The cabin was toasty warm—snow was an excellent insulator—but that warmth could become deadly if they didn't have enough fresh air to accompany it.

"Where should we start?" she asked, and it took a moment for him to realize she was talking about digging out of the snow, not about the things they had been doing under the covers.

"There." He pointed to the sunlight, and she turned her face to it. Her lips were swollen with his kisses. Her clothes were long forgotten in a corner of the little cabin. He wanted to see all of her, silhouetted in that mellow sunlight.

"Let's get it done so we can get back to other things," she said, and the promise in her voice was enough to make him drag himself from the warm, comfortable bed and find the shovel.

*　*　*

The snow began to melt outside. They shoveled around the doors and the windows, then Fletcher dug around the chimney, giving them the chance to fire up the stove. Once the flames were raging, the cabin warmed quickly. They did what they had to do, then crawled back in bed.

Water dripped from all corners of the roof, a melody that never stopped, day or night. They ventured from the bed only to stoke the fire or find something to eat. They survived on fresh water from the mountain, potatoes from the bin and the sustenance they drew from each other.

When their bodies were sated for a time, they talked. They discussed everything but the future. Somehow that topic had become taboo, probably because both of them knew the idyllic delight of their cabin hideaway wouldn't last past the early spring. She had a job to go back to, and he had—

Well, what *did* he have? That question kept Fletcher awake at night when she was sleeping beside him, both of them now in the single bed, cuddled under the same quilts. He had no doubt she would go back to her normal, everyday world, the very place he had abandoned.

What would he do?

He could imagine life going on as normal, chopping wood for the wintertime, planting a garden for sustenance, making a trip down to the ranger station once a month or so to pick up supplies and bask in the unusual presence of another human being. He would rock on his porch in the evenings, take long walks in the early morning light, and keep the raccoon company in this great stretch of wilderness.

He would be lonely.

He sat up beside her in bed one morning, soon after the snow had melted enough that the road was passable, and the temperatures were high enough that anyone could make it a reasonable distance without danger. She could go any day now, and he knew it. She hadn't mentioned it yet, but sometimes he saw her gazing off toward the end of the long dirt road, the question in her eyes.

He understood. She wanted to leave, but she didn't want to hurt him.

"Janine?"

She rolled toward him and stretched lazily, smiling up at him, purring like a cat. "Good morning."

Her body pressed against him, warm and cozy, even softer with sleep. He kissed her, a long, lingering kiss. He tried not to think about how many of those he might have left.

"I thought we might go up to the Ranger station today," he said. "Supplies and all that."

She nodded. Her eyes filled with tears. "It's that time, huh?"

Fletcher didn't know what to say, so he didn't say anything at all. He traced the line of her hip with one hand while he tried out different words on his tongue, but none seemed to fit.

Janine abruptly threw the covers back and climbed out of bed. She was naked, warm from sleep, and absolutely stunning. She was also caught in that space between furious anger and breaking down into tears of sadness. Fletcher watched the war in her eyes until it became too painful for him to see, then he looked out the window.

"I know better than to ask if you will come with me," she said. "But you could at least discuss it, Fletcher. It's not like the world is full of pariahs and you're the only one who isn't."

"I never said anything like that."

"Your attitude screams it."

He got up from his side of the bed and stalked to the make-shift closet—a dozen nails on the wall, where he hung the dozen pieces of his meager wardrobe. He yanked a shirt from the nail so hard that the fabric ripped. He put it on anyway, wondering where the sudden anger had come from.

"I don't know if I can go back there, Janine." He buttoned the shirt and stood staring at the wall. "I don't know if I can handle living in that world."

"It's the same world," she argued. "Just different corners of it."

He turned on her, and she shrank back from the fury in his eyes. He grasped at the one thing he knew he could hold between them. "Remember how you wound up here? I'm the hunted, and you're the hunter. Doesn't look so good from my standpoint, sweetheart."

Janine's face went blank. She carefully avoided looking him in the eye as she finished dressing in the far corner of the cabin. She walked slowly to the fireplace and put another log on, pushing it in hard, making the fire rage.

"If I had known . . ."

"If you had known, then what?"

She looked up at Fletcher with wide eyes. Tears spilled over and made silver trails down her face. "I never would have come here."

Fletcher yanked the door open. "Wait!" Janine called, but he didn't hear what she had to say after that. It was lost in the slam of the door and the roaring of his broken heart.

* * *

The walk to the hiking station was made in silence. The phone there actually worked, and the ranger promised to send someone out. They had about thirty minutes before their time together came to an end, but even so, Fletcher couldn't find the heart to say anything to Janine. He couldn't say anything at all.

He felt her watching him, those eyes that saw right through him, and wondered what she was thinking. She sat quietly on the rough-hewn bench outside the station, watching him from under a toboggan that was far too big for her. They listened to the sounds of the mountain, and once watched an eagle arrow through the sky, but when she turned her eyes back in Fletcher's direction, he found something interesting to look at just over the ridge.

When they heard the truck in the distance, Janine spoke in a rush. "I didn't mean what you thought I meant," she said. "If I had known how leaving you would break my heart, I would still have come here. But if I had known I would break yours . . ."

Fletcher looked at her then, and despite all his admonitions to himself, tears sprang into his eyes. They froze on his lashes before he could dash them away.

"I never meant to make you cry," she said.

The pleading in her voice was enough to send him over the emotional ravine he had been fighting so hard all morning. He dropped to his knees in the snow in front of her, held her hands in his and looked up at her, knowing he didn't want to be alone on that mountain anymore, but also knowing he couldn't go back to the world he had already given up for dead.

"I don't know if I can go back," he said slowly, as the truck pulled into view at the top of the lane. "I just don't know, Janine."

"Do you want to be with me?" she asked.

There it was, point-blank, putting him on the spot he had so carefully avoided. Did he want to be with her? Or did he just want to be with somebody? Was it about this woman, or was it about having someone on the mountain with him, to stave off the long and lonely nights?

Asking those questions was nothing more than trying to justify a way out. Fletcher might have been stubborn, but he wasn't the kind to play games with himself.

"Yes."

Janine's eyes flooded with tears. "Then come with me. Come to New York with me."

He shook his head, his heart breaking. "I can't."

"You can. You're saying you won't."

Fletcher tried to push away from her, but she held him tight, not letting him go anywhere. She pulled him closer, and he gave in. His head rested against her belly. He felt her sigh, and shudder, fighting tears. The truck pulled up a few yards away from them, and the driver honked the horn.

"If you don't try," she whispered to Fletcher, "Then you'll never know for sure."

A week later, spring came to the mountain. The trees shook off the last of their snow and blossomed anew. The rivers began to run again, then spilled over their banks. The avalanche was just a distant memory—but Janine's memory was still so fresh, so vivid, sometimes Fletcher reached out in the middle of the night to touch her, only to find she wasn't there.

The hike back to his cabin was hell without her. He had watched her climb into that truck, then had watched as it disappeared over the horizon. He kept standing there, rooted to the spot, listening to the engine until even that vanished. Fletcher sat heavily on the bench at the ranger station as he realized she was gone—really, truly gone. Not one given often to tears, he buried his face in his hands and cried until his body felt hollow.

That week he cleaned up the cabin, airing out every piece of fabric, washing down every wall, cleaning out every nook and cranny until the place smelled just as fresh inside as it was outside. He fed the raccoon when the old boy came around, but the visits were few and far between, which didn't help his loneliness one bit. Fletcher sat in front of the fireplace at night, now with only a small fire to cut the lingering chill, and he stared at the flames, his mind thousands of miles away.

One day, he found Janine's camera. She had lost it in the fall and both of them thought it gone forever under the snow, so neither had thought to search for it. The avalanche had stripped clean the trees at the top of the ravine and carried them down the valley, but somehow the forces of nature had seen fit to leave her camera only a mile or so from where she had dropped it as she fell into his life.

The case was battered and the film inside certainly destroyed by the months of ice, snow, and rain. When he held it in his hands, knowing she was the last one who had touched it, the onslaught of vivid memories stole his breath. He longed for pictures of her, something to look at from time to time, and wondered if she ever looked at pictures of him.

The thought of pictures made him think of the tabloid photographs that were taken of him, back when he was a part of the same world Janine inhabited. Living on the mountain was like living on his own little planet, but Janine had found him. And if she had found him, someone else could, too.

As he turned the camera over in his hands, he wondered what he would do when that happened. Was it best to be on the offensive, or was it best to call the shots himself? And what better reason to head off the inevitable, than to give Janine the chance she had asked him to give?

He took the camera to the house and put it on the kitchen table, where he stared at it while he considered doing the one thing he had sworn he would never do.

Everything in New York City moved fast. The lights, the cars, and the people—it was all a sea of getting somewhere quick. In the middle of it all was a man in the back of a cab, fresh off the plane, scared to death of what he was doing there, but certain he had no other choice.

"Manhattan," Fletcher said to the cabbie.

When Janine saw him standing at her office door, her eyes widened with shock. Her face went pale, and her hands began to tremble. She looked different in colorful clothes, with her long brown hair pulled back into a ponytail, color on her cheeks and soft pink lipstick on her mouth.

Then she smiled, and it transformed her into the Janine he knew.

"You're here," she said, disbelief radiating from every inch of her.

"You said I would never know until I tried," Fletcher said. "Can I still try?"

The tears in her eyes spilled over as she nodded, too overcome to speak. Fletcher strode behind her desk and wrapped his arms around her, lifting her off the ground. Her high heels dropped to the floor as he kissed her. Coworkers gathered around the door, looking in at this strange man with Janine, the one who had made her cry and laugh at the same time. Fletcher ignored them, caring for nothing but this woman in his arms, the one he had missed so much, it had damn near driven him crazy.

"You wanted a story," he whispered into her ear. "You got me instead."

Janine held on as if she would never let go. Outside her big window several stories up, the sun was setting. For the first time in years, Fletcher watched the final rays burst over something other than his mountaintop and marveled at how pretty it was. He cradled the woman he loved in his arms and smiled over her shoulder at the glorious Manhattan skyline.

 GWEN MASTERS writes all the time: in her sleep, in the car, even in church. Hundreds of her stories have appeared in dozens of places, both in print and online. Her latest novel, *One Breath at a Time*, hit shelves in the spring of 2008. Gwen hides away in a sleepy little town, writing novels and working on the century-old home she shares with her journalist husband. For more information on Gwen and her works, please visit her website: www.gwenmasters.net.

It's Not the Weather

by Alison Tyler

Winter

"I hate this," Roger groaned. "I fucking hate this miserable fucking weather."

I glanced outside the floor-to-ceiling windows of my living room, taking in the bright sunflower sun, crisp Crayola-blue sky. Even better, there were only two days left before the twenty-fifth. We were destined to have sunshine on Christmas day. From the international weather report, ever-present on Roger's open laptop, I could see that the East Coast was socked in with the type of storm we won't have unless hell literally freezes over. California looked like the place to be.

But not to Roger.

"Winter is supposed to mean snowdrifts and sleigh rides. Caroling and Christmas shopping." He watched with extreme distaste as I dropped my bubble-gum pink towel and slid into my favorite winter bikini—the emerald one with the scarlet straps. Carefully, I tied two tight bows at the hips, then slipped into my jade-colored knee-high socks. I perched on the edge of the sofa to slide on my rollerblades, before neatly doing up the licorice-red laces. Roger couldn't accuse me of not being into the holiday spirit.

"Don't you miss the snow?" he asked, staring as I adjusted my perky little red-and-white hat. I stood and caught a glimpse of my reflection in mirror over the mantel—*Santa, eat your heart out*, I thought as I tilted the cap down in the front, then adjusted my dark ponytail to hang low down my back.

"I've never lived in snow," I reminded him. There were two stockings pinned to the mantel, over a bricked-in fireplace that would never sport flame.

"But you realize that winter's *supposed* to be cold, right? You're a weather girl, after all."

"*Meteorologist,*" I corrected him, knowing already from our month together that there was zero sense in arguing when he was in this sort of a mood. "I'm going Rollerblading. We can find a snowdrift to fuck in later."

Roger didn't laugh.

I stared out the window while he continued to mourn the weather on the computer screen. When you're from Southern California, "cold" is anything under 78 degrees. Even though I had the day off, I knew the weather report for the following twenty-four hours. Today, the temperatures were supposed to soar to the mid–90s, and the beach was certain to be beautiful, like almost every day of the year.

"I'll be miserable with you later," I assured Roger, planting a kiss on his forehead in my attempt to be a properly sympathetic girlfriend. "I promise."

In a San Francisco—like fog, Roger returned to his bong and my sofa bed. He had brought out a thick velvety comforter with a frolicking red reindeer pattern leaping against a glistening green background. I watched skeptically as he tried to enjoy wrapping himself up in the fuzzy blanket, but the room was far too hot for the wintry weight. Too hot for anything but bare-naked skin and sun-drenched skies. For melting cherry-flavored Popsicles on each other's body and licking along the trail of icy red water. For taking cold showers together, pressing up against the slick colored tiles.

One look at me in my bikini, and most men would have tossed me onto the mattress, undoing the sexy little ties at my hips with their teeth. But Roger wasn't like most men. Was that what attracted me to him? I hadn't decided yet.

I blew him one last kiss and sailed out the door, bikini strings flying behind me like the kite tails out in the clear Santa Monica sky. As I skated, I worried about my new man. We'd met four weeks earlier at a premier party for his sitcom, a laugh-a-minute farce called *Wish You Were Beautiful*. I'd been hired early on as a consultant because the main character was a weather girl— "meteorologist," I'd told the creators, although they'd ignored that note. "*Weather girl* sounds so much sexier," they'd said. Roger had been imported from New York at the tail end of the project as a pinch-hitting writer, and he'd charmed me throughout the night with quips.

"I don't have to wish *you* were beautiful," he'd said over drinks.

"And I don't have to wish you were here," I'd teased right back.

There'd been an ice fountain spouting champagne and a clear moonlight sky, perfect for outdoor kissing. Roger had admired all the right things—my lips, my eyes, my laughter—while his hands had wandered ever so cautiously down to my ass as we danced.

When the pilot was picked up, Roger had been hired full-time. And our little fling had turned real, as *Velveteen Rabbit* real as cute meets like that can be in the make-believe world of Los Angeles.

But now, thirty days in, the mood was changing, if not the weather. Roger's attitude seemed frostbitten as he huddled over his laptop, shades drawn against the sunlight whenever I wasn't there to fling up the blinds, dark clothes matching his scowl. The closer we got to Christmas, the bleaker the forecast of his emotions.

I rolled out of the apartment complex toward the pedestrian path, my skates sliding on the smooth concrete surface glistening with silver sparkles like crushed diamonds. When I rounded the bend, I caught my first panoramic shot of the beach. There was nary a snowdrift in sight. Instead, the gold-sanded beach glowed with festive parasols and the world's most attractive people. Los Angeles attracts beauty like a magnet. That was an integral part of the sitcom Roger was writing. The weather girl in the story was a beauty who had fallen for an average Joe of a guy. The conceit of the sitcom was that this perky little meteorologist actually *could* change the weather, as if in a modern-day version of *Bewitched*.

I wished this was magic I could perform, as well.

My new beau had grown up back East, with Technicolor foliage and honest-to-goodness seasons. I'd heard him wax poetic about the way trees actually changed colors, heard him describe the seductive crackle of fallen leaves under his boot heels, the need for different clothes throughout the year. Roger seemed to feel that one shouldn't enjoy picture-perfect weather without first paying the price, as if so many uninterrupted days of sunshine in a row was something obscene.

"You can't wear a bathing suit in December in New York City," he'd said solemnly the night before as I'd paraded around in my brand-new two-piece from Powder Puff Pin-Ups, a blue bikini adorned with rhinestone-studded snowflakes. "You need scarves and hats, overcoats and earflaps."

Earflaps. I'd shuddered.

"At home, I have three winter coats in various thicknesses—mild, snowstorm, and blizzard—along with stripy scarves, gloves, galoshes . . ." Roger had spoken the words with pride, like a Boy Scout describing hard-earned badges.

The truth was that although I tried dutifully to understand Roger's dismay, I loved my closet—filled with tiny little sundresses, stiletto sandals, and a different bathing suit for every day of the week. My work outfits were admittedly a bit more subdued—mostly pastel-hued skirt suits—but off camera, my clothes were my own. While Roger described his jackets in terms of the type of storm-protection each one offered, my clothing could mostly be divided by levels of transparency—sheer, diaphanous, translucent. I owned tiny crocheted sweaters in ice cream colors to wear whenever a chill crept in.

"Chill," Roger had said with scorn. "Try a windchill factor of negative forty. Jesus, Michelle, it's not even *positive* forty here. It's sixty-nine. You can't be cold."

"Sixty-nine," I'd said, grinning, "the perfect temperature for fucking."

But Roger had remained in his unhappy place, flicking from one weather report to the next, and I'd had to warm up myself. Retreating to the bedroom, I'd imagined that I was a snow bunny, that Roger was watching me make snow angels, that he fucked me in that sea of powdery pearlescent whiteness. The snow was sublime in my daydream, glittering like shaved glass, soft as eiderdown. And then there was me . . . Naked? No.

All Roger's talk about weather gear had put a momentary crimp on my fantasy. Then my mind conjured up a comely lilac snowsuit, with a zipper that ran from neck to the split between my legs. The teeth of the zipper were a dark fuchsia, matching the panties I had on beneath. Hot pink against my tanned skin—a delicious contrast.

Behind my shut lids, I'd imagined Roger undoing the zipper with his teeth, slowly revealing my skin inch by inch, his scruffy five o'clock shadow scraping dangerously against my soft flesh. Then he spread open the suit and kissed my breasts, licked my nipples until they stood up hard as gumdrops.

I didn't stop to worry why the Roger in my fantasy looked so much like Jeremiah Cooper, the handsome actor-slash-bartender who worked at 5th Avenue, my favorite Santa Monica bar. At least, I didn't worry at first. I simply accepted the fact that tall, green-eyed Jeremiah was serving me a round of pleasure the same careful way he served me and my best friend drinks every Friday night. His long wheat-blond hair felt silk-soft against my thighs. His strong fingers danced over my clit in a way that brought an instant moan to my lips.

God, he was good.

Jeremiah had on snow gear of his own, a pair of those sexy oatmeal-colored long johns that look delicious on trim, hard bodies, and mirrored wraparound shades to show me my own reflection. Watching my lips part, my eyes widen, turned me on in my daydream almost as much as the imaginary feel of Jeremiah's body against mine. But as the tempo speeded up, my own fingers working through my satiny bikini panties, I tried to push his face away, replacing Jeremiah's long blond mane with Roger's short brown curls, transforming Jeremiah's light green eyes into Roger's dark blue ones, exchanging Jeremiah's strong body with . . .

No, it wouldn't hurt to keep Jeremiah's body for the little jill-off session, would it? That didn't make me too superficial, did it?

In my dreamworld, I imagined Roger fucking me hard, driving into me, the way he had when we'd first gotten together. Our first night had been the fabric of dreams, with Roger driving me in his rented convertible up to the Hills. We had made love outdoors, staring down at the flickering lights of Hollywood. I hadn't been introduced his distaste for the weather then, had admired his writing, devoured his uncanny comedic beats. He'd looked East Coast intellectual, which has always been exotic to me, since I'd grown up surrounded by surfer boy sloths. But now, he'd taken that look to the extreme—becoming pale-skinned and hollow-eyed, boycotting the sunlight as if he might melt.

"Sitcom writers don't have to be pretty," he liked to say, apparently striving to prove his point.

"Neither do weather girls," I always shot back, then laughed because we both knew that wasn't true.

My cell phone rang—"Cold as Ice." I'd programmed the song to make Roger happy, to show him we were in the season together. Wistfully, I slowed to a gentle roll, then pulled the tiny device from the strap on my skate and looked at the number, hoping Roger had shaken off his storm clouds, that he was wooing me back for an afternoon romp in the middle of the living room. But it was my best friend, Carolyn.

"Roger still in a funk?" she asked.

I zigzagged to avoid some tourists—clearly out-of-towners because of the unattractive zinc oxide each one sported. "It's sweet that he's so emotional, right?"

"If I hear those carols again when I come over—'Let It Snow.' 'White Christmas.' 'Winter Wonderland,' someone's going to get a jingle bell shoved up his—"

"I've dated worse," I reminded her, thinking about my recent string of losers: the high-rolling gambler who'd made a bet with himself that he could fuck my last roommate. He'd won the bet and lost me. Or the yoga instructor who could bend himself into all sorts of erotic difficult-to-master shapes, but didn't want to screw me because it would mess with his *chi*. "He's simply one of those people who's affected by the weather," I said into Carolyn's meaningful radio silence.

"It's not the weather that's the problem," Carolyn said emphatically before ending the call.

I knew she thought I should cut my losses and move on. But I'd moved on quickly my whole life, my relationship history a colorful blur like a ride on a whirligig at an amusement park. I'd sworn after my last devastating break-up that I'd give my next relationship a chance. Twelve months to succeed or fail. With 100 pecent of my effort, windchill factor or no.

As I rounded the loop and turned back toward home, I developed a new idea. Perhaps if I could make Roger see how lovely a sun-drenched winter could be, I'd be able convert him. Maybe he could turn his back on his beloved East Coast, become an expatriate, like Hemingway in the Paris of the 1920s. Only instead of sitting in precious French cafés smoking Gitanes and drinking absinthe, he would grow his hair long, buy some board shorts, wear a Sex-Wax T-shirt

I cruised into the apartment like hell on wheels.

"Fuck me on my blades," I begged. "Pretend you're doing Mrs. Claus, if that will help you any." But Roger didn't even glance my way. He was staring fixedly at a movie on his computer.

"Come on, Rog," I urged. "You can spin me any way you want. You can do me up against the window, and let people watch. All you have to do is pull the ties on my bikini, and I'll be naked."

No response.

When I got closer, I saw that he was watching *Alive*, watching with a look of utter dreaminess, as if this were a travel infomercial for Aspen rather than a tragic tale of cannibalism in the Andes. Peeking over his shoulder, I followed along with him for a moment, and a real shiver worked it's way down my spine. Roger didn't notice. He seemed totally mesmerized by the scenario.

"Look," he said softly. "Look at all that snow."

* * *

"What is it about the winter?" I asked Roger the next day.

"Women are all dressed up. You don't know what they look like underneath. Here in L.A., it's like a skin parade twenty-four-hours a day. There's no mystery. No wishful thinking about spring when the short skirts come out, when the girls strip off those outer layers and let their real selves show through."

Wow. Here was the first man I'd ever met who didn't like women displaying their bodies. He was unique. That's what I told myself. He was special.

"There's no cuddling by the fire. No hot chocolate or hot toddies. No chestnuts, Shelly. There's no fucking chestnuts." His deep blue eyes pleaded with me to understand.

So I tried again. I borrowed winter gear from Carolyn, who likes to go to cold places as much as I like to stay in warm ones. I dressed myself up in layers upon layers, ending with a purple-and-orange stripy scarf and a hat with earflaps. I checked myself from all angles. I've dated my fill of kinky players in the past, but this was a whole new appearance for me. I no longer looked like Michelle. I looked like the Michelin Man.

I put the finishing touches on the apartment and waited for Roger to arrive. While I stood there, flushed all over, the sweat pooling at the base of my spine, I thought about what would happen when Roger arrived: I would open the door. Roger would see me all bundled up. He would undress me slowly, carefully, unzipping my down jacket, unwrapping the scarf from around my neck, pulling the turtleneck over my head, removing the heavy outerwear until he discovered the cotton-candy pink bikini beneath all of that wool. That was my way of remaining true to myself—the bathing suit under the winter gear, like a pearl inside a Gore-Tex-wrapped oyster.

The thought got me wet. Did Roger have a point? Maybe L.A. women *are* too loose with their bodies. Maybe mystery *was* the way to go. After all of those years of draping myself in diaphanous outfits, perhaps what I ought to have been doing is dressing more conservatively, so that my admirers might ogle me in opaque, fantasizing about the slow striptease reveal.

Burning up with heat, I jumped at the sound of Roger's fist knocking on the door. I whipped open the front door and stood before him.

"Michelle?" he seemed confused.

"I did what you said." I grinned, hoping I looked seductive and not like a bright blue marshmallow.

Roger blinked. Then he sneezed.

"I know that neither of us can take time off to go East," I rushed on as Roger continued to stare at me, apparently dumbfounded. "So I brought the snow to us."

"That's *not* snow!" he said, growing visibly more alarmed by the second.

"Well, I couldn't actually get snow," I explained as patiently as possible. "Or make it snow," I added, hoping he'd remember I wasn't the magical character in his sitcom. "So I used feathers."

"I'm allergic, Michelle," he was backing out of the apartment as he spoke.

"I'm sorry," I squeaked as he left, his blue eyes streaming. "I had no idea."

"Call me when it's clean," he yelled from down the hall.

I sprinted after him, moving as fast as I could all bundled

up like that. How did people walk in snow clothes? I could sail along blithely on my blades, but this was different. Still, I managed to catch up with Roger at the front door of the apartment building. He was sneezing uncontrollably now, and he seemed to be trying to find his car by the sound of his alarm beeper, pressing his thumb on the round button on his key ring and pointing randomly out at the street.

"It's not the same when it's a hundred degrees outside," he said, eyes watering.

Dejectedly, I reached into my pocket and handed him the tin of chestnuts, and he gave me a sad little half-smile through weepy eyes and said, "Not water chestnuts, Shelly. Not water chestnuts."

Back in my apartment, I spent fifteen minutes getting my own self out of the silly outfit before calling Carolyn. This wasn't how my dream date was supposed to end. My buddy, who had loaned me the gear without questions, now seemed filled to the brim with them.

"Explain it again, Michelle. What did you do?"

"I wanted to be like the queen in that fable who tucked a tiny pea under twenty tall mattresses. I hid my body beneath all these layers of clothes. All he had to do was peel me."

"You're a woman," Carolyn interrupted. "Not a banana."

"I hate winter," I added despondently, planning on spending the rest of the evening vacuuming my pad. But Carolyn insisted I meet her for an emergency drink at 5th Avenue. Feathers or frilly cocktails? That was an easy decision.

"Why would you go to all that trouble?" Carolyn wanted to know.

"I thought maybe he had that type of disease people get in Alaska, where the sun doesn't come up for six months and they have to wear those hats with little lamps on their heads."

"Yeah, *that's* his problem," Carolyn snorted into her empty glass.

"No, I think Roger has the reverse," I told Carolyn. "He needs a hat that snows."

"He needs a kick in the—"

"Seriously," I interrupted her.

"I'm *being* serious," she countered quickly as Jeremiah brought over our second round of drinks, Flaming Flamingos made pink by raspberry vodka and a hint of cranberry juice. I blushed when I saw him, remembering the clinch I'd had in my fantasy—Jeremiah starring as the sexy snowboard instructor, and me, his own personal snow bunny. It had seemed so dirty that he'd left his shades on the whole time, so that I watched myself in the mirrored reflection as the pleasure built. Now, I shifted on the round leather seat as I recalled how he'd unzipped my pale purple snowsuit, how he'd flipped me over and fucked me doggy-style against a snowdrift that would never, ever melt.

My breath caught when Jeremiah leaned over the bar and plucked a wayward feather from my long dark fringe. Was it my imagination, or had he just programmed the Terry Jacks's ballad "Seasons in the Sun" on the jukebox?

"Roger's miserable," I told Carolyn, trying to push thoughts of Jeremiah from my mind. "He can't work. Can hardly get out of bed. Can't do anything but moan."

"He's a schmuck," Carolyn insisted. "Ditch the dude and move on."

But I didn't. I couldn't. I loved him.

While I sipped my second drink, I thought about the way he'd looked at me in the moonlight at the premier. About the way he'd kissed my hand and held me close while we'd danced.

"He'll be better in the spring," I told Carolyn, certain.

"Only if he's a groundhog."

Spring

California is breathtaking in the springtime. To everyone, that is, but Roger.

"In New York, it's raining," I told him. I'm the weather girl on channel 23. I had my facts straight. I'd been waiting impatiently for today to arrive. March twentieth. Spring equinox. No more would I hear about the wonder of snowbanks, the sweet smell of roasted chestnuts. Plus, I had a secret weapon with me, spring in a bag, and I couldn't wait for Roger to stop working and come play with me.

"I'd be at Tony's Coffee Shop, writing in the back booth, listening to the rain."

"But it's gorgeous outside," I said, "just look. And it rains in L.A. sometimes, too. Maybe you're simply homesick. Have you ever thought that? Maybe it's not the weather."

Roger shrugged and went back to his laptop. He was working on a new episode. I wondered how someone so miserable in real life could be so funny on paper. I stared at his serious face, at the way he looked pinched when he focused, and then I peered at his screen. Had I just caught sight of the word *feathers*? Was Roger using our relationship as fodder for his sitcom?

He blocked the screen with his hand, gave me an annoyed grimace, and then waited for me to move aside before he continued typing. Morosely, I headed back to his bedroom with the satchel still unopened in my hand. There were rose petals in the large paper bag. Thousands upon thousands of rose petals. I'd spent the whole morning picking them carefully off the green stems, and I had the thorn marks on my thumbs to prove it. The idea had been building in my head for weeks, a way to kick-start our relationship, coinciding with a way to celebrate the official first day of spring. I hadn't stopped to consider that Roger might not like California in March any more than he had in December.

Now, I would be celebrating without Roger. I emptied the bag out on the bed and stared at the mounds of individual petals. I smoothed some out with my palm. They felt so light beneath my skin. Like silk rather than plant. Without thinking, I pulled off my tiny sweater, then drew my semisheer sundress over my head. My panties were the same hue as the scarlet petals. I'd chosen them on purpose, wanting to compliment the flowers rather than clash, and on a whim, I decided to leave them on.

Gingerly, I climbed on top of the mattress, but I didn't call out to Roger. Instead, I imagined Jeremiah walking in, finding me, kissing me from my lips to my toes. He had full lips; I'd noticed that each time he greeted us at 5th Avenue. He sometimes seemed to be lost in thought when I walked through the front door, and he'd bite his bottom lip for a moment before saying hello.

God, that was sweet, I always thought. That little-boy-lost expression. It made me want to find him, or help him find his way home. And by "home," I meant the split between my legs.

Oh, Jeremiah, I thought as I stroked myself through my satin panties. *Put down the cocktail shaker and get over here.* I had the distinct feeling that he wouldn't push me away if I snuggled against his chest, that he would admire my bikini-clad body if I Rollerbladed into his arms.

The flowers caressed me, light as fairy wings. My fingertips pressed more firmly to my panty-clad clit. When playing solo, I've always loved to start by stroking myself through a barrier, that sensation of almost, but not quite, touching. Now, I worked slowly, hearing the *tip-tap* of Roger's fingers on the keyboard in the other room, but seeing Jeremiah in my head the whole time.

Around and around my fingertips skated, making daring little diamonds, sweet circles, stretched-out ovals, exactly the way I like. Pleasure burst through me, until I was breathless, not caring so much about being quiet. Not worrying whether Roger heard me or not. I rolled on the mattress, my body releasing the scent of so many roses into the air. I thought for one last moment of beckoning Roger, of having him find me like this—spread out on the blanket, roses surrounding me, my cheeks as pink as the petals. But Jeremiah winked at me in my fantasy, and I closed my eyes and let myself go.

Carolyn had said that Jeremiah was my own form of light-hat therapy. She claimed that if I thought Roger needed to wear a snow hat, then I should try to wear Jeremiah. "He'd look good on you," she assured me.

I had to admit, he was appealing. That boyish grin. Those great green eyes. The way he always had to push his hair off his forehead with an impatient flick. I wanted to push the hair away for him, with my lips. I wanted to sit on the top of the bar and have him make a drink out of me.

But I'd done the bartender-cum-actor before, as well as the waiter-cum-actor, grocer-cum-actor, Porsche-salesman-cum-actor I knew that type of relationship tended to expire before last call (or after the last "cum"). I still had hopes of making things work with Roger. "Relationships take effort," I told Carolyn piously.

"I think Jeremiah would go down easy," she countered.

He did in my fantasy. Spring showers raining down on us. The two of us clinched on a bed of petals. His strong, hard body against mine. I shut my eyes tighter, breathed in the perfume of the roses, kicked off my panties, then spread my own petal lips and danced my fingertips ever more powerfully over my clit. There was no pushing Jeremiah out of this fantasy. He fit right in.

His body pulsed between my legs, letting me feel his cock, dipping in once, just to show me how wet I was, then deeper, to show me how hard *he* was. He pushed forward and stayed, rocking his hips slightly to let me feel those secret places inside me come magically to life. I moaned, then realized I'd made the noise aloud. Had Roger heard me? I paused, listening, caught the sound of a chuckle from the living room.

Quickly, I rolled over, pressing my fingers deep inside my pussy now, fucking myself fiercely as I crushed those vibrant red petals, coming as I heard Roger muttering his own dialogue.

"Not *water* chestnuts, Weather Girl," I heard him say.

Summer

"Summer's muggy in New York," I reminded Roger. "I called your mother. She said if she could be anywhere in the world, she'd be here, right by the beach, enjoying the non-muggy weather."

"Summer is Coney Island," he got a glazed look in his eyes.

"We've got the pier."

"It's not the same."

It was becoming more difficult now for me to remember exactly why I'd liked Roger in the first place. He had made me laugh. He had called me beautiful. We'd shared one of those perfect meets at a premier, where the stars shone not only over head, but all around us. When I concentrated hard enough, I could see the way he'd dazzled me. Our first month together had been bliss. But the image was growing faded at the edges, like a vintage postcard kept too long in a top dresser drawer. The edges bent. The paper brittle.

"I live right near the beach," I reminded him, pointing out the window. We could hear the waves crashing against the sand. The surf was up. But not for Roger.

"It's on the wrong coast."

"Wrong coast," Carolyn echoed with distaste. "What's *that* supposed to mean, Shelly? Like you're going to bring the Atlantic Ocean to him? He really *does* think you're the character in his stupid little sitcom, doesn't he? He thinks you're Weather Girl. 'If you don't like the weather, change it.' Right? Isn't that the tagline?"

Carolyn was too serious to appreciate sitcoms.

"He's an artist," I told her, groping uselessly for another excuse. "He feels things other people don't."

My best friend shut her coffee-brown eyes, clearly trying to focus on my words. I could tell I was reaching her. If only I could reach Roger. This is what I thought as I made my way to the ladies' room. Jeremiah was in the hallway, heading toward me. He had a carton of liquor bottles in his arms, and I had to flatten myself against the wall to let him squeeze by. Was it my imagination, or did he press himself closer to me than he needed to? I sucked in my breath as he moved by, becoming as lean as possible, and winning the spice of his skin, the fresh mowed-lawn scent of his hair. My willpower nearly evaporated when he gave me his trademark wink. What I wanted to do was knock that box from his arms, replace those bottles of Cointreau and Amaretto with something far more decadent: me.

But I'd promised myself to be good. To behave. In the ladies', I splashed cool water on my cheeks and tried to remember every nice thing Roger had ever said to me. When I sat back on my stool, Carolyn looked meaningfully at Jeremiah, and then back at me.

"It's not the weather," she said, and I sighed and shook my head.

"Do you remember Kai?" I urged, the man who hadn't thought fucking strippers was cheating. "Do you remember Gerald?" a dog walker who had used our bedroom as his puppies' own personal lavatory. "So Roger is a bit weather-sensitive. It's perfectly reasonable for him to be with me, isn't it?"

Carolyn repeated her mantra, dolefully, singing along with the Bob Dylan song Jeremiah had programmed on the jukebox.

"You don't need a weatherman, Michelle, to know which way the wind blows."

Fall

"You *have* to like the fall," I insisted; I was getting desperate. We'd been together nine months now. I only had three more to convince Roger not only to love me, but to love lush, green California.

"The trees ought to be gold," he said, and turned away. *Autumn in New York* was on. He sighed meaningfully as the leaves in the trees fluttered down to earth. I stared at the screen without seeing the picture.

I had an image, or really a fantasy. One more Jeremiah fantasy in a long list of favorites. Fall to me meant candles. And candles meant hot wax. Wax that might spill slowly over the lip of the ivory candle to create pretty patterns on my skin.

"*Oooh,* I like that," Carolyn had said when I'd told her. "That's kinky."

I didn't confess to Carolyn that in my fantasy, our favorite bartender was pouring the wax, tipping the candle and watching me flinch at the instant pain and pleasure that would follow. I could wear a bikini, I thought, and Jeremiah wouldn't mind. He wouldn't say that you couldn't wear a bikini in New York in the fall. He'd said, "Bad girl, wearing a bikini to Happy Hour. Get over my lap so I can spank you."

The thought was difficult for me to push away. Whenever I passed a store with candles in the window, I thought of what it would feel like to have the wax on my skin. Whenever I saw Jeremiah, I wanted to ask him if he'd ever played with hot wax. Wanted to see if there would be shock in his green eyes, or interest. It took every bit of strength that I had not to give in, not to break up with Roger and throw myself in front of Jeremiah. But I've got willpower. And I used every last drop preparing for my biggest effort ever.

"I'm bringing fall to Roger," I gushed to Carolyn.

"Why bother?" Turned out that she'd liked my candle fantasy only because she'd thought I was going to pour hot wax on Roger. The thought of my beau in pain gave her intense pleasure. "I've never seen you spend so much energy on one man before," Carolyn said. "And he's not even that handsome." She looked meaningfully over at Jeremiah. "I mean, he doesn't hold a candle to Jeremiah."

Candles. She had to say candles. I shut my eyes for a moment and swallowed hard. How would that wax feel? Would I be able to stand the sensation without crying out? Maybe crying out would be the best part. I thought of the fat candle flame dipping low. I thought of Jeremiah telling me that if I didn't hold still he would have to tie me down.

"Looks aren't that important to me," I said finally, admiring Jeremiah's body in that tight-fitting ocean-blue T-shirt, in spite of myself. When he bent over to get something from a low shelf, I had to suck in my breath. "Roger's got brains."

"But they're all in his ass," Carolyn sniffed, as I savored Jeremiah's sweet rear in his form-fitting Levis. "He doesn't appreciate you, Michelle. Remember the feathers?" Carolyn demanded.

"This is different. I've got leaves. Autumn leaves in different colors."

"You imported leaves?"

"I cut them from paper."

"How many?"

I didn't want to tell her. It had taken me weeks. Sitting in front of the TV late at night, watching reality shows while I traced and cut colored-paper leaves to spread around our room. This was my penance for fantasizing about Jeremiah. Each paper leaf was a way to show Roger that my heart was all his own.

I'd bought woodsy-scented candles to light around the room. I'd bought satin sheets that were the brilliant hue of gold-flecked autumn leaves. My new comforter had maple leaves stamped all over it. We would make love in this fantasy fall, and Roger would see, he would finally see how beautiful California could be.

"California?" Carolyn asked. "Why do you want him to love California? It's like you're applying for a job with the tourist board of Southern Cal."

"I want him to love me *and* California," I shrugged. "We sort of go together."

I didn't confess the most important part. Roger would look into my eyes and see everything that I wanted him to do to me. He would touch me softly through my panties before slipping them down my thighs. He would press his lips to my naked split and drink from me. He would take over from Jeremiah in my fantasies, pushing the bartender-cum-actor back behind the counter where he belonged.

Guilt had made me giddy.

Unable to stop myself from running with a theme, I bought a coppery-colored negligee. I wore stockings that had gold fibers woven through the sinuous sheer fabric. And I lit every single candle I owned, placing them strategically around the room— on windowsills, coffee table, shelves, the floor.

Roger arrived a little past nine, in his normal dour mood. He tossed his flannel shirt onto the sofa. "I heard *Sweet November* is on," he said, not sparing me a glance.

Was it my imagination, or did Roger have rancid taste in movies?

"This way," I instructed, beckoning him.

He clicked the remote, but nothing happened. I'd thought ahead and removed the batteries. "Pretend it's a power outage," I told him. "Like the ones when you were little, when the wind blew down a line. Pretend we lit the candles because there weren't any lights."

Roger sniffed. "What's that smell?"

"I baked an apple pie," I told him, continuing to lead him down the hall to the bedroom. He seemed amiable for once, and interested, but he was still sniffing.

When we got to the bedroom, he reacted immediately, but not exactly as I'd hoped. "You set the place on fire!"

I stamped out the solitary smoldering leaf. "It got too close to the candles, I guess." I was hoping he would be able to look beyond, to see the rest of what I'd done, but Roger appeared incensed at my carelessness rather than wooed by my creativity. I couldn't give up, though, and so I snuggled against him.

"I'm not in the mood for sex, Shelly," he said with a tone of bleak finality in his voice. "We could have gone up in flames."

"I'd rather have you light my fire," I murmured, pointing to the flat-screen TV on the wall. I'd bought a special disc featuring an ever-burning fire in a marble fireplace, but Roger was gone, back to watch movies on his computer—fall-flavored fiction, while I was left to sweep up the leaves.

Sighing, I clicked the remote, changing the fire on the flat-screen TV to a tropical fish scene. I wondered what Jeremiah Cooper looked like in a bathing suit.

Winter

Then it was winter. Again. But this winter brought me a brand-new misery of my own. And the misery came directly from the weather. I'd finally taken Carolyn's advice and broken up with Roger. But because everything in L.A. reminded me of him and my attempts to turn him into a converted Californian, I'd applied for a new job in New York. I was weather girl on a cable station, an upgrade from my previous early-morning position, but a downgrade in the lifestyle I had become accustomed to.

Snow had always looked so postcard pretty to me. Now that I had to slush through the white wetness, I saw the dirt, the grit, the way city snow only remained pure for an hour or two before real life came in and destroyed the crisp white blanket.

Soot. Slush. Salt. Sand.

My expensive leather boots were trashed the very first day, my jackets soiled, and my bikinis languished—untouchable. Unworn. "You can't wear a bathing suit in New York in December," Roger had told me, and he'd been right.

How had this happened? I had wound up in Roger's Winter Wonderland, without Roger. He was still hating life in Southern California, without me. Neither one of us could change the weather. His sitcom had been canceled, but he'd landed another gig, had taken over the lease on my apartment by the beach. He was in my own paradise, and I was trapped in the snow.

And was that *sand* in the hall? Had some imbecile dragged in sand off the street?

I was thinking dark storm-cloud thoughts like these when I entered the hallway of my building, hat still pulled down nearly to my chin, striped muffler wrapped past my nose, gloves on, trench coat, no skin showing. I felt as if I were being smothered by my own clothes, and I could never get rid of the chill in my bones, no matter how many layers I piled on. Miserably, I worked my key in the hole, stamping my feet to get warm, surprised when the door opened from within.

Fear sprang inside of me. I'd been taught never to enter an apartment with the door opened. But it had been locked seconds before. Someone had opened the door from inside. Confusion took over, and I blinked rapidly, not sure that what I was seeing wasn't some sort of mirage. Because there in my living room stood Jeremiah Cooper.

In a Speedo.

The furniture—what little I'd had time to buy—had disappeared. The whole floor was covered in pure white, ultrafine powdery sand. Heaters stood glowing red in every corner, and a beautiful aqua terry-cloth bath sheet was spread under a lovely paper parasol. One wall had been covered in a photo mural of the Santa Monica Pier—carousel and all—sunset breaking over the water.

I blinked and looked at Jeremiah, in his neon-blue flip-flops, pushing Wayfarers to the top of his head, long blond hair spilling to his broad shoulders, tan as gingerbread all over. A chill ran down my spine.

Was I dreaming? I had to be. Maybe I'd slipped on the ice and hit my head. Maybe I'd wake up under a snowdrift and have to claw my way to the surface, creating my very own scene from *Alive*.

"Are you cold?"

I shook my head. "No," I said, realizing suddenly as I said the word that I was the opposite. "I'm hot." I started to peel off my clothes, the scarf, hat, gloves. Next came the Michelin Man–style jacket, so puffy I felt as if I couldn't breathe right when I was zipped into it. My mind was trying desperately to make sense of the nonsensical scene, even as I felt the warmth of the heaters surround me. "How did you . . . ?" I started, working on my sweater, then turtleneck. "I mean, how could you know . . ."

"*Carolyn.*"

We said the word together, and I shook my head, still in a daze. Was this just one more of my multiple fantasies? The ones I'd harbored guiltily for more than a year? Couldn't be. The heat was so real on my face, and when I finally stripped off my cashmere socks, I could feel the warm sand beneath my bare feet.

"When she told me how much you missed California, I thought I'd bring California to you."

I remembered the feathers I'd spread for Roger. Rose petals

in the spring. The cutout paper leaves in the fall. I thought about the DVD of the everlasting fire, the time I dressed head to toe in winter gear in spite of the 99-degree temperature. Thought about the fancy tin of water chestnuts.

"But how?"

He grinned at me and took a step closer. He was watching me carefully, those mesmerizing green eyes never leaving my face. "I used to eavesdrop while you told Carolyn about your boyfriend, the idiot."

"Roger."

"Whatever."

He was right next to me then, tilting my face up to his. "And I would imagine what it would be like to have a woman as sweet as you setting up those scenes for me. Dressing up in winter gear so I could unwrap her layer by layer. Spreading paper leaves all over our bed in the fall."

"I set them on fire," I confessed.

He just laughed. "I had this image of playing with candles," he told me, eyes bright. "Of tilting one of those candles over you, so that the little drops of wax would drip slowly . . ."

I shivered again.

"You sure you're not cold?"

"No," I told him, nearly breathless. I was so wet. Could he sense that? "I'm hot. I'm really hot."

"So when Carolyn came by one night and told me you were lonely, that you missed California, well, the news couldn't have come at a better time. Because I landed a spot on a soap. Recurring. So . . ."

"You're here?" I asked. "To stay?"

"If you'll have me."

The words weren't out of his mouth before I was in motion, pushing him onto the towel. Kissing him all over. His mouth, his neck, his chest. I worked my way down until I had my lips pressed to his vibrant blue Speedo. He was rock-hard under the filmy fabric, making a line I could easily trace with my tongue, mouth with my lips. I made a wet spot on the fabric, leaving lipstick kisses all over that shiny blue before pulling the flimsy bit of nylon down his muscular thighs. Oh, sweet Jesus, he was hard, so damn hard. Finally, I pressed my mouth to him, tasted his warm skin, like summertime, like Santa Monica beach. Like everything I missed about California.

Jeremiah let me devour him for a moment, seemingly shocked by the overwhelming force of my response. But happily so. Then he began to move his hands on my own body, stroking me smoothly, running his fingertips over the line of my collarbone, spreading his fingers wide to slip down my flat belly.

"You're so pretty," he breathed, a heavenly sight. "I knew you were. I mean, I always thought so. But naked, God. You're stunning." His words melted over me, like water drips from an icicle, and I pressed my body even more closely to his. I wanted to seal myself to him, to be one with him. Jeremiah wanted the same thing.

He gripped me by the hips, slid me up and then down, slowly on top of his cock, as if taking me for a ride.

A ride I never wanted to end.

Each fantasy I'd had for the past twelve months seemed to flash through my mind in fast motion. And then a voice inside my head said, "It's not a fantasy, it's real."

As real as Jeremiah's cock inside of me, thrusting hard, filling me up. As real as Jeremiah flipping me onto my back, using his hands on my wrists, pulling my arms over my head, holding me steady. He kept me in place with his body as he worked me, and I had to force myself not to close my eyes, worried that if I squeezed my lids shut, the scene would dissolve. That I'd find myself back in Santa Monica, basking in the warmth with Roger. Being in a blizzard with Jeremiah was better than any sunshine-filled beach I could ever imagine.

Jeremiah gave me a half smile as he bent to kiss my neck. "I've been dreaming about this for so long," he murmured, pulling out slowly and flipping me so that I was facedown on the towel. How could I be imagining this? The terry cloth was so soft under my skin, and when I put one hand off the edge of the giant bath sheet, I could trace circles and diamonds in the sand decorating the hardwood floor.

But who would go to so much trouble? Who would work so hard to re-create a world for a lover? That was easy to answer. *I* would. Although I couldn't believe Jeremiah had done all this for me, I'd spent most of the last twelve months doing similar crazy things for a man. Why couldn't my own fairy tale come true?

That was the thought in my head as Jeremiah gripped my hips and slid into me from behind. Inch by inch by inch.

"Oh God," I sighed, loving the way his warm skin felt on mine.

His body found that perfect rhythm, and he slid one hand under my waist, parting my nether lips with his fingertips, stroking my clit as he fucked me. The sweet pleasure of almost coming surrounded me. That sensation of being so close, so damn close, but not quite reaching the finish. Jeremiah knew how to keep me teetering. He worked his fingertips in my juices, using my own lubrication to twirl and slide in.

"You're so wet," he whispered, and I shuddered all over. "So fucking wet."

I could hardly breathe from the pleasure, and when he gripped onto my long dark ponytail and pulled, I came. They say no two snowflakes are alike, but I'd amend that to say no two orgasms are, either. This one was earth-shattering, my body trembling all over, my breath coming hard and fast, as Jeremiah reached his own limits, as he shuddered hard and called out my name.

"Michelle. My Michelle."

Ever the conscientious bartender, my new man brought me a glass of spiked lemonade afterward, then wrapped me in his strong arms. Together, we watched the snow fall outside the window. Crisp, perfect, white pristine flakes. For a moment, I could understand Roger's nostalgia, his homesickness for this type of weather.

"It's not the weather," Jeremiah said, as if reading my mind. He drizzled a handful of coconut-scented Tropicana oil on my belly. "It's the boyfriend."

 ALISON TYLER, called a "trollop with a laptop" by the *East Bay Express* and a "literary siren" by Good Vibrations, is naughty and she knows it. Her sultry short stories have appeared in more than seventy-five anthologies, including *Sex for America* (HarperCollins), *Sex at the Office* (Virgin), and *Best Women's Erotica 2008* (Cleis). She is the author of more than twenty-five erotic novels, and the editor of more than forty-five explicit anthologies, including *Naked Erotica* (Pretty Things Press). Please visit www.alisontyler.com for more information or myspace.com/alisontyler to be her friend. Although she thinks that snow is lovely to look at, she's a California girl through and through.

Baby, It's Cold Outside

by Marilyn Jaye Lewis

The Philadelphia Flyers had come into the new hockey season ranked down at the very bottom of the Eastern Conference, but Connor Moore, a die-hard Flyers fan, knew there was still plenty of time left in the season for them to get back on top. He was determined to get to the arena in plenty of time for today's face-off—the Flyers were playing the New York Rangers at five o'clock. Another snowfall was heading toward Hellertown, but Connor was undeterred. They would make it to Philadelphia come hell or high water—or even more snow.

Kaylie Moore, Connor's wife, was less than a die-hard hockey fan. She didn't hate it; she simply didn't love it. But she did love Connor and after three years of marriage and two years of steady dating, she'd gotten used to his devotion to the Flyers, to his love of the sport. She saw the home games as a way to spend time with her husband, if nothing else. Still, sometimes his fanaticism drove Kaylie a little nuts. Here they were, already getting into the car.

"Don't you think that two o'clock is a little early to be leaving, Connor? The game doesn't start until five. We're only about an hour away."

Connor slid into the driver's seat and pulled the car door closed. "I'm leaving plenty of time for bad weather and—I thought I'd surprise you."

This piqued Kaylie's interest. "Really? Surprise me how?" She fastened her seat belt.

"We're taking the scenic route. I thought I'd take 611 the whole way instead of the freeway. How does that sound? And we can stop at that old barn thing you like—that farmers' market."

It was a very nice surprise. Kaylie was amazed that he'd even thought of it—on a hockey day, no less. "I'll bet 611 will be beautiful in this snow, but I don't think the market is open in the wintertime, Connor."

"Sure they are." Connor put the car in reverse and backed down the long graveled driveway to the semirural street they lived on, Fullerton Way. "There must be something farmers can sell in the winter. You know, stuff they ship in from California that we could buy cheaper just about anywhere else. It's the ambiance we're after here and I'm sure they're well aware of it, even in winter. Farmers can be pretty shrewd."

Kaylie smiled in spite of herself. "Pretty shrewd" was her husband's pat way of describing anyone whose crafts, food, folk art, or furniture were packaged in just the right way to get Kaylie to part with her hard-earned money. The Amish, the Quakers, and now, apparently, the farmers were all "pretty shrewd."

"You're sweet," she said. "Thank you for thinking of it."

"I just wanted to make sure you knew that I wasn't *totally* self-centered. I know I've seemed like it lately."

"It's not that, Connor. I don't think of you as self-centered."

"As what, then—afraid? Is that how you think of me?"

"Yes, maybe a little afraid." She was quick to add, "But that's okay."

"It's okay because I'm a man, you mean? We're all afraid of having children?"

"No, I didn't say that."

"Then it's not the children we're afraid of, per se——" Connor drove east on Fullerton Way, past the old filling station that was now called Rosie's Bar & Grille. "It's the *cost* of children, the permanence, the unending responsibility of them; that's what we men are afraid of, right?"

Kaylie looked away from him and made sure not to sigh. Sighing usually made Connor feel guilty and then this never-changing discussion they seemed to have almost daily now would morph into an argument, and Kaylie didn't want that, least of all today, when he was trying so hard to be a good egg about everything.

"You're allowed to respond, you know, Kaylie; you don't have to sit there and just stare out the window. We can talk about this, can't we, without getting into a fight?"

It was such a loaded topic that Kaylie couldn't help but sigh.

"What?" he said, sounding exasperated already. "I know you want to have a baby."

She looked at him. "*We* want to have one."

"Right. *We* want to have one. Just not——" Connor caught himself before he said it but it was too late.

"Just not now." Kaylie finished his thought for him.

"I didn't say that."

"What are you saying then, Connor? Just tell me."

"I'm thinking about it. That's all." Kaylie thought this was either very promising news—that he was seriously thinking about it, about being agreeable, finally, and trying to make a baby with her—or it was merely another stalling tactic. She decided to think positive and leave well enough alone for now. No reason to push him if he was indeed trying to be agreeable. "Thanks, Connor," she said. And she thought it would be best to change the subject for a while. "So how are the Rangers ranked right now?"

"Third."

"Wow. This should be a good game."

"It sure will," Connor agreed. "I'm excited." At the flashing yellow traffic light, he veered left, toward 611 and the Delaware River; it would be the river and trees and then pastoral foothills from here on out, and all of it, except the madly rushing river, was frosted with a light layer of still-white two-day-old snow.

Kaylie loved snow, and she loved taking the scenic route anywhere. She hated freeways. She especially loved taking 611, following the bends in the river. In the early days of their marriage, she and Connor used to take a lot of drives along the Delaware, stopping for picnics or to take hikes along the old canal. They hadn't done anything like that in a long while. Now, seeing it all dusted with snow made Kaylie's heart happy; her perspective freshened on everything. And it brought back memories, to boot.

"Remember that time—" she began.

Connor cut her off. "Yes," he said, smiling. "I do."

She smiled back at him. She was feeling her hormones stirring but she didn't want to say anything about it. She was ovulating; it would be sure to lead to a huge argument as soon as he found out. Better to change the subject again, but she didn't feel like talking about hockey. She wanted to have a baby. In all honesty, it was all she thought about anymore.

Not privy to his wife's thought processes, Connor was still on the topic of memories. "We were pretty bold that day, weren't we? I mean, even for us."

"I guess so," Kaylie replied distractedly.

"You *guess* so? Jesus, Kay, that's understating it. You know, I think about that day from time to time and I still get off on it."

This took her aback; she thought she'd been alone it that secret pleasure. "You do?"

"Yeah, I do. That was so hot, don't you think? I get a lot of mileage out of that memory. You were such a wild little girl that day. Not that you aren't all the time," he added playfully. "You just outdid yourself that time—and in public, no less."

"It was hardly 'in public,'" she said, suddenly feeling shy about it. "We were simply outside."

Connor reached over and squeezed her hand. "Hey, you're blushing."

"I am not."

"Yes, you are."

The simple touch of his hand on hers gave Kaylie that spark, ignited somewhere between her heart and her belly, and the sudden clarity of the memory overwhelmed her in its intimate detail. They'd been walking along the towpath of the old canal that day; it was late spring, warm enough to be walking without jackets for the first time that season. The sky had been that perfect shade of blue; the clouds, puffy and bright white. The air was filled with the scent of the first May blossoms and the river itself had smelled of spring, a thing alive and fresh and full of new promises. It had made Kaylie feel hungry for life—insatiable for it, in fact. One minute, she'd been kissing Connor; the next, she'd felt ravenous for his tongue. They were *really* kissing then—passionately, right there on the old towpath, out in the open. She was clinging to Connor's neck and his hand was up under her T-shirt. The feel of his fingertips grazing her nipple, even through the lace of her bra, had set her on fire. She'd practically dragged him to the ranger station—a very small, very old clapboard house just off the main path—and thrown him down onto the grass behind the building.

For a mere moment, she'd confined herself to lying on top of him in the grass and kissing him like crazy. But it wasn't long before he had her shirt pushed up, her bra tugged up over her tits and her tits exposed to the air—her tender nipple suddenly in his mouth and swelling from the intense pressure of how fiercely he was sucking on her.

She couldn't stand it then. She'd reached behind her and unclasped the bra but even that had felt too constricting. She managed to pull the T-shirt and then the bra off completely. It had felt so liberating, she remembered; that was the exact feeling, to be suddenly topless in the warm spring air, with Connor so eager to devour her nipples. It had become quickly obvious that they were going to have to fuck—there was no doubt about it. She was too worked up.

Her hands were at his belt, unbuckling it. Abruptly, his mouth was off her. "Kaylie," he said. "What are you doing?"

"You know what I'm doing," she insisted—hurriedly, as she fumbled with his buckle.

"Not really." He was mildly alarmed when he felt his zipper coming down. "It could be a couple things," he stammered, feeling his cock spring out into the warm air. "Oh Christ, Kay." He gasped quietly; his head fell back into the grass as he surrendered to his wife's mouth in utter delight. Her mouth felt so hot and so wet, and she was so greedy about it. She was really sucking on it, creating too much pressure, letting the head of his cock nudge way back in her throat.

"Shit, Kaylie, I'm going to come."

It was happening too fast. Kaylie stopped. "No way," she said breathlessly. "Don't you do that to me, I'm too excited."

"Kay, what you are doing?" Connor watched his wife with mixed feelings of shock and absolute arousal as she stood up and unzipped her own jeans and then pulled them, and her panties, all the way down. She kicked off her sneakers almost angrily, as if she couldn't get them off her feet quick enough, and in a heartbeat, she was completely naked. Right out there in the open.

She looked so beautiful, so swept up in her own desire. Connor pulled her down next to him in the grass, then rolled on top of her and mounted her. Her pussy was soaking, completely ready for him. The slick hole opened around his cock and her heat enveloped him. "This is not exactly going to keep me from coming," he'd warned her, her lips kissing his cheek, his chin, and then even his mouth as he spoke to her. "I hope you know that."

"I know that," she insisted quietly. "Just fuck me, honey. Be quiet and fuck me. Come whenever you need to."

"You mean, *in* you?" he said in her ear, his voice sounding just as insistent, and just as breathless, as hers. "You want me to come in you? It's okay? It's not your time or anything?"

"It's okay," she'd half-answered, half-cried that day as he'd suddenly gone at her with vigor. "You can come in me," she'd said, "—*oh God.*" He was so hard and going in deep. She spread her thighs wider, hiked her legs higher, feeling him going *really* deep. "Connor, *shit*—oh God."

She gripped him tight in her arms and then hugged her knees close to him, letting him go at her very hard and very fast, while she whimpered and cried in his ear in rhythm to every repeated thrust.

Miraculously, he had kept himself from coming right away. Once he'd found his rhythm in her, he'd kept it going, entranced by the sounds of her pleasure. He'd gone at her harder than he usually did; he'd felt that caught up in the rhythm of her cries. He'd never known her to sound so full of lust before. It had finally overwhelmed him.

He came in her, and even though she hadn't come yet, she'd suddenly felt very exposed out there by the riverbank, on the grass behind some old ranger station—and she hadn't thought to check if it was occupied or not. She'd hurried to get back into her clothes. It was not a moment too soon.

Connor seemed to be keeping pace with her reveries. "Do you think that the park ranger had been watching us the whole time?"

When Connor spoke, he startled Kaylie back to the present,

back to the reality of the car, its heater on high as they drove along 611. It wasn't spring, it was winter. There was snow out there along the canal now.

Kaylie laughed uneasily. "I don't know," she said.

"He sure timed it right, didn't he? Coming around the back of that house the minute you'd finished putting your clothes on?"

"I'd wondered about that, too—his impeccable timing."

"And you'd been making an awful lot of noise. He had to have heard you."

She'd been making a lot of noise; for some reason, hearing Connor say that made Kaylie feel excited again. "Well, he was polite about it, either way," she said.

"I suppose he was." Connor gave the idea some thought: a stranger, a man in a uniform, secretly watching him fucking his wife. For a fleeting moment, Connor found the idea curiously appealing but then he let it go.

Kaylie pulled her coat more tightly around her and then snuggled down into the seat. She couldn't help it; she was horny. Remembering that whole episode had gotten to her. She'd been in a light swoon all day anyway. She tried to distract herself by looking out the window at all the snow-covered scenery: the dusted trees, the hills in the distance, the occasional swath of snowy farmland that would suddenly burst into view. But nothing helped take her mind off it: she wanted to fuck and she wanted to make a baby. In that order. Right now.

"What are you thinking about?" Connor asked her. "You're so quiet over there."

"Nothing," she said. "I'm just looking at stuff."

"The farmers' market is just here up the road, you know."

"Have we already gotten that far?"

"Yep. We've gotten that far."

Why is he looking at me so oddly, she wondered; is he reading my mind? No, she convinced herself. I have a guilty conscience, that's all. But why should I feel guilty? He's my husband. I'm allowed to want to have sex with him.

It was the baby stuff she felt guilty about. She'd been pressuring him a lot lately. She found herself unwilling to let him make his own decision about it anymore. For the first time since they'd gotten married, she was ovulating and hadn't told him. Why was that? Was she hoping to trap him, to assert her will over his constant stalling?

I can't do that, she told herself. That would be so unfair. He would never forgive me. Well, she realized, he would forgive me, most likely. But maybe he would never really trust me again.

"Kay?" he said. "Did you hear me?"

"No, I'm sorry. What did you say?"

"I said it's closed; you were right—look."

They had pulled into the farmers' market and sure enough, it was boarded up for the winter. Not just the outside stalls, which would have been expected, but the inside market was closed for the season, as well. The whole property seemed deserted. The dirt roads that led through the fruit orchards were still dusted in snow; they showed no tire tracks, no footprints.

Connor pulled the car up one of the roads, then stopped and put it in park.

"What are we doing?" Kaylie asked. "Did you want to take a walk in the snow?"

Connor looked at her for a moment. "Not really," he finally said.

"Connor, what is it?"

"Well, we have plenty of time now. And no one's here."

Oh no, she thought, feeling unnerved by that look in his eye. It was highly unlikely that this had been part of his plans for the day; he probably hadn't brought a condom.

"What do you mean?" she asked naively, stalling a little herself now.

He turned off the car. "You know what I mean."

"I do?"

He smiled at her sudden reluctance. He liked it when she pretended to be shy. "You do. Come on, should we take a little walk?"

"It's cold out there."

"So? It'll be a new adventure. Come on, Kay. Let's go." He unlocked the car doors. The sudden springing sound of it gave her a jolt. "What's with you?" he asked, opening his door. "Don't you want to?"

"I want to," she said. "It's just—"

"What? Are you afraid of a little snow?"

"No," she said.

"Then what is it? Are you afraid I'm going to fuck you so hard you'll come all over yourself—and me, I hope?"

Oh no, now he was going to start talking dirty to her. She was doomed. Just *say* it, she tried to convince herself. Tell him it's not a good time; that he's going to have to be careful because she could get pregnant . . . But then he'll lose the mood—and fast.

"Come on," he said again, getting out of the car. "Let's go. If it's too cold, we can always come back to the car instead and fuck like crazy teenagers in the backseat. Come on." He slammed his door closed. Kaylie didn't move. She watched him come around the front of the car to the passenger side; she watched him open her door. His crotch was at eye level; he had a hard-on inside his jeans.

She looked up at his face. "Surprise," he said, knowing she'd seen it, his erection nearly bursting open his zipper.

This time she knew she was blushing. "Christ, Connor."

"Come on, honey." He reached down and unbuckled her seat belt. "Let's go take a walk in the snow."

"But what about the game—don't you want to be there in time for the face-off?"

"We will. Don't worry about it." He took Kaylie's arm and helped her get out of the car.

The cold air felt sobering but it wasn't an icy blast; it was bearable. Kaylie took Connor's hand and they began walking— up the dirt road into the orchards. The trees were breathtaking in the light dusting of snow. And the sky was heavy with another imminent snowfall. It created a feeling of isolation, of being cushioned against the outside world.

Connor broke the silence. "No one's here," he said. "We are completely and utterly alone—look at this."

Kaylie looked, they were indeed alone. Quietly, in keeping with the solemnness of their surroundings, she said, "You're not really expecting me to take my pants off out here, are you?"

"I kind of was," he said.

"Connor, you're crazy."

"Kaylie, come here." Connor pulled her into his arms and they kissed, their down-filled jackets serving as a soft barrier between them. "This won't do," Connor insisted. "Here, let me undo that." He unzipped Kaylie's jacket and then unzipped his own. "That's better, isn't it?" He pulled her to him again and kissed her, this time the warmth of their bodies connected them.

Kaylie felt Connor's erection pressing up against her and it made her push back against him; she couldn't help herself. She was getting too worked up for him and it just wouldn't do, she had to hide it, to keep it locked up tight. It was going to be a lost battle, though, if he kept pushing up against her like this.

"Connor," she said quietly.

"What?"

She didn't say anything more; she returned his kisses, finding his tongue with hers, engaging him fully, and moaning in urgency when she felt his hand going up under her sweater. It was ice-cold, but she didn't care. She wanted to feel him touching her skin.

He didn't go up under her bra, not at first. He seemed content to feel the fullness of her breast while he kissed her. It was Kaylie who wanted her bra undone. She had her coat on, she figured, and her sweater was covering most of her. No one would see—if there were anyone watching them, that is. And there wasn't. She pulled up her own sweater, then, and tugged her bra up over her tits.

"Kaylie," Connor said eagerly. Kaylie's nipples were stiff points; her breasts looked too inviting as they rose to attention in the cold air. His mouth was on her in a heartbeat.

Feeling the warmth of his mouth, the pressure of his lips,

his flicking wet tongue tormenting her swollen nipple—Kaylie groaned in reluctant defeat. She was too aroused for words now. And words were exactly what she needed to tell Connor to stop, that it was leading them into murky waters; that they would soon be out of control.

"No," she whispered quietly, too quietly to be taken seriously. "Connor, don't." His mouth had left her nipple and he was kissing his way down her ribcage, down her belly. He was on his knees in the snow and his hands were impatiently pulling the waistband of her pants, then her panties, down over her hips. "Don't," she insisted again.

Her mound was exposed, and the light swirl of brown hair. Connor caught her scent immediately. "Why not?" he asked, looking up at her—his eyes on fire with lust already.

Kaylie couldn't resist that look. "I'm going to fall down," she said.

"Okay," he said, quickly rising to his feet. Leaving her exposed, he pulled her to an apple tree. "Lean against it," he said. He went back down to his knees again, only now he pulled her pants and her panties all the way down to her ankles.

"*Oh God,*" Kaylie squealed. It was really cold out. Before she could protest further, though, two of his fingers went up her hole. She groaned deliriously, in spite of herself and the freezing cold.

"Jesus, Kaylie," he said. "You are soaking."

"I know I am," she whimpered in defeat, succumbing quickly to the sheer pleasure of his steady fingers probing up inside her. And once again, words became too much to manage; she was nothing but moans and little whimpers of delirium as she leaned her weight against the apple tree. Connor's mouth was on her down there, all over the swelling, sopping lips, his tongue pushing against her aching clitoris, stroking it, his fingers continuing their steady probe.

"Oh God," she cried again. Her fingers clutched at the rough bark of the tree, her hips pushed her mound out, offering it as best she could to Connor's mouth. She was as good as naked out there in the winter air and it felt fantastic—her tits exposed, the full length of her aroused body on display, and Connor ardently pleasuring her between her legs. She didn't know which felt better: the way his fingers pushed up into her, circled inside her and opened her, making her wish she could spread her legs wide for him, or the way his tongue circled her clit, pushed up into its hood, then mashed against it, before circling it again.

She was going to come, but she didn't want to come like this. She wanted to explode into orgasm on his pounding cock. She wanted to feel impaled on him, ravaged by him while she came. "Let's fuck," she blurted.

"Okay," he agreed, out of breath, his mouth a slick mess now. His nose was filled with the thick scent of just how aroused she was and he could hardly contain his own excitement. "Turn around," he said, getting up. "Hold onto the tree. Brace yourself against it."

She did as he asked, turning around awkwardly, her pants still down around her ankles, when the rough bark of the tree suddenly scraped against her exposed tits. "Shit!" she cried, pushing herself away from the tree, steadying herself against the trunk as best she could while keeping her breasts clear of it. Her ass arched up, as if on instinct, readying her to be mounted from behind. And it didn't take long, a mere moment was all. Connor's cock was thick and warm and solid as it pushed right up into her sopping, eager hole. It felt incredible, the way it filled her. He felt harder than he'd ever felt to her before—was that even possible?

"Oh God," she cried, not sure she could take this kind of pounding without something closer to hold on to. "Oh God, *Connor.*" He had a firm grip on her hips, pulling her ass up higher, getting his cock into her hole incredibly deep, giving it to her with very hard, very quick strokes.

"Can I come in you?" he asked urgently.

"Oh God," she said again, moaning, her head swimming. It all felt too good, it overwhelmed her—and she wanted a baby, she so wanted a baby. Her ass went up higher, trying to get him all the way up her.

"Can I?" he asked again, his brutal rhythm increasing in her.

"Yes," she said deliriously. This, too, was almost too quiet to be heard—this lie, this deception.

He wasn't sure what she'd said. "Yes?" he asked. "It's okay to come in you?"

"Yes," she said. "Come in me." Then she whirled to her senses. She shoved him off of her with all her strength and nearly lost her balance. "No," she cried. "Don't come in me!"

"Christ," he yelled frantically. "I'm coming, damn it."

They uncoupled gracelessly, with Kaylie falling against the tree, scraping herself, and Connor trying to keep himself from falling by keeping his grip on Kaylie's hips. The unstoppable spurts of his orgasm spattered onto the snow.

He tried to catch his breath. "What the fuck was that, Kaylie?"

"I'm ovulating," she blurted out. "I'm sorry." She was too upset to turn around and face him. She felt ridiculous now, hugging the cold rough trunk of the tree, scraped up, with her pants down around her ankles.

Sheepishly, she bent down to pull up her pants. She still refused to meet his gaze. She could feel his anger and could imagine his humiliation. "I'm sorry," she said again. "I lost my head."

"Really?" he said—his voice heavy with sarcasm now. He tucked himself into his jeans. "Is that what you call it, losing your head? You didn't know it this morning when you consulted your little calendar like you always do every single day of the year?"

"I'm sorry, Connor. I really am." She turned to look at him now and he looked disgusted with her. A moment ago they had been entwined in such connubial bliss. *Damn it,* she thought. Why had she done it? Or nearly done it—and which idea was worse? They were both pretty lousy ones.

Connor zipped up his coat and turned to walk back to the car—without her; he left her standing there alone to straighten her clothes and feel like a fool.

"Aren't you going to wait for me?" she called out.

He stopped and turned and looked at her. "Come on, then. Hurry up."

She hurried. She pulled herself together and ran to him, searching his face for even the slightest clue that he didn't completely despise her. "That was pretty sucky of me, huh?" she finally said. "I'm just really confused, Connor."

He didn't reply; he started walking again.

Kaylie kept pace with him, afraid to say anything more.

When they reached the car, a light snow had begun to fall. Connor opened Kaylie's car door for her and held it. She slid into the passenger seat and then looked up at him, smiling hopefully. "Thank you," she said.

"You're welcome, Kaylie," he replied. He closed her car door and went around to the driver's side. He got in and closed his own door. He turned the key that was still in the ignition and—nothing. He tried again. "Great," he spat. "This is just great."

"What?"

"The battery's dead."

"Oh no, you're kidding."

"No, I'm not kidding." He tried the ignition again—nothing, just an ineffectual *click*. "Shit." Connor got out his cell phone. "Give me the number for the Auto Club; the membership card's in the glove compartment."

Kaylie complied, feeling that somehow this dead battery was her fault. "I'm so sorry, Connor," she said.

He took the card from her and dialed the number.

"I need someone to come out and jump my battery," he said into the phone. Kaylie stared morosely out the window while Connor gave the Auto Club their exact location. "You're kidding," he said. "Why so long?" A frustrated pause; Connor tapped his fingers angrily on the steering wheel. "Okay, then. Well, obviously, we'll be waiting."

He closed his phone. "It's going to be at least half an hour," he told Kaylie. "And probably more like forty-five minutes. There's no one closer. In the Auto Club's opinion, we happen to be out in the middle of nowhere."

Kaylie looked at him apologetically. "I'm sorry, Connor. I really am."

"Why should you be? You don't work for the Auto Club."

"You know what I mean. I'm sorry about the whole thing, about what just happened out there."

"And what did just happen out there, Kaylie?" He studied her now unflinchingly. "Do you want to explain yourself?"

"If you'll let me."

"I'm letting you. Who's stopping you?"

"You're not being entirely, well, you know—"

"What? I'm not being what—*considerate* of you?"

The way he emphasized the word *considerate* made Kaylie feel three years old. "Point taken," she conceded quietly. "That was inconsiderate of me, to put it mildly."

Connor sighed. "I *don't* want to fight with you, Kaylie. We were having such a great time. Why would you do that to me? Since when is this just your marriage, huh?"

She had no adequate answer for that.

"And not just the way you shoved me away from you so rudely—and never would I do a thing like that to you, Kay. But this baby thing—it's getting out of control with you. What were you trying to do, trick me into creating my own kid? Like I wouldn't want to be there with you if a thing like that could *maybe* be happening, after everything we've been through about this already?"

"I just . . . I don't know, I guess I was just . . . I'm *thirty-two years old* already, Connor," she finally sputtered in defeat. "I am so tired of waiting for you to be ready." *God that came out sounding mean*, she thought; *why am I being so mean?*

Connor fell silent. They said nothing more for a while. They sat and stared out at the falling snow. It had gotten heavier; their footprints into the orchard were already obliterated.

"It's cold in here," Kaylie finally said.

"I know it is. The heater's not on."

"I know that, Connor. I'm just saying that it's cold."

They both heard it and saw it coming through the snow at the same instant.

Connor said, "What the hell is that?"

"It's a tractor," Kaylie declared.

It was a tractor, all right, with a man in a bright orange cap driving it. He was coming toward them, down the dirt road that was now snowed over.

"I wonder if there's some sort of farmhouse up that way?" Connor said.

"I don't know," Kaylie said, "but maybe he can help us get this car started?"

"I hope so. I'll see." Connor opened his door and got out. He walked toward the tractor that was now coming to a slow stop.

The farmer called down to Connor, "I couldn't help noticing that you seemed stuck down here."

Connor wondered what else the guy hadn't been able to help noticing, but right now, all Connor wanted was to get the car started. "My battery's dead," he called back.

"I figured as much. I've got a charger up at the barn." The farmer got down off his tractor and walked over to Connor. "I can either bring it down here and give you an emergency boost that'll at least get you to a service station, or, if you aren't in too much of a hurry, we can take the battery up to the barn and leave it connected for a little while; it'll totally recharge you. You won't have to pay me anything. It's up to you."

"Where's the nearest service station?" Connor asked, noticing that the farmer didn't want to look directly at him. Christ, Connor thought to himself; he did see us. And then Connor wondered if the farmer had been alone, or if there had been other people watching Kaylie and him have sex out there in the bone-dead orchard, where there was not so much as a speck of a leaf clinging to any of the trees.

"Oh gosh, I'd say about eight miles," the farmer said. "If it's even open. It's not always open in bad weather. Rick, the owner, lives pretty far out and doesn't like to risk getting stranded down here in bad weather."

"I can understand that," Connor said. The snow was already clinging to Connor's hair, to his eyelashes, even.

The farmer said, "I got tools in the tractor. It's no big deal taking that battery out. Let's just take it on up to the barn and recharge it."

"You're sure it's no problem?"

"No problem at all. I take care of all my own vehicles around this place."

"Thanks," Connor said. "How long will a recharge take?"

"About an hour," the farmer replied. "Maybe a little longer. It's a pretty powerful little box. There's a gauge right on it, tells you when it's done."

Connor could see the Flyers game disappearing in the distance. Even if they made it to the arena on time, this was more than a snowfall, it was a storm. With the battery acting up, they'd be crazy to drive all the way to Philadelphia and back. "I guess I'll take you up on that recharge, then. Let me just double-check with my wife."

Connor opened his door, reached down and popped the hood,

and said, "Looks like we aren't going to Philly today. This guy's offered to recharge our battery for free, though. If you don't mind hanging out here for about an hour?"

"But *the game*—you already bought the tickets. You were so looking forward to it."

"It's too risky, Kay. We can't drive all the way to Philly and back in this weather. Besides, if I don't get the battery charged here, we'll just have to stop somewhere up the road and do it, if we can even find a place. And then we'll have to pay."

"I don't mind waiting here, that's all right with me. I just feel bad for you—missing the game."

"I'll get over it," Connor said. "Hand me that card from the Auto Club again, will you?"

Kaylie handed him back the card.

"I'm going to go up to this guy's barn with him, but I'll come back and sit with you while the battery's charging."

"Okay, honey." Connor shut the car door again and was gone from view. The snow had nearly covered the windshield now. Kaylie couldn't see anything anymore, and she could barely hear the men talking outside. Eventually she heard the sound of the tractor heading back up the road.

One more hour in the freezing cold car, she thought. Well, now they'd *have* to talk things out. She wouldn't be able to stand it, being stuck in the car, all snowed over, and the two of them arguing, or worse—not speaking to each other. . . .

With the car battery wedged under the tractor's seat, Connor road shotgun beside the farmer, clinging precariously to the slippery tractor. He didn't have gloves on and his fingers were freezing. As the tractor made its slow, steady way up the road, Connor could see, even through the falling snow that the farther one went up the road, the easier it was to see the damn orchard. It wasn't even that much of a hill, but it was enough of a steady incline to get a perfectly clear view of everything below.

Well, Connor thought, so what if he saw us? At least that clear view helped the guy see that we were stranded, and he was decent enough to come down and help us.

About fifteen minutes later, Connor opened the car door again and this time he reached in and popped the trunk. "I think we have a blanket of some kind in back and a roll of paper towels. Are you all right?"

He said it with such unguarded affection, Kaylie smiled. "I'm all right," she said. "Just a little cold."

Connor tossed his cell phone onto the front seat. "I canceled the service call. That farmer is going to call us when the battery's done charging. He offered to let us wait up in his barn, but under the circumstances, I thought we'd feel more comfortable just waiting here in the car."

"Under what circumstances?"

"I'm pretty sure he saw us, Kay. He was just too polite to say anything."

"Wow," Kaylie said uncomfortably. "That's kind of ironic, isn't it? The park ranger in the spring, and now some farmer in a snowstorm. We're not too good at this 'sex in the great outdoors' stuff, are we?"

Connor studied her face for a second before answering. "We do all right," he finally said. "Maybe we need more practice, what do you think?" Before she could answer, he'd closed the car door again.

Why had he said *that*, she wondered, and why was she feeling that spark again? Connor didn't seem angry with her at all now.

In a moment, she heard the trunk slamming closed. Then the back door opened this time. Connor tossed in an old blanket and a roll of paper towels, and then he slid into the backseat. Kaylie watched him unroll a wad of the paper towels. He began drying off his snow-covered hair.

"Well?" he said to her. "Aren't you going to get your ass back here? We had a little unfinished business, didn't we?"

"We did?" Kaylie couldn't believe her ears; was he talking about having more sex?

"We did; didn't we? I don't think you came yet, wouldn't you like to?"

Kaylie was delighted. "Yes," she said doubtfully. "But that guy . . ."

"Don't worry about that guy. I think he's already seen more than he cared to. To be honest, I think that's why he's calling me on the phone when the battery's done, instead of coming back down to get me in person: he must think we're a couple of sex addicts."

"Shit," Kaylie said, finding it funny now. "Do you think he really saw us?"

"I think he really saw us. I was up there, Kay, and it's a pretty clear view, even in the snow."

"Oh my God, I was practically naked!"

"I know you were. I saw, remember?"

Connor took off his wet coat and laid it over the back of the driver's seat. "I'm *freezing*," he said. "But I have an idea of how to kill an hour and get warm at the same time. Of course, the idea kind of hinged on you getting your ass back here already."

Kaylie couldn't refuse him when he talked to her like that.

"Besides, I have a little bone to pick with you," he went on, helping her slip over into the backseat.

"I know, honey," she said. "I'm sorry." Kaylie's heart was on fire again. Did he really mean to see this through? Was it going to happen? Of course it didn't mean she was going to get pregnant, but she sure as hell was going to try. "I guess the shared body heat will do us both some good, huh? It's pretty cold in this car."

"I think we'll manage," he said.

They were in an odd twilight. All the windows were snowed over now. It was neither light nor dark, and they seemed cut off from the world. Connor unfolded the blanket and tucked it over the two of them. They sat snuggled close together in the backseat. He said, "I can't decide . . ."

"You can't decide what?"

"If I should take off my pants or not. They're wet and very cold."

"Then take them off," she said. "What's to decide?"

"The thought of putting them back on again in an hour makes me feel even colder."

"I see. Well, if you take off yours, I'll take off mine; does that make you feel less cold? We'll kind of be in it together."

"Yes, together," he said. He looked at her seriously for a moment. "Kaylie, I want you to know I'm sorry."

"My God, for what? What do you have to be sorry for?"

"For letting you get so fed up with me dragging my feet all the time that it made you—I don't know—not trust me anymore. I'd made a vow to myself, you know? Of course not, how could you know? I never said a word about it, I tried to, but it never came out. It always got stuck in my throat. But I'd made a vow to myself that the next time you told me you were ovulating I wasn't going to start a fight about it. I was going to make myself be okay with it and just move ahead with this already. It really killed me—what you said before."

"What do you mean?"

"Before—when you said that you were thirty-two already and tired of waiting for me to be ready. You made me feel like a little kid, like an immature little kid. And I realized I'm thirty-five already; when the heck do I think I'm going to be ready to start a family with you? I love you. I *want* us to have a family. What is my problem? I was thinking about it as I was riding on that guy's tractor, going up to the barn. You are *so* ready and all I ever seem able to do is work and then obsess about hockey."

"That's not true, Connor. That's not all you do."

He tossed aside the blanket and kicked off his wet shoes. "You're right," he said. "That's not all I do." He unzipped his frozen jeans and began tugging them off. "You know, I think I'm actually less cold with them off?"

Kaylie watched as he took off his underwear, too. He wasn't erect anymore; he looked positively freezing. "Get back under the blanket. You'll catch pneumonia like that." She threw the blanket back over him.

"Aren't you forgetting something?" he said, snuggling under

the blanket again—it really was cold in the car. "Didn't you offer to make a little deal, pants-wise; or are you chickening out?"

"I'm not chickening out." Kaylie threw off her half of the blanket, kicked off her shoes, and then wiggled out of her pants and her panties. She was already so cold that the leather car seat didn't feel that much colder. "Are we crazy?" she said.

"I don't know. Maybe. *Now* what are you doing?"

"I figure I might as well, right?" Kaylie had taken off her down jacket and now she was pulling her sweater off over her head.

"I think you *are* nuts. Now you really will freeze."

"No, I won't. I'm planning on being under you, and you're usually pretty hot." She unclasped her bra and took it off. Fluffing her down jacket into a loose pile, she used it as a pillow for her head. She lay down on her side of the seat. She didn't mind at all that she was cold. With her knees up, her thighs open, she knew he had a perfect view, one that was likely to get him in the mood quickly. "Too bad we can't turn on the radio," she said. "This isn't very romantic, is it?"

"Maybe not romantic," he said, pulling off his own sweater in a hurry. He was already back in the mood, and he wanted to be completely naked with her. "But it'll be memorable. Besides, we can make up for the lack of romance later."

"Really? You already know you want to do it again later?" It felt like too much to hope for; he really was trying to make a baby with her.

"We'll be snowed in for at least the weekend, Kay." He stretched out between her legs, lying on top of her, trying to pull the old blanket over both of them. "We only have two days, three maybe, to surround that little bugger that's up inside you and nail it, right? Perfect timing, this snowstorm."

"Thank you, Connor."

"Please don't say it like that, like I'm doing you some huge favor. I love you, Kay."

She felt his cock coming to life against her belly. She didn't want to waste time with foreplay; she wanted to get down to business—get *life* going. She reached down for his cock and coaxed it to an erection. He leaned close and kissed her, feeling his whole body beginning to stir.

She said quietly, "This time, you won't have to ask me."

He didn't have to say "ask you what," because he knew what, and the thought of coming in her now was intensely appealing to him. This added dimension of new life, of creating life, of melding who he was with who she was, creating something entirely new and unpredictable that could stand alone from them and thrive on its own—it was suddenly too compelling, too unbelievable for words—making babies, how *crazy* and inexplicable it all seemed. But he wasn't afraid. Connor kissed her again, this time roughly, passionately, as he worked to get his cock up inside her.

She assisted him in his mission. Still holding on to his cock, she helped him ease it up into her. She was already wet—in fact, had been wet since the moment he'd told her to "get her ass into the backseat." She'd known this was coming, that she'd be lying under him, that he would be on top of her—the old-fashioned way. It suddenly seemed so erotic. Kaylie raised her knees high as his cock pushed in and opened her. She moaned sweetly. He was very hard now. She hugged him closer to her and held on tight. "Really fuck me, Connor," she said right in his ear. "Fuck me hard; I need to feel it hard today."

He didn't answer with words. He braced himself, his arms at either side of her head, taking the bulk of his weight. Now it was an adrenaline-fueled strength that compelled him to fuck her— to fuck her very hard. He pushed deeper into her, feeling the wet heat of her hole swelling around his fully erect cock, hugging his shaft at the same time that it made room for him.

How mysterious it all was, this fucking business, he thought, *this baby-making stuff; how mysterious and how entrancing.*

"Oh God," she was crying repeatedly, rhythmically. Her need for him delighted him, propelled him in his task to fill her—to make his presence in her good enough and hard enough and filling enough.

Oh God, oh God.

She kicked off the annoying blanket, spread her thighs wider. She pushed open her hole for him, so incredibly open. *Oh God.* He was going in deep. She couldn't remember it ever feeling this good, this incredibly enticing. She was so aroused and so insatiable for sex, for the feel of his cock invading her, going up into her all the way, until it made her cry out—the pain was so deliciously sweet. She kept wanting to feel that tender pain. Her body pushed itself open for just that feeling—that thrust of his cock way up into the center of her. She was hungry for it, that's what it was; starving for his cock, for him, to be filled with him. She clung to him tight as they both began to sweat.

In a burst of passion, his rhythm suddenly increased. "God, Kay," he said, panting. The thick head of his cock pushed way up

into her, into that place deep inside her that normally blocked
his path; now it too was swelling open for him, thick and fleshy
and soft. It felt too good, that place. His cock drove up into it
repeatedly, seemingly with a will of its own. It pounded into
her.

Oh shit, yes. I'm going to come.

Her body held itself entirely open now. She'd never felt this
impaled, this delirious with lust. *Yes, yes.* She could feel his whole
body stiffen, could tell he was going to come. His breath came
out in little explosive cries, that thin line of ecstasy and agony, as
his body jerked against her, propelling his whole world out and
up into hers. The constant hammering against her cervix shot
her into orgasm. And for a moment, Connor was entirely rigid,
except for those hard, quick, short little thrusts.

"Shit," he gasped, panting. "Shit. Oh man, Kay. Wow." In
an instant, his full weight collapsed on top of her. "Wow," he
said again. "That was good. Did you come? It felt like you were
coming."

Kaylie was panting just as hard. "Yes," she said, nodding her
head, feeling happy. "I came."

They looked at each other, wondering if that had been it, the
spark of life. And whether it was or wasn't, they still had the
whole weekend ahead of them. Connor couldn't wait until they
could get the car started, get back home and do it again.

"To think I was so excited about seeing the Flyers take on the
Rangers," he said.

Kaylie's hips still rocked gently beneath him, her breathing
steadier now, returning to normal. She didn't say anything. She
just looked up into his face, luxuriating in the sound of his

voice, in the feel of him on top of her, as he talked about hockey and about how little it really mattered in the grand scheme of things. *I am ready for this*, she was thinking, as if in some hypnotic daze. *The unimaginable mystery of life, of everything love is; I am so ready for it.*

Connor eased himself out of her and then sat up. "Christ, it's freezing," he said. "We should probably get dressed, don't you think?"

"Probably," she agreed. "We don't want to catch pneumonia."

"No," he said. "We sure don't."

They hurriedly got into their clothes and then snuggled back under the blankets. They did their best to keep themselves warm while they waited for the call to come. They talked about what they might have for dinner later, about what they had in the house, or should they stop at the store first before they got completely snowed in. . . . It was just as easy as that, really—without even knowing it, they were making plans for three now.

 MARILYN JAYE LEWIS (www.marilynjayelewis.com) is the award-winning author of *Neptune & Surf,* a trio of erotic novellas, and the coeditor of the international best-selling erotic art book, *Mammoth Book of Erotic Photography.* She has received many citations and awards for her erotic fiction, including being named a finalist in the William Faulkner Writing Competition and winner in the New Century Writers Awards. Her short stories and novellas have been published worldwide and translated into French, Italian, and Japanese. *Lust:Bisexual Erotica* (Alyson, 2004) represents her collected erotic short fiction from 1997 to 2003. Other anthologies she has edited include *Hot Women's Erotica; That's Amore!; Stirring Up a Storm;* and *Zowie! It's Yaoi!* Her popular erotic romance novels, *When Hearts Collide* and *When the Night Stood Still,* were reissued in Spring 2008 as *From Hollywood, With Love* (Magic Carpet Books). Upcoming novels include *Freak Parade; A Killing on Mercy Road; We're Still All That;* and *Twilight of the Immortal.*

Northern Exposure

by Isabelle Gray

It started as a game between them in a time when they thought they understood the meaning of the words, "I love you." *Ask of me what you will*, they whispered to each other, breathlessly after making love, softly while lying in each other's arms the next morning, hoarsely after a fight. "Ask of me what you will," Alana says to Gideon, as they walk through the woods behind their cabin. It is a cold November afternoon. Their breath is foggy in the chill of the afternoon and they can hear the snow beneath their hiking boots. Her hands, red and chapped, are shoved into the pockets of her jeans, and she walks slowly, with stuttered steps, trying to keep up. "Ask of me what you will," she says again, but Gideon pretends not to hear. Instead, he listens to a flock of birds flying south, the occasional report of a deer-hunter's rifle, the sound of the air. He is in love with November. He does not want her to disturb this moment.

The winters are long in North Country. Snow falls as early as August, and by November, cold has taken hold of the earth and won't relinquish its grip until late May. It is not the cold or the snow or the mere six hours of daylight that bother her, Alana is fond of saying, but the fact that she doesn't get to take advantage of her extensive shoe collection often enough during these long winter months. Instead, her feet are trapped in warm, heavy boots sturdy enough to brave the elements, the slippery ground, and more than three hundred inches of snow a year.

It hurts to breathe, but Gideon inhales deeply. He enjoys the sensation of the cold air bruising the delicate lining of his lungs. Alana grabs the sleeve of his jacket, pulling him toward her.

"Gideon, do you hear me talking to you?"

He nods, squinting as he stares into the distance. "I hear you."

"Ask of me what you will."

"There is nothing I want to ask of you." He turns toward her, brushing her hand from his sleeve. Her blue eyes flash angrily, her chin jutting forth. This is the first time he has asked nothing of her.

Their relationship has always been volatile—hot and cold. They met in an entirely different place than the one they find themselves in now. They were seniors at NYU. He was studying architecture. She was studying musical theater. One drunken night, after meeting over bingo at a hipster bar in the Williamsburg section of Brooklyn, they stumbled back to her fifth-floor walk-up. She poured them wine in plastic cups and as they drank, Gideon awkwardly kissed her neck and fumbled with her bra clasp, thankful he had remembered to bring a couple condoms before heading out. When they were sufficiently drunk enough to not be nervous around one another, she sat him on the edge of her bed, unbuttoned his jeans, and wrapped her mouth around his cock, thick and pale, lightly veined. Alana had no way of knowing at the time, but she was Gideon's first. The sensation of her tongue lazily sliding along the length of his cock, and the tiny sounds she made as she took him into her throat were more than enough for him to swear the rest of his life to her.

For the next five years they were inseparable, living the big-city lives they had always dreamed of. He earned a position at a successful architecture firm. While his particular work wasn't that exciting, there was room to grow and the senior partners were doing truly innovative work. Alana started in the ensemble and eventually landed a leading role in the company of a long-running Broadway show. Every night, Gideon would meet her at the stage door, waiting at the end of a long line of eager fans. He walked her home, listening to her talk about how her performance had gone, which cast member was sleeping with whom, the things that had gone wrong. When they talked about his day she listened intently, as if the design specifications of a window in a fifty-story building mattered. Alana would talk so fast, her face flushed with excitement, traces of stage makeup still marking the edges of her face. In these moments, Gideon would look up at the sky, the buildings towering over them, Alana's small hand in his, and his heart would pound so hard, he feared his ribcage would shatter.

Some nights, she would wait for him in her dressing room wearing nothing but her robe, a gift from Gideon on opening night, her skin still damp from the shower. Alana would close the door, lean against it, giving Gideon a *come hither* look, her thick black hair falling around her face. "You're about to fuck a woman who's going to be a star," she'd say. She believed in telling the story until it came true and so did he. She would let her robe fall open, revealing olive skin, the gracefully defined muscles of a dancer's body, the impossibly long lines of her legs, a little extra thickness in the thighs, her breasts full, set slightly apart, nipples dusted lightly with brown. She would close the distance between them, straddle him on the small love seat, and they would fuck until they were both sweaty and spent, her hands pressed against the wall behind them, his hands firmly gripping her ass.

But then things changed. Gideon's father got sick—the kind of sick that required him to move back home until the inevitable. When he told Alana he had to leave, she smiled, chewed on her lower lip for a moment, then said, "Let's get married." The next morning, with a few of their friends, they went to city hall, got a marriage license, and were married by a justice of the peace. After a tearful good-bye at JFK, Gideon flew to Minnesota, his father and the life he thought he had escaped—not a bad life, but certainly not the one he wanted for himself. Six months later, when her contract was up, Alana followed. They left a lot behind—more than they realized at the time.

The *ask of me* game started in the time when they couldn't keep up with all the thoughts they needed to share with each other. It started when they wanted nothing more than to do whatever would make the other happy. Now, Gideon wants to keep his thoughts to himself, because Alana is leaving him. The one thing he wants to ask of her she will not give. A year or two turned in to three or four and she's ready to get back to the lives they left behind. For too long, they hoped that if they pretended that things were normal, they would somehow become normal. Now, they have stopped pretending. If winter had not settled in already, she would have left weeks ago. Instead, she's decided to wait until spring. Things are always easier when the snow thaws.

She grabs his arm again. "Why don't you have anything to ask?"

Gideon grabs Alana by her waist, pressing her against a nearby tree. He holds her arms over her head and looks down at her. "I was under the impression that we were no longer in the position to ask anything of one another."

Before she can answer, he covers her lips with his, kissing her hard, the tightness in his chest growing. Her lips are dry, almost chapped. She is reticent at first, struggling to free herself from his grip, but soon, her mouth is open, her tongue playing with his. Gideon fumbles with his belt buckle, undoing his jeans, then hers. She is warm and sweet and in their kiss he tastes who they were when they first met. He slides his hands under her sweater, squeezing her breasts, then running his thumbs over her hard nipples. She moans, taking his cock in her hands, stroking until he's hard. Shivering, he lifts Alana and she kicks her left leg free from her pants before wrapping her thighs around his waist.

Alana gasps as he slides his cock inside her cunt, where it's humid, and entirely unlike the North Country. She grabs at his coat and he quickly shrugs it free, letting it fall onto the snow. Bracing himself with one arm against the tree, he thrusts until his cock is buried deeply. They stare at each other, until his breath catches and Gideon looks away. Alana gently clasps the back of his neck with one hand, sliding the other beneath his shirt. She has always enjoyed the sensation of his chest beneath her hands—sinewy muscles over his breastbone and a delightful softness at his belly. Gideon fucks her slowly, softly, tiny spirals of pleasure blossoming at the tip of his cock and quickly working their way through the rest of his body. Alana tightens the grip of her thighs and grabs hold of the tree with both hands. With each thrust, she rises to meet him. They no longer feel the cold. Instead, it is skin, the cadence of their voices, Alana's moans increasing in pitch as she nears climax.

After they come, Alana pushes Gideon away and dresses quickly. As she walks away, toward the cabin, leaving him alone, near a tree with his pants around his ankles, she says, "I'm not staying." She doesn't look back.

Despite it all, Gideon is in love with November.

During their first year together, they promised one another they wouldn't go crazy buying each other expensive Christmas presents. Instead, they would take trips to all those places in the world they had always wanted to visit. That first year, it was the Amalfi Coast of Italy and three weeks in a small apartment, drinking wine and making love until their bodies were chafed and sore. Gideon learned how to say *Non posso vivere senza te*—I can't live without you, which he tells her, on a beach, in the middle of the night because they cannot sleep. Alana covered her mouth with one hand. There were arcs of tears cresting along her eyelids. "I can't believe you're mine," she told him. She was wearing a thin sundress, and nothing underneath. Gideon slid his hand between her thighs, warm and gritty with sand. When he slid two fingers inside her, she covered his hand with hers, tossed her head back and whispered, *"Non posso vivere senza te."* With his thumb against her clit, and his fingers pressing against the soft doughy walls of her cunt, Gideon made her come over and over again. When her clit became so sensitive, so saturated with pleasure that even the lightest touch hurt, she collapsed in his arms. They fell asleep where they lay, on a deserted Italian beach, until a police officer woke them in the morning.

In Paris, two years later, they stood on a rooftop watching the City of Light alive and mysterious below. The air was warm and still. It was a perfect spring evening. Alana leaned back against Gideon's chest, enjoying his embrace. He whispered *Vous êtes l'amour de ma vie,* before nibbling on her earlobe.

"I don't know what you just said," Alana told him. "But it was lovely."

Gideon smiled in the darkness, pulled at her neck with his teeth. Alana reached for his hand, pulling it under her skirt, and beneath the waistband of her panties.

He chuckled softly. "Here?"

Alana motioned to the city below. "Is there a better place?"

Gideon sank to his knees, rolling Alana's tank top up over her navel, pressing his lips against the small of her back. Alana lifted her skirt around her waist and slowly, Gideon pulled her panties down around her ankles, kissing the backs of her thighs, the sensitive spots behind her knees, her inner ankles.

Gripping the low brick wall in front of her, Alana whispered, "Please, don't tease. Not tonight."

Gideon stood, and in one motion, he pulled his cock out and slid inside Alana where she was wet and waiting for him.

She reached back, holding his thigh with one hand, letting her fingernails dig into his skin. Gideon groaned, loudly, pressing his weight against her body. He slid his hand, fingers splayed widely, up her back and into her hair, slowly curling his fingers into a tight fist. He pulled her head back the way she liked it, the muscles of her neck straining. A sheen of sweat broke out across his forehead, and, clenching his ass muscles, he thrust hard, hard enough to push Alana forward. She braced herself with her free hand, her breathing rapid and shallow.

"Open your eyes," he told her.

Alana spread her legs wider, dug her nails deeper into his thigh. When she opened her eyes, she stared at Gideon, a hard expression in her eyes. *"Noubliez jamais ce moment,"* he told her.

He thrust again, his cock reaching for the deepest parts of her.

"That," she gasped. "I understand."

The year before everything changed, they went to Hong Kong and stayed in a gorgeous hotel on Victoria Harbor. The chaos, the lights, the millions and millions of people—Gideon and Alana couldn't help but marvel at a place so different from the world they knew. The next year, they decided, they would return to Hong Kong and the skyline and the mountains in the distance.

But there will be no trip this year, and there's no real reason to exchange gifts. Nonetheless, Gideon buys a small tree, which Alana decorates on Christmas Eve, draping it with silver and red strands of fabric. She does this to pass the time, she tells him, and for old time's sake. Outside, it is snowing, fat ornate flakes piling up and covering every visible surface. It has been snowing every day for two weeks, and there is no end in sight. Each morning, Alana goes outside with a measuring stick to see how much of the stuff has fallen overnight. She wants a record, for posterity. As she makes coffee, she gives Gideon the daily report, liberally peppered with profanities about godforsaken places. Sometimes it's three inches, other times it's thirteen or more. Her displeasure is palpable and mutual. To cope, she spends her days online, instant messaging her New York friends, reading Broadway gossip sites—carefully measuring how much sanity she will need to endure this final winter, hoping she has enough. Gideon spends his days staying out of her way, clearing snow from the driveway, checking in on the hardware store his father owns, and making sure his father is as comfortable as can be expected. They know their lonely routines well now. They both have their roles to play.

On Christmas morning, Gideon awakes early and watches Alana sleeping. They still share a bed because the nights are cold and bitter. Sleeping alone in a chilly room is one indignity his wife is unwilling to suffer. Her breathing is shallow, her back turned to him. The pale shafts of light breaking through the clouds cast shadows across the expanse of her back. She shifts and he quickly turns away. He hopes that his memory can hold enough of these images to sustain him when she's gone. That night, after a dinner of glazed ham, roasted red potatoes, and a spinach salad, Gideon quietly hands Alana a small package, wrapped with a single red bow. Inside are old Playbills from the shows she wanted to star in had she been alive fifty years ago. The last Playbill is custom made with a picture of Alana on the cover. *For when you're a star,* Gideon wrote inside the cover. She fingers the edges of each booklet, carefully turning each page.

"Oh, Gideon."

She shakes her head almost imperceptibly and leaves the room. He finds her in bed. She is naked, leaning against a stack of pillows, one hand resting across her stomach. Gideon kneels at the edge of the bed and takes his shirt off, throwing it on a nearby chair. He starts to say something, but she presses one finger to his lips. "I'm not staying," she says. "But I do want to wish you a Merry Christmas."

Alana pulls Gideon toward her and gnaws his lower lip with her teeth while sliding her fingernails down his back. He is instantly hard. She shifts and turns onto her stomach. He closes his eyes, kissing the backs of her thighs, dragging his tongue alongside the curves of her ass. For now, they're not in a small, drafty cabin on his father's property. They're in their Manhattan loft, sweaty and tangled in sheets and one another. Instead of the silence of snow, they can hear the city beneath them, the low wail of an ambulance in the distance. Gideon massages his way up Alana's body, placing moist kisses along her spine. She raises her ass slightly and his cock jumps. He nudges her thighs apart and Alana pulls her knees toward her breasts. She is open and wet, so wet he can smell her. Holding his cock, Gideon traces the edges of her pussy lips, teasing her by pressing just the tip inside her. She hisses, pulling the loose sheets into her hands. He penetrates deeper, presses two fingers against her clit, stroking hard. When she tries to move toward him, he stops her. He wants this moment to last.

Tossing her hair to one side, Alana looks back at Gideon, her eyes hazy with desire. "Please, fuck me," she asks. Her voice is raw and low. She knows he likes it when he brings her to this place where she wants nothing more than to ask for what she knows he will eventually give. Gideon bites her shoulders softly, strokes her clit a little harder. He can feel bone just behind that slick flesh. Her legs twitch. He lightly smacks her ass and she buries her head in the pillows. He smacks her ass again, harder this time, leaving a light red blush that he traces with his fingertips. When she moans, "Please," again, he lets her have a little more of his cock, gives her ass another tap. Alana's thighs tremble.

"You may not be staying," he says. "But I want you to admit that there's no place you'd rather be right now."

Alana stills, and moans loudly.

Gideon pulls back, his cock hovering against her pussy lips.

"Fine," she mutters. "There's no place I'd rather be."

Gideon slaps her ass. "Say it like you mean it."

Alana looks at her husband over her shoulder, her hair covering her face. She turns away and softly, ever so softly, ever so slowly she says, "There is no place I would rather be."

It is a small victory, but for now it is enough. Gideon takes hold of her ass, and inches his entire cock into her cunt, quickly settling into a steady rhythm. Their moans are punctuated by the damp sound of their bodies coming together and falling apart. He tells himself that he doesn't need her to stay, that these moments are enough. She tells herself she doesn't want to stay, that these moments are not enough. But with each stroke, she rears to meet him, clenches the sheets in her fists until her knuckles are white. Alana comes before Gideon, feels the overwhelming sharpness that starts just below her clit and quickly spreads throughout her body until she is shaking uncontrolla-bly and a gush of wetness explodes from her cunt. As her body spasms around him, Gideon comes and falls on top of his wife, his sweat mingling with hers. When he tries to roll away, Alana shakes her head and starts crying softly.

"Don't move, not yet," she says.

Gideon kisses her shoulder, sliding his hands along her arms until his hands are covering hers. "I'm staying," he says.

New Year's Day is not a good day. Gideon's father is disori-ented, and angry that his body and now his mind are failing him. Alana and Gideon sit with him, trying to pass a few hours away. She has more patience for this kind of vigil than Gideon because she lost her parents at a young age and wishes she could have had this time to say good-bye. She sings her father-in-law old show tunes and he smiles at the songs he recognizes, barks profanities at other times, thinks she's his wife, eyeing her with a toothless grin. When Gideon can no longer stand witness to his father's frailty, he steps onto the back porch and lights a cigarette. He had quit years ago, at Alana's insistence, but since moving back to Minnesota, he had been sneaking a few smokes a week, huddled behind the cabin like a common criminal. It is a dark afternoon, and all he can see are trees and huge bluffs of snow. In the distance, he hears the nasally whir of snowmobilers shredding snow. When he hears the metal screen door creak behind him, Gideon flicks his cigarette into a nearby mound of snow, shoving his hands into his pockets. Alana leans against his back, her chin resting just below his shoulder.

"You've been smoking," she says with a small laugh, sliding her hands into his coat pockets.

"I needed to relax, get my mind off things."

Alana intertwines her fingers with Gideon's. He can feel the cool metal of her wedding ring against his skin. The realization is bittersweet.

"Come inside," she says.

Gideon breathes deeply and follows her back into the house. They stand in the doorway between the kitchen and the living room. The television in his father's room blares loudly, and occasionally, Gideon hears his father's laughter. Alana looks up at Gideon and smiles.

"Things will get better."

"You can't promise that," he says.

Alana leans against the doorjamb, hooking one foot around Gideon's calf, pulling him closer.

"I can help you relax," she tells him. "And I won't kill you."

He arches an eyebrow. "That remains to be seen."

Alana smirks. "Funny."

Gideon shrugs out of his coat and leans against the opposite doorjamb, tapping the toes of her boots with his. "You can go back to the cabin, if you want."

"I'm not leaving you alone today. Don't get all maudlin on me."

He smiles. "Maudlin?"

Alana winks at him the way she used to at curtain call, searching the dark audience for where he was seated—a private moment they could share in plain view.

Alana gently brushes her lips across Gideon's. Wordlessly, she unties her boots, sets them neatly just inside the kitchen. Barefoot, she steps onto his boots, places her right hand against his back, her left hand on his shoulder.

"Dance with me?"

Gideon leads her in a lazy waltz as she hums a random tune. She rests her head against his chest, idly fingering a hole in his sweater. "I don't remember the last time we danced."

"Birdland. We were at a concert at Birdland. When the band started playing 'Moody's Mood for Love' . . ."

"I pulled you onto the dance floor, despite your protests, and made you dance with me," Alana finishes.

Gideon holds Alana tighter. "*Protest* is a strong word."

Their lips meet again, in a tender, almost shy, kiss. Alana slips her tongue between her husband's lips, finding the hard edges of his teeth. Her fingertips tingle as she clasps the back of his neck with one hand. Gideon responds eagerly, swaying from side to side with Alana in his arms. Every so often they pause, pull apart just far enough that their lips are barely touching.

"What are we doing?" Gideon asks.

Alana silences him with another kiss, memorizing every groove of his lips, the lower one slightly fuller, the subtle ridge at the center from a skateboarding accident. Their tongues wrestle until they are grinding their bodies against one another. She can feel his cock, erect, straining against the seams of his jeans. When she pulls away again, Alana tries to catch her breath and turns away for a moment. She slides her yoga pants around her ankles. Underneath, she is naked, and the sight of her pussy, covered in a neatly trimmed pelt of black hair, excites Gideon. Placing her hands on Gideon's shoulders, she pushes him onto his knees and leans back against the doorjamb. Gideon sighs, slides her threadbare NYU T-shirt up just below her breasts, rests his cheek against the bare flat of her abdomen. They stand like that for a long while, Gideon listening to her breathe, the steady beating of her heart, the strange, intimate sounds her stomach makes. Alana runs her fingers through Gideon's hair— it is one of her favorite things about him—wild and curly, refusing to behave.

Gideon draws a thin trail of saliva from Alana's navel to just above her pussy. She continues to play with his hair, occasionally massaging his scalp with her fingertips, her eyes closed. Gideon places his hands between her thighs. She shivers, but follows his direction, widening her stance. With his thumbs, Gideon spreads Alana's pussy lips and leans forward, lightly flicking his tongue against the spot just above her clit. His cock throbs, aching for relief. He leans back against his heels, slides one hand around Alana's body, taking firm hold of her ass. He traces the outer edges of her pussy lips, which quiver ever so slightly at the touch, and then he blows lightly, letting his breath fall against her. Alana pulls one ankle free from her pants, perching it over Gideon's left shoulder. Gideon slides his left hand up her body and slips two fingers into her mouth. His wedding ring presses against her chin. It is a bittersweet sensation. She takes hold of his wrist, and, looking down at him, she swallows his fingers into her mouth until her lips reach his knuckles. Gideon rests his forehead against her mound, the soft hairs tickling his skin, enjoying the sensation of her mouth working along his fingers.

When they are thick with wet, he pulls his hand away and slowly slides the moist fingertips inside her ass. Alana gasps quietly, her stomach muscles tightening. Gideon waits, slides his fingers deeper.

"Put your mouth on me," Alana whispers. Gideon wraps his lips around Alana's clit, hard and swollen. He hums with his lips, and the curious sensation sends sharp shards of pleasure up Alana's spine. With his tongue, he suckles insistently, increasing the pressure as Alana's breath quickens. When he senses Alana is about to come, he stops, slides his tongue between her pussy lips to her cunt, thrusting his tongue in and out, exploring the mysterious folds just past her entrance. His fingers work deeper into her ass, the tight muscles clenching around him. Alana covers her mouth with her hand, trying to stifle her moans. Her heel digs deeper into his back, her thigh muscles straining as she tries to resist the intense waves of joy and sadness washing over her. Slowly, Gideon pulls his fingers back until her ass puckers around the fingertips, penetrates again, allows the rest of the world to fall away.

All he concentrates on is Alana—how she tastes and smells and responds to his mouth and his fingers. When she can control herself no longer, Alana pulls Gideon's head back slightly, and rocking her hips back and forth, grinds her clit against Gideon's tongue. He submits, allows himself to be used. Her gasps grow louder, her thigh muscles tense further, a burning sensation settling around her hips. As she comes, Alana allows herself to groan loudly, just once, her body shuddering, her legs rubbery and weak. Gideon thrusts his fingers hard, deep into her ass one last time, then pulls them out, the thin membranes reluctant to relinquish their grip. She accidentally slams her head against the doorjamb and winces. Wiping his hands on his pants, he falls back and stretches his limbs, staring at the ceiling. Her pussy juice covers the lower half of his face, quickly drying into a fragile, thin layer. Alana slips back into her pants, then lies down next to him, licking the palm of her hand before sliding her hands beneath the waist of his jeans. She brushes her thumb across the tip of his cock, and carefully wraps her hand around the shaft. She strokes him from base to tip. Seconds later, he comes, with a violent thrust of the hips, his cock spasming in her hand. She licks the silvery strands of come from her fingers, rolls onto his chest, and kisses him deeply. They taste each other on one another's lips and wonder, as they have for the past several months, if this will be the last kiss they share.

"I'm sorry," she finally says, rolling away and sitting with her knees pulled up against her chest.

Gideon rolls onto his side, leaning on his elbow. "What are you sorry for?"

Alana studies the antique ceiling fan above, admiring the intricate detail on the woodwork and the Tiffany glass dome. "For all of this. Us. Your father. He's not getting worse but he's not getting better. I know seeing him like this hurts you."

"Seeing us like this hurts more," Gideon says.

Alana presses her forehead against her knees, rocking back and forth. "It hurts me, too," she says softly.

Four evenings a week, Alana gives voice and dance lessons at a small studio she rents in town. The space is not so much a studio as it is a large, poorly lit room with a piano and a wooden floor, but it's something. The work gives her something to hold on to, she says. And it helps keep her in shape for getting back to her life in the city. When the last of her students have left, she'll often stay in the studio by herself, working through old sheet music or practicing dance routines. Before one or two years became three or four, Gideon used to arrive early to pick her up. He loved watching the ease with which she moved her long dancer's body and the pure joy radiating across her face. But then, he stopped watching because it was plain to see that there was neither as much joy nor as much ease in the way her body moved from one corner of the room to the other because her heart was no longer in it.

On Valentine's Day, Gideon is at home, studying blueprints from the last project he worked on before he left New York. Alana is at her studio. She left early in the morning, with a note on the refrigerator that she would be gone all day. At the bottom of the slip of paper, she scribbled, "Happy Valentine's Day." Gideon crumpled the note in his hands and watched it burn while he stood in the backyard smoking a cigarette. Around nine, the phone rings. At first Gideon ignores it because few people have the number but when the caller persists, Gideon sets the blueprints aside and looks at the caller ID screen.

"Hello?"

"It's me," Alana says. "It's a long story but I've locked myself out of the studio and the gas line in my car has frozen. No one seems to be around town and I'm freezing my ass off."

He looks out the window above the drafting table. The night is still, but he can tell that the air is frigid because of the frost lining the edges of the glass panes. "I'll be right there," he says.

Five minutes later, Gideon pulls up in front of the studio.

Alana is hunched over in the doorway, facing away from the wind, her dance bag resting at her feet. Gideon turns the heat to high and quickly helps her into the car.

"What happened?"

Alana holds her hands over the heating vents. "Just take me home."

Back at the cabin, Gideon quickly starts a fire and sits Alana in front of it, wrapping a warm wool blanket around her shoulders. He steps into the kitchen and returns with a mug of hot tea. Alana is shivering uncontrollably, and in the orange glow of the fire, he can see that her fingertips are bright red.

"Take this," he says.

Hands trembling, Alana takes the tea, cupping the mug with both hands. Gideon sits next to her, rubbing her thigh.

"Feeling better?"

Alana shakes her head, her teeth chattering.

Gideon slides behind her, wrapping his arms around her shoulders, trying to share some of his body heat. Alana tenses, then relaxes against him. For a long while they are silent, watching the fire, listening to one another breathe.

Gideon perches his chin over her shoulder. "How did we get here?"

"I don't know," Alana says. "But I don't want to be *here*."

"Neither do I," says Gideon. "But he's my father. I can't leave him alone."

Alana swallows the last dregs of tea and sets the mug down. "I didn't ask you to."

Gideon pulls away. "You've made that clear."

Alana turns and kneels between Gideon's thighs. When he

tries to look away, she holds his face between her hands. "There's nothing for me here."

"I'm here."

Alana kisses Gideon softly, then rests her forehead against his. "I never understood what people meant when they say that love isn't enough, but now, I think I know."

"You are impossible."

"Put your arms up," Alana says.

Gideon complies and she removes his sweater and the long johns he is wearing. She quickly slides out of her clothes and helps him remove his pants. Lying atop his body, she says, "They say that the best way to help someone with hypothermia is to lie naked with them."

"You're changing the subject," Gideon says.

Alana kisses Gideon along the column of his throat and the hollows above his collarbone. She slides one hand between their bodies toward his cock and slowly traces each of his nipples with her tongue.

"What are you doing?"

Alana takes a nipple between her teeth, and mutters, "Stop talking."

Gideon covers his eyes with the palm of his hand. Despite their best efforts, they come back, over and over again, to this place where they make love instead of facing the difficult truths of their relationship. Alana works her way lower, until her lips are at the tip of his cock. She traces around the tip, then inside the slit, already wet with salty silver. With her eyes closed, she remembers the night they first met, and how nervous Gideon was, sitting on the edge of her bed. She cups his balls in one hand, squeezing until he groans. When she feels his hand against the top of her head, she traces the base of his cock with her tongue, then back along the shaft, tracing each vein and the thick ridge along the underside. Squeezing his balls harder, so hard that Gideon arches his back, raising his hips to her mouth, Alana starts working her lips down the length of his cock until her lips are pressed against the base. She gags slightly, then breathes and relaxes her throat. Gideon holds her head between his hands as she starts to bob up and down, every muscle in his body taut.

Before he can come, Alana straddles Gideon's waist, pulling his hands to her breasts. He squeezes them, rolling them upward, then to the side. Without ceremony, Alana lowers herself onto Gideon's cock, planting her hands on his chest. Tonight she is open and slick; his cock fills her easily. Back arched, eyes closed, she pitches herself back and forth, sometimes moving her hips in a lazy, sensuous circle. Gideon rolls her nipples between his thumbs and forefingers with increasing pressure.

"Yes," Alana says. "Harder."

Gideon squeezes harder, bringing Alana just past the brink of pain, pausing, squeezing harder again. Alana rocks her hips faster, with shorter strokes. Her hands slide to Gideon's shoulders, and she claws at him with her fingernails, leaving mean red marks from his neck to his elbows.

"We have to stop doing this," Gideon stutters, his hips jerking to meet her with each thrust.

"I know," Alana says through clenched teeth, continuing to ride him, clenching the muscles of her cunt tightly.

"I'm coming," Gideon pants, as the intense pressure between his thighs erupts and he pulls Alana to his chest, lessening the distance between them. His body continues to spasm as Alana slows the motion of her body, until she is perfectly still.

"I'm warmer now," she says.

They lay in front of the fire, Gideon pulling the blanket over their bodies until she falls asleep. He kisses each of her ten fingertips, and carefully extricates himself from her embrace.

"I'm not staying," she says when he is halfway up the stairs. "Not because I don't love you or because I don't want to but because I can't."

Gideon stops, tries to think of an appropriate response, but says nothing.

The blizzard comes out of nowhere as Gideon is driving back from a meeting in Minneapolis in late March. What starts as light flurries quickly becomes sheets of snow blowing back and forth across the two-lane highway, wind howling at a distressing pitch. He leans forward in his seat, his hands gripping the steering wheel. There is no visibility in any direction. When he tries to use his cell phone, there's no signal. A mile ahead, Gideon spots a truck stop, the neon lights glowing faintly through the thick clouds of snow. He pulls into the nearly empty parking lot and, wrapping his coat around his body, heads inside. The place is populated with a few bored-looking truckers and other commuters who, like Gideon, had actually believed the weather reports. He finds a local newspaper, orders a pot of coffee, and takes a seat in an empty booth, hoping to get back on the road soon. The waitress, Nicole, her name tag reads, comes to take his order. She is short, pleasantly curvy, with fiery red hair and dark eyeliner around her eyes.

"You get caught in the storm?" she asks with a wide smile.

He nods, rubbing his arms instinctively. "It's pretty bad out there."

She gestures around her. "It's pretty bad in here, too, but you're definitely different from the guys I normally meet."

Gideon sips his coffee, gagging quietly. "And what kind of guys do you normally meet?"

Nicole leans back on her heels. "You know. Truckers, loggers, miners. Guys with dirty hands who like to stare at my ass. But you," Nicole says, grabbing hold of his hand and inspecting his fingernails. "You have clean hands. I like that."

"I did, however, stare at your ass."

Nicole laughs, a loud, vulgar laugh that thrills him. "You're married, I see."

Gideon cocks his head to the side. "Technically. It's complicated."

Nicole slides onto the bench across from him, continues holding his hand. "I also like complicated."

Gideon smiles, enjoying the fluttering in his stomach and the attention of a woman he knows nothing about and will never see again. He glances at his watch and remembers that Alana is probably wondering where he is. "I have to make a phone call," he says politely.

Nicole grins. "You do that. The phones are over there," she says, pointing to a dark corner.

Gideon slides out of the booth slowly, his knees aching. Along a narrow, dimly lit hallway, there are three pay phones between two bathroom doors. The air is dank and sour. He stares at the phones, fingers his pockets for change, leans against the wall with a heavy sigh.

"Are you going to make that call?"

From the corner of his eye, Gideon can see Nicole standing, one hand against her hip. "I'm not sure."

Nicole takes hold of his collar and pulls him into the men's restroom, where the dank smell is stronger, and one of the fluorescent lights overhead flickers. The sink is dirty, covered with matted paper towels and cigarette ashes. "You should never do things you don't want to do," she says.

"Why is that?"

"Life is too short."

Gideon laughs. "This from a woman working in a truck stop?"

Nicole slaps his chest. "I do what I have to so that other times, I can do what I want."

Gideon draws a finger down Nicole's neck and between her breasts. "And what is it that you want?"

Nicole sinks to her knees, lowers the zipper of Gideon's khakis and pulls his cock out. "Not bad," she says.

"I do what I can."

"I bet you do."

Without ceremony, Nicole pulls his entire cock into her mouth. Gideon grits his teeth and tries to relax but when he looks down, all he can see is his wife on the floor of her fifth-floor walk-up, and the way her eyes flash when she has him in her mouth. He pushes Nicole away.

"I can't do this."

Nicole arches an eyebrow, wiping the corners of her mouth with her middle finger. "I have a room in the motel out back if you'd be more comfortable there."

"That might be good," he says.

Gideon puts himself back into his pants and helps Nicole to her feet. She slips a key dangling from a large plastic key chain etched with the number *three* into his pocket and tweaks his chin. "I'll meet you in a little while. My shift's almost over."

As he returns to his booth for his coat, Gideon looks around the truck stop, imagines that Alana is at the far end of the room, eyeing him with disappointment. He rubs his eyes, gathers his things, and heads out the back door, trying to maintain his balance as he wades through the snowdrifts covering the small parking lot. Nicole's motel room is clean but sparsely deco-rated—a sagging but neatly made queen bed, an old television, two night tables, one with a lamp and alarm clock, the other holding a vase of plastic flowers and several picture frames. In the bathroom, a spare uniform and panty hose are hanging from the shower curtain. Gideon sits on the edge of the bed and turns on the television. The last thing he remembers is chuckling as he listens to the newscasters discussing the unexpected nature of the blizzard raging outside.

He wakes, groggily, to a firm hand on his shoulder, shaking him. He opens one eye and looks up. Nicole is sitting next to him, wearing a knee-length purple negligee, one leg crossed over the other. "Aren't you supposed to fall asleep afterward?"

Gideon blushes, sits up so fast he becomes dizzy. "I must have been more tired than I realized."

"I'm just teasing you," Nicole says. "And the good news is that I'm off work now."

"What time is it?"

"A little past three in the morning." Nicole swings her legs onto the bed, leans back on her elbows. "I think we should continue where we left off."

Gideon stretches alongside her, resting one hand across her belly. Nicole raises her lips to his, kisses him shyly, lips slightly parted. Gideon's hand slides to her breast, which he cups lightly, as he slides his knee across her thigh. He tries to clear his mind, give himself permission to make love to another woman, but this is too much for him. Alana is the only woman he has ever been with.

"I really can't do this," he says.

"Is it me?"

"Not at all. You're sweet and beautiful. My life. My wife. It's complicated."

The waitress smiles a sad little smile. She pats Gideon on the chest, just over his heart. "Isn't it always?"

When Gideon finally makes it home several hours later, Alana is pacing the hallway by the front door. "Where the hell have you been?" she shouts as he closes the door behind him. "You were supposed to be here last night."

"Can I at least take off my boots?"

Alana glares. "I was worried. You weren't answering your phone and the weather . . ."

"I didn't realize we were still worrying about each other."

She nods, just once, crossing her arms across her chest and pursing her lips. "Sometimes," she says. "You can be a real asshole."

Gideon stomps the snow from his boots and starts peeling off the winter layers—scarf, hat, gloves, coat, sweater, and boots. "That makes two of us."

Before her hand can connect with his face, Gideon leans to the right and grabs Alana's wrist.

"I almost slept with another woman."

Alana wrests free and stares at him with a blank expression. "What am I supposed to do with that?"

"I wanted you to know."

Alana starts pulling on her coat and boots from the closet. "I can't even look at you right now," she says.

Gideon stands in front of the door, his hand on the knob. "You're leaving me, or have you forgotten? And I stopped before I did anything that couldn't be undone."

"I'm leaving here," Alana shouts, her forehead pulsing. "I'm not leaving you for anyone. If you can't see the difference, I don't know you at all."

She slips behind Gideon and yanks the front door open, a blast of cold air making her cough. "And I'll have you know that I haven't even considered being with another man. I can see now what a waste that's been."

Gideon tries to close the door, but she ducks under his arm and heads for the main house.

"Alana," Gideon calls after her. "Let me explain."

"Go to hell," she shouts back.

In North Country, April snow is what truly breaks your spirit. The mild days give you hope, but then, one morning, a morning after a beautiful forty-degree day, you wake up to eighteen inches of fresh powder and the painful realization that winter will never end. Gideon's father passes away on one such morning in mid-April. One moment he's sitting up in bed, smiling at a black-and-white picture of his wife. The next, his eyes are closed and his brittle chest is no longer rising and falling. For hours, Gideon holds his father's hand, the skin dry like paper. He cries with loud, ugly sobs not because his father is dead, but because he is relieved. This is how Alana finds her husband, alone with his father in a dark room, his shoulders heaving. Holding back her own tears, she sits on Gideon's lap, and lets him cry against her shoulder, his tears quickly spreading across her thin blouse.

"It's okay," she says over and over.

When he has no more tears left to cry, Gideon looks up. "I don't know what to do."

"I'll take care of things. Go home and wait for me."

Two hours later, Alana returns to their cabin. Gideon sits at the cluttered kitchen table, staring into the distance. She draws him a bath in the old claw-foot tub and sits on the edge, keeping quiet company as he lays in the hot water until his skin is bright red.

"Join me?" he asks.

Alana undresses, then sinks into the water across from him until she is almost entirely immersed. She rests her feet against his thighs, wiggling her toes playfully.

"How are you feeling?"

Gideon idly runs a washcloth across his chest. "I don't know, yet. So much has happened."

"You were a good son to a good father. That much *I* know."

"This doesn't change anything, does it?"

Sadly, Alana shakes her head. "No, my love. It doesn't."

Gideon nods curtly, and they stare at each other until Alana is forced to look away.

* * *

It is a warm May afternoon. Alana and Gideon stand on the tarmac as she readies to board a puddle jumper to Detroit and then on to New York. The ground is wet with melting snow, but the sun shines brightly overhead. She squints, holding one hand above her eyes as she looks up at him. Gideon stares at his feet and shrugs as she brushes her fingers across his hand.

"I should be going now," she says.

He nods. "Do you have everything you need?" It's a rhetorical question, really. She boxed up most of her things and had them shipped back to their loft several weeks ago. She already has several auditions scheduled and will waste no time picking up her career where she left it. Alana and Gideon said their good-byes at the cabin to avoid a *scene*—to end things as neatly as possible. In a few weeks, when he has finished handling his father's affairs and the sale of the hardware store, he too will return to the city, sleeping on a friend's couch until he can find a new apartment. He'll find a job at a new firm and try to start over.

Alana stands on the tips of her toes and draws her lips from his ear to the corner of his lips. They hold each other's hands tightly but avoid making eye contact. They still wear their wedding rings.

"Non posso vivere senza te," Gideon whispers into her hair.

She starts to murmur a reply but changes her mind, angrily brushing away stray tears.

"I can't do this," she says.

She spins on her heels and heads up the stairs. Halfway up, she stops, tensing her shoulders. Without turning back, she asks, just loud enough for Gideon to hear, "Ask of me what you will."

Gideon inhales sharply, lowers his head, a loud ringing in his ears.

Alana turns around, balancing between two stairs. "Ask of me what you will," she repeats, saying each word carefully.

Gideon turns the palms of his hands upward and looks up. "Stay," is all he says.

 ISABELLE GRAY is the pseudonym of a writer braving North Country winters. Her writing can be found in *First Timers; Best Date Ever; Iridescence: Sensuous Shades of Erotica;* and many others. She can be found online at www.pettyfictions.com.

Hidden Treasure

by Sophie Mouette

When Brenda was a girl, her widowed mother had worked at Frogmorton House, and, promising always to be good, Brenda had been given the run of the estate. She never touched any of the antiques as she wandered through the folly of a Germanic castle, pretending she was a princess in the turreted tower and believing that the narrow servants' staircase was a secret passageway.

When she was older, she fell in love with the romance between railroad magnate Winthrop Frogmorton and Austrian Henrietta Ströbel. Henrietta had claimed the Adirondacks reminded her of her beloved Alps, so Winthrop commissioned her a castle of their very own.

By the time she hit college, Brenda was beyond notions of girlish romance and obsessed instead with history, particularly the Victorian era of upstate New York. When she finally returned and took on her dream job as curator of Frogmorton House, it had been her idea to have the staff dress appropriately, to give visitors the full experience of the *schlöss*-like manor.

She'd never admit aloud that one of the reasons she'd hired

Sean as a security guard last month was because she guessed he'd look mouthwatering in a proper Victorian policeman's outfit of dark blue wool.

She'd been right about that. Oh, had she ever been right.

Now, as the lights flickered ominously, she looked up from the computer screen, aware that she hadn't been seeing the membership newsletter in front of her. She'd been fantasizing about Sean again.

Still, she automatically hit Save, just in case they lost power. The battery backup should mean she wouldn't lose anything, but you never know with computers.

She slipped off her narrow black-rimmed glasses, surprised to see how dark it had become. Had she been woolgathering that long? Somehow, not surprising when it came to thoughts of Sean.

They'd gone to the same high school, but she'd been bookish and involved, and he'd been distant and sporty and a little shy, his bangs always tumbling into his eyes when he ducked his head.

Now his silky black hair was shorter, but tousled and untamed on top. He'd enlisted after high school, he told her when he started work at Frogmorton House, and by God, now that he was out, he was growing his hair again.

He was no longer shy, no longer a boy. His shoulders had broadened; his brilliant blue eyes held depth and experience. His grin was roguish, his stride confident.

And Brenda appreciated all of that. A lot.

She also appreciated the way his wool pants snugged over his tight ass cheeks. Her hands itched to cup the muscled curves, pull him close . . .

Shaking herself back to the present, she flipped on the antique banker's lamp on her desk and glanced at the clock, certain it would be time to close up the House and head home to her thermal lounging pajamas, leftover homemade pizza, and her Welsh corgi, Mort.

But it was only 3:00 p.m.

She glanced out the window. All day they'd had menacing gray clouds, as ominous a sign as the flickering lights. She'd known they were due for a storm, and by all accounts it was going to be a humdinger.

She just didn't expect the world to be white already.

The snow swirled down in gusts and eddies, the flakes dancing like manic fairies. She couldn't even see the evergreens just outside the window.

The lights flickered again, this time going completely out for a few seconds before returning. Brenda saved the membership newsletter file again, copied it onto a flash drive, then shut the computer down. It had been an excruciatingly slow day already, and in this weather they weren't going to get any more visitors. Best to close early and get out before the roads got too slippery.

She grabbed the walkie-talkie off the desk. "Sean, this is Brenda."

No answer.

"Sean? Pick up, please."

She gave the walkie-talkie an exasperated shake. Cell phone service was seriously dodgy in the Adirondack Mountains as it was, but Frogmorton House was nestled in a little valley that defied the reach of any cell tower. Sean should have his walkie-talkie on. . . .

She'd just have to go find him.

Not that seeking him out was such a bad thing. Brenda slipped her burgundy velvet fitted coat over her deep green wool and cashmere dress, glad for the extra warmth—Frogmorton House was drafty even in the height of summer, and today's storm was rattling the beautiful but ill-fitting windows, the glass wavy from over a century of excruciatingly slow gravitational slide.

She smoothed the velvet down the molded line of her torso. Even on quiet days like this, when time dragged and she didn't get to share her passion for Victoriana with another soul, her job still thrilled her. How many people got paid to hang out in a castle and wear a glorious late-Victorian outfit, complete with corset, to work?

Plus, a well-made corset was incredibly comfortable. Not to mention the pleasing way it nipped in her waist and plumped up her breasts.

She'd definitely noticed Sean ogling her cleavage.

Sean could ogle her cleavage any time. Do more than ogle, if it came to that, which she hoped it did.

During his interview, his sensual lips had curved into one of his roguish grins when she mentioned the required policeman's uniform and the formal butler's outfit he'd don when he helped at fund-raisers.

"Bonus," he'd said. "Halloween every day. I always loved . . . trick-or-treating." His tone was light, but his voice deepened suggestively on the last words and hit straight between her legs. She felt herself flushing and bit back an urge to offer all sorts of treats (and an assortment of tricks), right on the spot.

Thank God Hank, their bookkeeper, had been looking down

at Sean's résumé at that moment; his proper elderly brain would have caught fire from the looks shooting back and forth between them.

The heated glances and flirtatious remarks had been piling on ever since. But they simply hadn't had time to do anything about it. First the series of Victorian Christmas teas for the local schoolkids, and the holiday fund-raising cocktail party (Sean had made the kind of butler who'd have had real Victorian matrons consorting with the lower classes in a heartbeat), and then getting the house undecorated, and getting year-end thank-you letters out in time to make the IRS happy, and trying to sort through the Whitney bequest . . .

Plus all the maintenance issues that kept Sean busy because, let's face it, a lot of the time there wasn't a lot for a security guard to do except just be there, but the house itself could devour all your time if you let it. And like Brenda, Sean would let it.

One more reason she liked him.

She left her office, which was in the parlor off the foyer, so she could hear when tourists arrived.

Frogmorton House's pale stone hearkened to its Austrian and German inspiration, and it had round towers and clusters of narrow windows and a meandering, wandering layout that didn't make a whole lot of sense, really. The unconventional design made the House seem vaster than its two-stories-plus-basement-and-unfinished-attic. From the outside, it looked like it should be the setting for a ghost story or a Gothic tragedy, but Winthrop and Henrietta had lived into chubby, philanthropic old age, surrounded by a passel of children and grandchildren who, unusually for the era, had all survived to adulthood. The place was homey as well as grand, with a large nursery and elegantly framed children's drawings proudly displayed next to the Sargent portrait of Henrietta.

Brenda loved the place with an unholy passion.

She found Sean emerging from the basement into the kitchen. His dark hair was mussed—then again, it always had a mussed look to it, like he'd just crawled out of bed, and that was a lovely image because then he'd probably be naked—and a few cobwebs clung to the crisp navy blue wool of his uniform. The brass buttons shone as if he'd just buffed them, though.

"There you are," Brenda said. It was sort of a stupid thing to say, but for a moment there, the spicy smell of his aftershave had glued her tongue to the roof of her mouth. "I was trying to reach you, but the damn walkie-talkie . . ."

"Needs new batteries, I think," he said with an apologetic smile. "I'll pick some up tonight. But if you wanted me to check the fuse box, I just did. Replaced the fuse for the left tower, but the rest survived the power surge okay. Fuses. *Sheesh.* You wouldn't have an electrical upgrade scheduled any time soon?"

"It's tricky with a historic house—and expensive." She shrugged. "Maybe after we re-slate the roof so it stops leaking into the Birch Bedroom." Frogmorton House was luckier than many small museums—some of the numerous Frogmorton descendents had inherited Winston's generous spirit and knack for business—but money was still a constant struggle.

"Maybe we should check out the Birch Bedroom, make sure it's not snowing in there?" Sean raised one heavy dark eyebrow in a way that would have done a movie star playing a wickedly naughty hero proud. If Brenda had any doubts that his mind was in the gutter—and she didn't, because hers had descended right along with his—his smile made it clear he wasn't thinking about protecting the William Morris wallpaper or the delicate dressing table.

"Oh no," she blurted. "That bed frame's already damaged."

Oh God. She felt her face suffuse with heat. Had she actually said that aloud?

Yes, and despite the rush of mortification, she couldn't say she regretted it.

Not from the look on Sean's face, which had gone from flirty-but-work-safe to something that wasn't safe anywhere, and certainly not at work. Especially not when your workplace boasted seven bedrooms, six of which had sturdy, comfortable, downright decadent Victorian beds.

Heat coiled from her flushed face, tickled her nipples, spread down to her sex, which pulsed in appreciation of the images racing through her mind. Her. Sean. One of those Victorian beds—not the one in the Birch Room, which was only a single anyway, but maybe the grand canopied Frogmorton matrimonial bed.

Her lace-trimmed silk drawers caressed her thighs as she shifted nervously back and forth, rubbed against her suddenly damp and sensitive cleft. The corset held her like an embrace.

Her nipples felt like they were drilling through the now-confining corset.

Sean took a step forward.

The lights flickered again as the wind let out a howl like a tortured soul.

In the brief darkness, Sean's arms slipped around her, pulled her close.

His lips brushed hers. Soft, an inquiry, but with the promise of so much more behind them. He smelled good, like bay rum and something slightly musky that she thought was just him.

They'd kissed once before, back in high school, when Brenda had been inexperienced and she guessed Sean had been, too. He hadn't gone to the prom, but crashed the party by the lake. Of course there'd been drinking. At some point she'd turned on the log where she sat and he'd just been *there*, and their lips had touched, and then he'd eased back and for a moment she saw the fire reflected in his eyes, and then he was gone.

He kissed like a man now, and she was woman enough to appreciate it.

She had a dim memory, however, that she'd come to find Sean for reasons other than snogging him, but damned if she could remember what they were. She'd been thinking about his sculpted mouth for a long time, and it felt just as good on hers as she'd imagined.

Better, even.

The lights came back on all too soon, though, and with it, some semblance of reason.

Damn.

She licked her lips, aware of how provocative the action was by the way Sean's nostrils flared. "Uh . . . don't know if you've noticed, but the snow's coming down pretty hard. I'm declaring us closed on account of bad weather."

Suddenly serious, he nodded. "Plan. Do you want to ride back into town with me? At least if we get stuck, we won't be alone."

Brenda's Outback was fine in snow, but he did have a point. Being alone out there if something went wrong would be *not good*.

If it had been anyone else, she might have suggested he just follow her so they could keep an eye on each other—get both cars back to town, all that.

But she liked the idea of a ride home with Sean. More to the point, she liked the idea of asking him in once they got there, and having him meet the dog, share the pizza, maybe open a bottle of wine—and see if they could build on the promise of that kiss. "Sounds good. You lock up the back. I'll grab a few things from the office and meet you out front."

Brenda made sure everything was shut down, changed the message on the answering machine to say they were closed, and grabbed her flash drive. The one thing she'd wanted to get done this afternoon she could do at home just as easily (assuming she didn't let Sean sweep her off her feet, that is).

Very little of what Mrs. Whitney had left the house was directly useful—some Victorian-era family photographs and papers and a few nice pieces of furniture. But some of the more modern stuff looked like it might be collectible and she'd been combing eBay and other auction sites, looking for information.

Good God, that wind was terrible. She swore it wasn't just rattling the windows, but penetrating the stone walls.

Then she looked out the window.

Damn.

The world was a solid wall of white.

She went to open the front door. It opened a crack and then stopped. Too much snow piled in front of it.

Double damn.

"I think we're stuck."

Sean's voice made her jump. He'd sneaked into the room;

when she turned, she saw he was in his stocking feet, as if he'd left wet, snowy boots in the kitchen. Snow clung to his pant legs, all the way to his thighs.

Normally the idea of snow on the irreplaceable and already worn peacock rug would trigger her anal-retentive tendencies, but it was hard to get into full preservationist mode while staring at Sean's thighs—the snow was almost up to his crotch. The carpet had survived several generations of Adirondack winters, when various Frogmortons had presumably tracked in snow on a regular basis. It could handle a little more.

"You can get out through the kitchen door," he added, "but the snow's knee-deep—or worse—already. We could dig my Jeep out, but we're not going to get far. Even if they're keeping up with the main roads, no one's touched Frog Hollow."

She picked up the house phone. "I'll call the plow guy. Maybe he can push us up on the schedule. Assuming his cell phone's working." Frog Hollow Road was private, more like a long driveway than an actual road, and they had arrangements with a neighbor with his own plow to keep them dug out.

The plow guy answered his cell, all right—from the hospital, where his wife was in labor. ("Great timing, eh? I can already see this kid's gonna be trouble.") He had backup, but she had a day job to get home from and her own plowing clients to hit. "Best make some coffee and get . . ."

A loud crackle made Brenda jump and hold the phone out from her ear as if it were a live mouse.

When she moved it gingerly back to her ear, it was dead.

Well, wasn't this interesting? Snowed in *and* incommunicado. On one hand, poor Mort was stuck home alone—she just hoped he'd have the courtesy to do his business on the tiled bathroom floor when he got desperate. (Or better yet, that the next-door neighbor who'd walked Mort for her when she was working late would be clever enough to notice she hadn't made it home and come to the poor dog's rescue.)

On the other hand, she'd daydreamed about spending the night in the romantic old mansion. Spending the night in the romantic old mansion with a devilishly handsome man was an even better idea.

Especially a devilishly handsome man who'd already kissed her once and showed every sign of wanting to kiss her again. And more.

Oh yeah, especially more.

The next gust of wind was so hard she half expected the stained-glass window sporting the Frogmorton utterly ridiculous faux coat of arms (which included, perhaps unsurprisingly, a frog salient, or leaping) to blow in. Which would be a shame. Fundamentally tacky it might be, but it was part of the house's history.

"It's warmer in the kitchen," Sean suggested. "And that's where the coffee pot is."

"And the food. We might as well use the microwave before the power goes out. Because face it, the power *is* going to go out."

Sean took her hand. "*Oooh,* I'm scared of the dark. Will you protect me?"

"Jerk." She smacked him playfully on his ass (his very fine ass). But she didn't let go of his hand while she did it.

And when he took advantage of that fact to reel her in for another kiss, she decided that inconvenience and potential carpet-cleaning and all, being snowed in was just fine with her.

His lips were warm, but his cheeks were cold from his foray outside, a contrast that made Brenda shiver with delight.

The first kiss had been tentative. Questioning. This one started that way, too, with featherlight brushes and tiny flicks of his tongue against her lips like snowflakes against bare skin, only hot.

Brenda was more than happy to encourage him to the next level.

She threaded her fingers into his hair, which was damp from the snow, and boldly deepened the kiss, meeting his tongue with hers and then dipping farther, between his lips, to find the sweetness beyond.

A sharp intake of breath. His body tensed. Then he leaned in, his fingers massaging the muscles just inside her shoulder blades as he pulled her closer.

This version of the kiss sent tingles right down to her toes and back up to where they mattered the most.

The lights flickered again, actually going out for enough time to plunge them into darkness, where the only thing that existed was the feel of him touching her, mouth to mouth, chest to chest, thigh to thigh, and a delicious hardness of his pressing against the softness of her lower belly.

Power restored itself, with no promises of how long it would remain, or whether the next time would be The Big One. It took all of Brenda's willpower to pull away from Sean enough to say, "Um. We'd better get something to eat while we still have electricity."

Sean's grin was fiendish, and they were halfway to the kitchen when it occurred to her that he'd interpreted "something to eat" in an entirely different way from how she'd intended it.

It was her turn to grin. Oh, she liked the way his mind worked.

When Jeremy whined, "It's *co-old*," for the third time, it was all Clyde could do not to undo one of his snowshoes and smack it into his friend's kisser.

"It's not that bad," he said for the third time. "I heard once that when it's really cold, it can't snow. All this snow means it's not really cold."

"I don't get it," Jeremy said. "It snows in winter, and it's cold in winter. Snow is cold."

Clyde didn't understand it, either, but he'd lived in the Adirondacks for all twenty years and three months of his life, and he'd noticed that sometimes it was colder when it wasn't snowing, so cold the hair in his nose froze up.

It wasn't that cold right now, a fact for which he was quite grateful.

The snow fluffed and fluttered around them and poofed up beneath their snowshoes. Their breath lingered in the cold air like pot smoke in the shed behind the high school.

"It's not my fault you didn't dress warmly," he snapped, finally giving in to his exasperation. He regretted it almost immediately when he saw Jeremy's face fall.

Still, he couldn't keep from adding "Like I told you to."

"I didn't know it was going to be this *far*," Jeremy protested.

Apparently Jeremy had thought they'd be driving to Frogmorton House, as if they were going to make a triumphant entrance and demand the property that was rightfully Clyde's.

Clyde didn't think that would go over well with the people who worked there.

"It's no farther than the deer blind on the other side of Cascade," he pointed out.

Jeremy heaved a sigh. "But we have beer stashed there."

"I will buy you a case of Pabst when we get back, I swear," Clyde said.

A smile crossed Jeremy's wind-red face. "Really?"

"Cross my heart," Clyde said.

Mollified, Jeremy started off again. Really, the long underwear top and down vest and jeans should keep him warm enough while they were moving. Clyde felt almost too hot in his own layers, which included a checked red-and-black hunting shirt and thermal socks his grandmother had given him last Christmas.

God rest her soul.

Then again, it was all his grandmother's fault he and Jeremy were out in the middle of the woods right now.

She may have gifted him with thermal socks, but she'd denied him his birthright, and as God was his witness, he was going to claim what was rightfully his.

Before or after he pitched the whining Jeremy into a ravine.

Sean put on a pot of coffee to brew while Brenda explored the fridge and cabinets for something resembling a light supper. The rich aroma made her mouth water as she set out her findings.

Bagels and cream cheese left over from a Chamber of Commerce breakfast. A frozen pizza stashed by Sean in case of a dire lunch emergency. Energy bars and green tea drinks. A handful of ketchup packets—not at all useful right now. A tin of instant hot chocolate with mini-marshmallows. (Possibly dessert.)

Best of all, far back in a cupboard, a dusty bottle of decent champagne left over from some long-past benefit. Brenda tucked that into the fridge for later.

She'd always believed in thinking positively, and positive thinking right now included the idea that by the end of the evening, they'd have something to celebrate.

From the pantry she dug out a pair of the nothing-special-but-looked-properly-historic heavy silver candelabra they used for parties. Soon candles were flickering over on the counter, making the kitchen both cozy and romantic. She hadn't intended that.

Okay, maybe she had. Just a wee tiny bit.

Sean had his flashlight at the ready, too. But when the power went out for good, they didn't reach for the flashlight. They reached for each other.

The candle flame sent Sean's cheekbones into sharp relief, made his eyes just that much more deep before he pulled her in for another kiss.

First little nibbles on her lower lip that made her shiver with delight, but set a fire deep inside her. Shivering but hot. Nice.

Her lips parted, and his tongue brushed the inside of her mouth, exploring the surfaces, sparking more delicious sensations.

Once again, she laced her fingers in his hair, holding him as if he might escape. Not that he was showing any sign of wanting to escape.

Sean kissed away from her mouth to her ear (which made her giggle, even though it tickled in a very, very sexy way), to her throat, until his lips were brushing against the handmade lace ruffle just at the base of her throat.

Sean found an extra sensitive spot on the side of her neck, half hidden by lace. When she moaned, he seemed to decide that lace and a little bit of wool were tasty enough as long as he could reach her through them.

More shivers. More fire. Throbbing nipples and a pussy that pulsed in time with her heart.

Pure need.

Damn, why wasn't she wearing her ball gown? Sure, she'd have been freezing with her arms and cleavage bare, but it would give him so much more skin to touch and kiss. She pressed herself against him, trying desperately to feel more of his body. It wasn't easy through layers of skirt and petticoat—she'd gone for the layered effect because it was both authentic and warm, but damn, right now she was regretting it. As much as she was regretting her authentically high neckline.

Her hands slid down his broad back to his ass, cupping and gripping it, pushing him closer so she could push herself against the hard bulge in his crotch.

Not enough. Not nearly enough.

He slipped a leg between hers and still it wasn't enough contact.

It wasn't just the fabric in the way, although that was a problem. She wanted to feel his skin. No, she wanted him inside her skin—inside her, yes, but under her skin too, and she under his.

At the very least, she wanted to start unbuttoning his crisp uniform jacket—but she'd have to pull away to give herself room to work, and that would mean less delicious contact.

Decisions, decisions.

"Too many damn clothes," Sean said, barely lifting his mouth from her skin. "I love the way you look in the Victorian outfits, but they get in the way."

"They do come off, you know."

He pulled back enough that Brenda could see his face. His grin was even more wicked by candlelight. "A little at a time, though. We've got all night, and I'm getting off on seducing the lady of the mansion . . . who quite likes slumming it with a policeman."

She resisted the urge to note that in the Victorian era, "slumming" referred to counterfeiting.

Resisting had less to do with actual thought than with the way Sean's big hands slipped her velvet coat off her shoulders and then went to work on the tiny buttons on her bodice.

He paused to run his fingertips lightly over the top of her breasts, where they swelled over the corset. She gave up on thinking altogether and just felt.

Clyde stopped. Jeremy went right on by him before he realized it, and stopped as well, scootching backward carefully.

"What is it?" Jeremy asked.

Clyde jerked his head, indicating forward. "There it is." As if Jeremy couldn't see it.

Dusk had fallen. The air was the midnight blue of twilight, when everything seemed possible. Around them, the wind was the only sound. The snow still tumbled down.

In the gloom, the house loomed before them. Clyde had expected to see some lights on, even after the staff left, but the entire place was menacingly dark. He was glad he had a Maglite in his backpack.

"*Whoo-ee,*" Jeremy said. "Crazy-lookin' place, ain't it?"

Since the land around Frogmorton House was owned by the museum trust, there was no hunting on the premises, but their usual hunting grounds skirted the area, so they were familiar with its bulk.

Even though hunting season was long past, Clyde had brought his shotgun, just in case. Never know when you might come up against a bear, grumpy at being woken early from its hibernation.

"Guess they went home early," Clyde said. "Better for us anyway. Won't have to wait."

Jeremy rubbed his hands together, his ski poles dangling from straps around his wrists. "Can't wait to get my hands on some treasure."

Clyde tossed him a silver flask. "I'll drink to that," he said.

Sean moved from the left nipple to the right, drawing it into his mouth, making her arch so he could take more in. The bereft left nipple puckered in the cool air, pressing against the slightly damp linen of her corset cover. He didn't let it get cold for long, though, tweaking it between his thumb and forefinger.

Tit for tat—or was that tit for tit? Brenda pinched his nipples, which stood out dark behind the not very Victorian, but eminently practical, white T-shirt he wore under his uniform.

True to his word, he was taking his time. Her dress was open to the waist, but he decided he liked the lace-trimmed corset cover and had worked her breasts above the corset without taking it off. And while her skirt was pushed up, showing off her silk drawers—she was perched on the kitchen counter at this point, with her legs wrapped around Sean's waist—he wasn't rushing to get the drawers or his pants off, either. (Although, thank goodness, he'd taken off his gun belt—that had been a little distracting.) Never mind that he was hard as a steel rod, threatening to pop the fly buttons on his trousers, and never mind that her drawers were so drenched in the crotch that they must be transparent, or that they were both trembling with want.

When was the last time someone had taken the time to explore her this way? Never, not that she could remember—and Brenda was damn sure she'd have remembered it.

Remember being this aroused, this sensitized, so much so that Sean's breath on her skin felt like a touch. Remember being this wet and open and needy. Remember her sex pulsing around emptiness, yearning to be filled. Remember reaching for a fly with an achingly hard cock behind it and being turned away with a playful reproach and a passionate kiss.

Her mother always said patience was a virtue.

And in this case, Mom was right—up to a point. But damn, if Sean didn't pick up the pace, she might catch on fire.

"I want to be naked with you," she whispered, running her hand down his chest and taut belly to his fly. One of the relatively few brain cells that wasn't focused on her rising need pointed out that there might be a better location for doing so than where they were. Someplace with soft surfaces and warm blankets. "And not on the kitchen counter, either."

"Spruce Bedroom?"

The master bedroom with the fully made-up bed, very comfortable bed, including an impressive, if perpetually dusty, em-

broidered velvet coverlet and canopy? "Hell yes." The sheets
were Irish linen, still sturdy despite their age. And if by chance
they destroyed them, well, it would be a shame, but they had an
entire closet full of similar sets.

Before she hopped down from the counter, he cupped her
mound at last, and that pressure was almost enough to drive her
over the edge.

Almost. Not quite. "Please?" she moaned, feeling ridiculous
to beg but needing it so badly that she didn't care.

His grin grew. He looked like a fox, or maybe it was just foxy.
Delicious, in any case. "I like hearing you beg."

Brenda writhed under his hand. "Please. Pleasepleaseplease-
please . . ."

He started circling his fingers, slowly but with just the right
pressure. "Yeah. That's it. Perfect . . . so close . . ."

She took a deep breath, sensing that within seconds she'd
need it to scream.

And in that instant of silence, they heard the distant sound
of shattering glass.

She might have thought she imagined it, except that it was followed immediately by the shrill droning of the burglar alarm.

Jeremy jumped back as if the house had bitten him. He started
to run—and promptly fell down because in his panic, he forgot
he was wearing snowshoes. It would have been hilarious except
for the alarm screaming at them.

"Clyde! There's an alarm!"

"Asshole. Of course there's an alarm. And you just tripped it
by breaking the window."

"Then how were we going to get in?"

Honestly he'd been hoping that there wouldn't actually be an alarm, but he wasn't about to admit that. But he did have a plan. He reached into his pocket. "I have instructions! How to disarm an alarm system."

"Really? Where'd you find that?" In the last of the fading light, Jeremy finally looked interested.

"On the Internet. You can find all kinds of shit on the Internet." It occurred to him belatedly that he'd never tried them out and they might be just as fake as the boobs on a porn site.

What the hell. The window was broken anyway, the alarm was going off. Might as well just crawl in the window the old-fashioned way. If the alarm was sending a message to the police station, well, the cops couldn't get there before morning at least, and by then they'd be long gone.

He propped his rifle against the wall and leaned down to remove his snowshoes. Then he shimmied out of his backpack and tossed it inside before clambering in after it.

It was, of course, pitch-black inside, but he got the flashlight on just as Jeremy fell through the window and landed with an audible thump.

"Just a broken window," Brenda said, hoping Sean would put any quiver in her voice or shake in her hands down to sexual frustration.

Which was definitely part of it. Whatever this emergency was, the timing couldn't have been much worse. Although maybe it wasn't all bad. She'd probably feel even more anxious if every nerve in her body wasn't too busy screaming for relief to register the influx of fight-or-flight hormones.

"It's really windy," she added. "Probably a branch or a roof slate or something blew through." She was buttoning every third button of her bodice as she spoke. Getting them all would take way too long, but she'd be damned if she'd face down an intruder—or even deal with a simple, drafty, broken window—with her tits hanging out.

"Let's hope." Sean fastened the gun belt around his hips, grabbed his big flashlight, then gave her one last quick, hard kiss. "You stay here. I'll go check."

"No way. I'm going with you."

"I'm the security guard. It's my job."

"And it's my museum, dammit."

"Your museum?" He glared at her, his thick eyebrows drawing together. He did fierce awfully well for someone with such a gorgeous smile. But not well enough to make her back down.

"I'm responsible to the board for anything that happens . . . and I know this place like the back of my hand. Better than you do." She took a deep breath and decided to admit to the truth. "And if I have to sit here alone, I'll go nuts. I'll leave any tackling of burglars up to the person with combat training, but I can't just sit here."

Sean nodded. "Good points, all of them. Let's go." He headed for the main door.

She shook her head as she grabbed the candelabrum. "Servant's hallway. If there's anyone in the front rooms, we can surprise them coming that way. And shut off the damn alarm while we're at it."

They'd made it to the front of the house. Clyde poked his head in one room, but it was being used as an office, and he didn't see his target.

"What are we looking for again?" Jeremy asked.

Something resembling a brain in your head. Clyde gritted his teeth. "My grandmother's writing desk. You remember, the one that used to be under the window in her living room."

"I don't remember," Jeremy said, as if he hadn't sat in that living room a million times eating Clyde's grandmother's home-made peanut-butter thumbprint cookies like he was one of those starving kids from Africa.

"It was kind of a reddish wood, with carving along the front—roses or something. Stood about this high." Clyde held out his hand, palm down. "She usually had a vase of fresh flowers on it, and a framed photo of my grandfather."

Jeremy squinted. "Okay," he said finally, reluctantly, as if he maybe didn't really remember but he didn't want Clyde to get angry.

At Christmas a few years ago, Grandma had gotten tipsy on eggnog and told Clyde something very, very important.

She'd told him the desk contained a special treasure.

When he'd asked what sort of treasure, she'd smiled a smile he'd never seen before (and even though he couldn't quite explain why, it kind of squicked him out) and patted him on the head and told him he'd understand one day. And Clyde had taken that to mean that she'd be giving the treasure to him.

Then she'd upped and croaked and left everything to Frogmorton House, including the writing desk—which, as far as he was concerned, they could keep—and the treasure she'd promised him.

"We'll split up," he said, because Jeremy had done one thing right and remembered to bring a flashlight of his own. "You go upstairs; I'll look down here. Look for anything that looks like the desk I described. We'll meet back here in—" he checked his watch "—fifteen minutes."

He felt compelled to add, "Don't break anything else. Don't even touch anything," as Jeremy clomped toward the stairs.

He shone his own flashlight left and right. Right seemed to be the dining room, and he doubted the desk would be in there. Left, then.

At the top of the stairs, he heard a bang and an *"Owdammit!"* from Jeremy. Then Jeremy's faint voice wafted down, "S'okay! Didn't break anything!"

Clyde went left.

As Sean fiddled with the alarm box, Brenda leaned out the broken window, careful not to brush against a fragment of glass. "They came on snowshoes," she announced. "Two pairs. There's a rifle out here, too."

"Good to know they didn't bring it inside," Sean commented into the blissful silence left when the ringing stopped.

"They could have another one," Brenda said. She stepped back, her shoes crunching on the glass. She was pretty sure the window hadn't been an original, but she was still pissed off that the slobs had broken it.

"We'll cross that bridge when we come to it."

They continued on. At the end of the servants' hallway, in the dining room, Sean signaled a halt.

Brenda halted all right. She felt a little ridiculous with her long gown and her candelabrum, like the ditzy heroine of a vampire movie.

At least she wasn't going to make the ditzy-vampire-movie

heroine mistake and run off on her own. Face it, neither the master's in history nor the certificate program in nonprofit management had covered How to Deal with Intruders.

"Flashlight," Sean whispered, making almost no sound at all. She had to lean in to hear him, which brought back the scent of—oh God, *herself,* on his fingertips. The reminder of her arousal made her clit tremble again.

"What was that?" she whispered back, sure she'd heard something.

"Voices. Couldn't hear what they said. I think you're right: there's two of them."

"Good odds," Brenda said, even though she wasn't much sure she was a match for one of them. She'd been desperately trying to remember the self-defense course she'd taken in college. That had been a long time ago, and she and her friends had spent most of the time ogling the instructor.

Why hadn't she paid attention? Nobody said she'd actually *need* that information being a curator.

"Stay behind me," Sean said. In any other circumstances she would have gladly done so just to look at his ass, but now she actually paid attention to the matter at hand.

They crept through the dining room and entered the foyer just in time to see a faint light moving away from them, toward the sitting room and library.

Sean had loosened his jacket so he had easier access to his gun, but he left it in its holster. Brenda hoped he wouldn't have to use it.

She was appalled that someone would break in. Yes, the place was brimming with antiques, but most of it was heavy furniture. The knickknacks were all discreetly marked and everything, down to the silver, was obsessively categorized and photographed. If the thieves tried to sell anything, they'd get caught, no question about it.

Sheer mindless vandalism, then? It wasn't out of the question, but it didn't make a whole lot of sense. They usually had problems on the Fourth of July or around graduation time, when stupid kids got stupid drunk and came up with stupid plans.

Surely nobody was stupid (or drunk) enough to want to come out here in the middle of winter, in snowshoes, just to smash things up.

The snowshoes, Brenda decided, meant they'd planned this.

That made her even madder. She felt like a mother partridge puffing up to protect her young.

Although didn't mother partridges pretend they were wounded to draw predators away from their chicks? Might not be a bad strategy here, if it came to be needed.

Following Sean, she was impressed at how smoothly he slipped through the rooms. Victorian decorating called for a lot of furniture to be jammed into small spaces—and don't even mention the knickknacks and lace and frippery. It was all utterly lush and romantic, but it made it hard to walk in a straight line.

Sean moved like a panther, lean and silent. And Brenda knew where every stick of furniture was placed better than she knew her own apartment.

The man (she assumed it was a man) they followed, on the other hand, had neither of their skills. He wasn't crashing into things, at least, but he was moving slowly and bumping into the occasional side table, chinking the curios and ornaments against each other.

At this rate, they could have followed him blindfolded, just from the noises he was making.

They caught up with him easily in the vaguely leather-scented library, which had looped them around almost back to the foyer. Brenda had the vague sense that they could have just waited for the perp to come back to them, but it was too late to contemplate that now.

"Freeze!" Sean shouted.

Brenda jumped. She pressed a hand to her pounding chest as the thief whirled and his hand shot into the air. His flashlight made crazy patterns on the ceiling.

"Don't shoot!" he said.

"What are you doing here?" Sean demanded, training his own flashlight on the thief's face.

Wait a minute . . . Brenda stepped from behind Sean, squinting in the gloom.

"Clyde?" she said. "Clyde Whitney, is that you?"

Clyde started to bring his hands down, but Sean's sharp "Hey!" made him rethink that. "Yes, ma'am, it is."

"What in God's name are you *doing* here?"

Sean shot her a look that clearly said, *Who's in charge here?* but she ignored him. The situation was back in her territory now.

"It's Clyde Whitney," she told him. "His grandmother left Frogmorton her things when she passed. I know him from when I subbed at the high school. You graduated two years ago, isn't that right, Clyde?"

"Yes, ma'am."

"So why *are* you here?"

"The things my grandmother gave you," he said. "She wasn't supposed to give you everything. The treasure was supposed to be mine."

Treasure? "What treasure?"

"In the writing desk. She *told* me."

"I'm sorry, Clyde, but I think she was mistaken. She gave us a detailed listing of everything she was donating, and she didn't say anything about something being in the desk."

Clyde let his hands drop, not threateningly, but as if he'd forgotten he'd been caught. "But—"

And that's when they heard the voice behind them. "Clyde, I think I found it! It's in the big bedroo— Oh, crap."

The speaker loomed right behind Brenda. Without thinking, she turned and nailed the stalker across the head with the heavy silver candelabrum.

The young man blinked once, then crumpled to the floor.

Most of the candles went out, but one dislodged and went flying. With a shriek, Brenda dove after it, stomping out the flame before it caught anything alight. She winced at the thought of wax on the hardwood floor, but she knew several different secrets to removing it.

Then, in the near darkness, she ran her hands over the candelabrum to check for any dents or nicks. It may have been an everyday one, but it was still a part of Frogmorton House.

"Nice job," Sean said, admiration in his voice.

She straightened her coat. "Thank you."

Sean gestured to Clyde. "Come on."

Clyde's eyes widened. "Where are we going?"

"You two can cool your heels in the basement until morning.

The cops won't be able to get here till tomorrow, and we can't let you go off tramping around the countryside."

"What about my treasure?"

"There's no treasure," Brenda said.

"But—"

"But we'll check the writing desk, just in case. Okay?"

"Okay." Clyde's shoulder's drooped.

Sean made Clyde help him lug the half-conscious and moaning Jeremy to the basement. Brenda grabbed an armful of wool blankets from the linen closet. It would be chilly down there, but they wouldn't come near to freezing to death.

In the light of the freshly burning candelabrum, Brenda found the secret compartment in the back of the writing desk within minutes. Sean whistled his admiration.

"I never thought to check for a false back," she said. "Hello, what have we here?"

She drew out a packet of papers, tied with a red ribbon and smelling of cedar and lavender.

She examined the envelopes. "They're letters," she said. "From Mr. Whitney to Mrs. Whitney, and vice versa."

"Love letters?" Sean said with a chuckle. "Grandma's secret treasure was her love letters? *Aw*, that's sweet." Then he smiled, and it wasn't the roguish, flirty grin that Brenda had come to lust after. It was a softer smile, still sexy as hell, but almost . . . wistful.

So, naughty Sean was a closet romantic? Brenda told herself firmly it was too soon to obsess about the ramifications of *that* bit of information—although they could be very nice ramifications—and filed the knowledge away for future reference.

She'd meant to take a quick glance at the letters, then put them away and get back to more interesting matters, but the first few lines she read intrigued her so much that she kept reading, not even bothering to sit down.

"Oh my. Not just love letters. *Steamy* love letters. Listen to this." She scanned the letter until she found the passage that had caught her eye.

"'I miss you. All of you: your eyes, your laugh, your toes, that mole on the back of your leg, your beautiful breasts, your round little bottom, and every other bit of you. But right now, I really miss being inside you, feeling you so tight and wet and hot around me. When I get home, I'm going to kiss every inch of you, from your forehead to your cute painted toes'—*hmm*, seems Mr. Whitney was a bit of a foot fetishist—'and then I'm going to lick you until you beg me to fuck you. But I don't just want to fuck you. I want to make love to you. I want to make love to you so we can't tell where I end and you begin.'"

Brenda looked up. Sean's eyes were shining, dark blue and wide.

"Hot stuff," he said. "As long as I don't think about Mrs. Whitney playing bridge with my grandmother, at least."

"Let's not go there, okay?" Brenda laughed. "God, Clyde would die, knowing we're reading his sweet old grandparents' smutty letters. Hell, knowing his grandparents *wrote* smutty letters."

Brenda shuffled through the papers. "Here's another good one. 'I know I'll be home in a week. I may even get home before this letter gets to you. But a week's too long. When I'm alone in my hotel room, I take out my cock and play with it, trying to pretend you're touching me instead, imagining your hands, your lips, your sweet, greedy cunt. And I come. Oh, do I come. But even while I'm coming, all I can think about is how much better it is when I'm making you cry out and tighten around my cock. Do you touch yourself and think of me? I'm sure you do, because you're a naughty girl and that's part of why I love you so much, but write to me about it. That way, the next time I travel, I can read it and imagine you lying in the dark touching yourself and imagining it's me.'"

"Did she?" Sean asked.

"If he was half as sexy as he sounds in these letters, I bet she did. It looks like he traveled a lot on business."

"I mean write him about it." Sean had moved in behind her now and was reading over her shoulder while he unbuttoned her dress.

Brenda leaned back against him as she flipped through the packet. "Found it! 'You want to hear how I keep from going crazy while you're away? You want to know how much I miss you? I miss you so much that my fingers aren't enough sometimes. I can make myself feel good that way, but it's not the same without you inside me. I hope they're feeding you well in Indianapolis, because you're going to need your strength when you get back here.'"

"Lucky man. I bet he got a warm welcome home."

Sean pushed against her as he spoke. Even through her layers of skirt, Brenda could feel how hard he was.

It pretty much matched how wet she was getting again, between the steamy letters and Sean's hot body pressed against hers and the memory of their play down in the kitchen.

"It gets better. 'It got so bad that today I went to the market and found a cucumber about the right size. It wasn't the same at all, but filling myself up with something made it easier to think of you inside me. So imagine me so desperate for you that a cucumber looks pretty good. Imagine me pushing that cucumber in and out of me and calling your name and . . .' "

She stopped. "I actually can't read the rest because . . . well, it looks like he did imagine it. Often. This letter's pretty beat-up."

Sean let out a shuddering breath. "Jesus, that's hot. Just knowing she was so horny and so far away must have made her husband crazy." He pushed her dress off her shoulders, forcing her to set the letters down on the desk so he could work the narrow sleeves down her arms. "Have you ever been that horny?"

She turned in his embrace, letting the dress slither off her hips as she did. "Not until tonight. And it's all your fault. Hope you're planning to do something about it."

Another of those roguish grins that made her insides quiver and melt. "I don't know . . . I kind of like the idea of watching you getting yourself off." He paused just long enough to get her concerned about the evening's plans, then added, "Sometime, if you'd be into it. Not tonight. Tonight I want to be inside you when you come. Want to feel you exploding all over my cock."

Brenda slithered the rest of the way out of the dress and got her petticoats and corset cover off in record time.

Sean stopped her when she was down to corset and drawers. "Let me look at you," he breathed. "Just for a minute. Damn, you look good like that."

She made a show of unpinning her hair, shaking it out so it tumbled around her shoulders. "No fair. It's cold. Besides, I want to see you, too."

"Fair enough." He opened his fly teasingly, one button at a time. The purple head of his cock peeked out the top of his purple briefs.

She couldn't resist. She sank to her knees and kissed it before working the trousers and underwear down.

Enough teasing. Enough playing. She wrapped a hand around the base of his cock and took him in her mouth.

Salty and delicious and just the right size, thick and meaty. Perfect to suck and even better to fuck.

Sean groaned as she moved her lips up and down his shaft. God, she wanted this moving inside her, filling her, making her scream. She wanted to milk him so he exploded inside her, wanted to come and come and come on this delicious cock, but damn, he tasted so good it was hard to resist continuing to suck.

He was the one, in the end, who pulled away. "Let me help you with the corset," he said huskily, "and get on the bed. I want to be in you."

She was already turning around so he could reach the laces, even as she teased, "I thought you liked the corset."

"I do, but I want to feel you. See you. The corset's sexy. But you're gorgeous."

It wasn't necessarily easier having him help with the corset—she'd gotten good at managing on her own and it seemed to be new to him—but it was certainly more fun.

Onto the bed then, with a mountain of covers pulled over them, the linen sheet cool underneath her and Sean lying over her. Like Mr. Whitney had promised his bride, he kissed his way down her body—suckling her nipples until she moaned and rolled her hips with need, exclaiming over the corset marks on her hips and belly and licking them "to make them better."

He reached the reddish curls of her mound, buried his face there, took a deep breath as if enjoying the bouquet of a fine wine. Brenda made a small noise, half crazy with arousal, and put her hand on his head.

She didn't think he'd needed the hint, but he certainly took it.

Brenda didn't have time to enjoy a full demonstration of Sean's oral skills, though—after the long tease and the hot letters, a few flicks of his tongue were all it took to send her into convulsions of pleasure.

There was a brief interruption while Sean fished a condom out of his wallet. (She was amused—and a little relieved—to catch him checking the expiration date on the packet. He might be sexy as hell and a big-time flirt, but he hadn't needed the "just in case condom" in a while.) Even with the interruption, she was still twitching with aftershocks when he repositioned himself between her legs, the head of his cock pressing against her pussy.

He'd said he enjoyed hearing her beg, hearing her admit just how much she wanted him. And since she did want him, and the hotter she made him, the hotter she got, and so on, she opened her legs a little wider, rolled her pelvis, looked into those amazing blue eyes, and whispered, "Please. Please fuck me."

"Sure you wouldn't rather have a cucumber?" He pressed against her as he said that, teasing at her already sensitized clit with his head.

She smacked him on the ass. To her surprise, the yelp he let out sounded awfully happy. "Sounds like you liked that."

He shook his head, a bemused look on his face. "I think I did. Who knew? We'll have to talk about that. Later. Much later."

He pushed into her slick pussy, just the head at first, giving her a few seconds to appreciate how thick he was, how delicious he felt there, how much she wanted to feel more.

Wonderful as the long teasing had been, she'd have to be superhuman to be patient any longer. She raised her hips, grabbed his ass, said "Now," and gave him a push all at once.

"The lady desires something?" he purred, and slid the rest of the way in.

He froze, buried to the hilt inside her. His eyes widened, looking impossibly bluer in the flickering candlelight. His mouth opened. He looked like he was striving to make the perfect clever, wicked remark, but couldn't find words.

Then he started to move.

Oh God, did he start to move.

He was like the blustery weather outside, fierce and elemental and inexorable. He was howling like the storm and cutting through all her defenses like the wind cut through the walls. He was wild and dangerous and beautiful as the snow. But he wasn't cold. In the freezing room, he was fire, and she was burning with him.

After his earlier delicacy and restraint, he was letting himself go crazy now. Each stroke jarred her to the core, but in the most pleasurable way, raising her up off the bed and throwing her down again. Each stroke touched someplace new, someplace wonderful, sending another wave of icy-hot ecstasy out to drown her. The storm was raging and she was raging, gouging at his back and ass with her nails, urging him to fuck even harder even though if he did he'd break her in two—or at least break the antique bed.

She came, and it didn't end. Not multiple orgasms, because that implied stopping at some point and then starting again. This was one long spiral of pleasure, rising higher and higher without respite, without conclusion.

It was almost too much, but at the same time it wasn't enough.

It wasn't enough until Sean's face, already red, contorted to something beautiful but scarcely human, some god or nature spirit, maybe the face of the storm itself. "Yes . . . Brenda . . . ," he cried and she almost didn't recognize her own name, but she recognized the way his muscles clenched and released, the way that even with the condom between them he seemed to surge into her.

They fell asleep tangled in each other and woke to early light peeking between the velvet drapes. Brenda crawled reluctantly away from Sean's warmth, wrapping herself in her velvet coat, to look out onto the white world. The snow had finally stopped, but it didn't look like they'd be going anywhere for a while.

Not that she minded (although she'd be happy when the police could come out and take charge of the two idiots in the cellar—maybe she should toss them some bagels). Sure, the house was chilly, but she suspected she and Sean could find ways to keep warm. Something about watching her play with herself, for one, and something about spanking him, for another. They could probably make the spanking go both ways, because she was curious about being on the receiving end herself. So many possibilities—and for once, so much time.

And now, in the light, they could really see each other.

Brenda crawled back under the covers, snuggled close to him and kissed him on the shoulder. "Wake up, sleepyhead."

"I was awake. I was just about to roll over and grab you when you got up."

"It's a beautiful, cold snow-covered day and it looks like we're stuck with each other."

"*Aw,* damn. Whatever shall we do?" He rolled over and grabbed her, and for a few glorious minutes there was nothing but his body, his mouth, and his clever hands.

Then he stopped, pushed himself up on his arms, and looked down at her. "Brenda, I have a confession to make."

She froze. She couldn't tell if he was serious or not, couldn't read the dense blue velvet of his eyes, couldn't read what lay behind the sudden absence of his usual grin.

The silence lasted longer than she liked. Finally he spoke. "I applied for the job just knowing it was for a security guard."

Brenda nodded. It had been a blind ad; she knew because she'd written it, hoping to get at least a few applicants who weren't dreamy kids who just wanted to work at the "castle" and would fall apart at the first sign of a real problem.

"But I took it because of you."

Gulp.

"I had another offer, from a resort out by Blue Mountain Lake. Paid better and I could have lived on-site. But after I saw you again at the interview, I knew I'd have to take this job and then ask you out like I didn't have the nerve to do in high school."

"I refuse to believe you pined for me since high school."

The roguish grin came back. "Not exactly. But you intrigued me, and I thought about you. Wished I could go back in time with what I'd learned since then and sweep you off your feet—or at least really get to know you. So when I got a chance, I took it. Plus you grew up really nicely."

"You, too." Brenda breathed an inner sigh of relief. "At least we both had ulterior motives. So I don't have to worry about a sexual harassment lawsuit?"

A snort. "No way. But I hope you don't mind if I harass you for sex every chance I get."

She grinned. "It's only harassing if one of us doesn't want it. And I don't think we'll have that problem. So what kind of harassing for sex did you have in mind this morning?"

He stretched. "I'm not sure yet. So many possibilities. I know—why don't you grab those treasure letters and we'll see if we find anything inspirational?"

 SOPHIE MOUETTE is the pseudonym for two widely published writers of erotica, romance, and speculative fiction. Sophie's first novel-length erotica, *Cat Scratch Fever*, was published in 2006 by Black Lace Books. Sophie's short erotica has appeared in *Best Women's Erotica 2005* and *2007*, various *Wicked Words* anthologies, including *Love on the Dark Side*, *Sex in Public*, *Sex with Strangers*, *Caught Looking*, and *H is for Hardcore*. For more information, see www.cyvarwydd.com.

Sweet Season

by Shanna Germain

Six thousand dollars. Six thousand and fourteen dollars to be exact. How much maple syrup would she need to make to come up with that much? Dulcie started to do the math in her head but gave up when the numbers started to come clear. A lot, that's how much.

Before she'd died, her grandma had asked Dulcie to keep the family maple syrup business alive. Dulcie had said yes, of course, but now it seemed an impossible task. Not only was the business in debt, but Dulcie hadn't sugared since she was teenager—she wasn't even sure if she'd tapped the maple trees properly. And would she be able to turn the sap into syrup? She had no idea.

Dulcie stepped through the snow in her grandma's old barn boots. If she was back in Syracuse now, she'd be, what? Sitting in her tiny little apartment, grading her students' essays on *Jane Eyre* and *Paradise Lost*. Drinking a bottle of wine likely—she'd gotten in the game of taking a drink every time a student wrote the words *orphan* or *torturous*.

Now, she was back in the place she thought she'd left behind. Her fingers were freezing, she was wading through the woods in knee-deep snow and she was mucking up her grandma's last wishes.

"Fuck," she said into the gray air. Her breath made a cloud of white against the bark of the maple in front of her. Well, at least her tap was still in the tree. And there was even sap in the bucket. Maybe she was doing something right.

Dulcie poured the sap from the tree into one of her collection pails. Not even half full. Not even half enough. She put her hand on the rough bark of the tree in front of her. "C'mon baby, you have to do me good this season," she said. "Please . . ."

"Well, I can try, but I can't make any promises."

Dulcie's heart cranked in her chest. A man stood near the hedgerow, dressed like a hunter, in camouflage pants and coat. He had big brown eyes, like a doe, and his wool hat was pulled down nearly to his brow.

Cold air swept over Dulcie's tongue, and she realized her mouth was open. She forced herself to close it. She didn't see a gun, but she hefted the half-full collection pail in her hand. She'd hit him with it if she had to, even if it meant spilling the sap.

"This is private property." She tried to make her voice bigger than she felt. "And it's not even close to hunting season, so you might want to rethink whatever it is you think you're doing here."

He grinned beneath his hat. Deep dimples curved into his scruff-covered cheeks.

"Don't remember me, *huh?*" he asked.

"No, do I know—"

But then he pulled off his hat, and she saw the long thin scar that ran through his right eyebrow up to his forehead. The scar she'd given him when they were, what, fourteen? Fifteen? God, how he'd bled. She'd been the one who'd cried.

"Jesus, Travis? You scared the hell out of me. I was going to take you out with my pail."

"*Hmm,*" he said. "Not the welcome I might have expected."

"Expected?" Dulcie tried to look at him without being obvious about it. He was taller than she remembered, although she wasn't sure that was possible, and wider, too. She couldn't see much of what he looked like, under all those clothes, but she guessed that he still spent a bit of time chopping wood or gardening or something. He had a country build, through and through.

"I heard you were back," he said. "Figured we'd run into each other at some point."

Jesus. She hadn't seen him, in what, seven, eight years? Who was she kidding—she knew exactly how long it had been. Eight years and two months. And still, when he said that, her body did that thing, like all her cells were straining toward him.

"Your hair's longer," she said.

He touched the ends of it, the dark blond strands that nearly reached his chin. "Yours is shorter."

She put her fingers up near her earlobes self-consciously, wishing she'd worn a hat. Or that she'd never chopped her hair into what she'd thought was a respectable teacher's cut.

"I mean, it looks good," he said. "I like it."

"You don't have to say that," she said.

"I know."

They stood and looked at each other while Dulcie's heart thumped in her chest. The sound was so loud she thought she should be able to hear it, but there was only the crack of tree limbs bending beneath the snow. She wondered what he'd been doing while she was gone, if he'd gotten married, if he still loved apple pancakes.

Travis moved closer, and for the first time, she could smell him, above the crisp cleanness of the snow. He smelled of woodsmoke and cider, and something else that she couldn't name, something wet, like wool.

"They still call you Dulcie?" he asked.

Dulcie could only nod. She couldn't tell him about her teaching job in the city, how the students had called her Miss Becker or Sara. She thought of herself always by the nickname Travis and her grandma had cooked up for her, even though no one had called her it for years. Not even her grandma had remembered in the end.

Travis pulled off his glove and held out his hand. After a second, she took it. His palm was warm and soft against her cold skin. The touch sent sparks through her, like accidentally hitting an electric fence, only nicer. She felt her face flush at the state of her knuckles, cracked and raw from working with the maple taps.

"Dulcie, pleased to meet you," he said, like they'd never met. Like she'd never beaned him with her grandma's pitchfork. Like he hadn't leaned over and kissed her one summer afternoon, their lips stained blue and sticky sweet from raspberry ice pops.

She had to laugh and try to pull her hand away. But he didn't let go.

"Listen," he said. "I'm sorry about your grandma. Ada was . . ." He swallowed.

Dulcie's stomach cramped into the ache she'd been keeping down with too much worry and work. She pulled her hand from his and pressed the back of it to her eyes, feeling the winter sting of tears starting. She refused to cry; she hadn't yet and she wasn't going to start in front of him.

Travis made his lips into a circle. The whistle that came out was long and loud. For a second, she thought he was whistling at her, but then she heard the sound of paws through the snow. A short black and brown dog appeared, his legs so short or his ears so long that the tips of them brushed against the snow.

"Agate," he said, when the dog bounded up to brush against his legs. "Meet Dulcie."

When Travis looked at Dulcie, she thought she saw that his dark eyes were wet at the edges, too. "Agate's good for sadness," he said. Agate ran around Dulcie's legs twice, and then licked a bit of snow from her boot. "And a little comic relief."

Dulcie put her pail down and went on her knees to pet Agate, and when the dog licked her face, she knew what that other smell was on Travis. Not wet wool, but clean wet dog.

Dulcie could have stayed there all day, with the warmth of Agate's fat back beneath her hands and his nose stuffed into her neck, but eventually she stood.

"Thank you." She raised her pail. The way it sloshed was how her stomach, her whole body really, felt. She tried to keep her voice light. "I'd better get moving. Maples to go before I sleep, isn't that what Frost said?"

"Something like that." He smiled before he reached down and gave Agate a scratch. The dog whined, low and soft, her belly against the snow. "How goes the maple syrup business?"

"I have no idea," the words came gushing out of her, as though his question had opened a tap she didn't even know she had. "I'm sure I'm driving it into the ground, and it's only my first season. The sap's not really running yet. Not cold enough. And I nearly broke my thumb putting the taps in and I can't remember how to do this and there's the money and does anyone even buy handmade maple syrup anymore?"

"*Whoa*," Travis said. "Breathe."

Dulcie took a breath. "Holy crap," she said. "I don't know where that came from. I don't know what I'm doing."

"Sure you do," he said. "You know, you can tap all the trees on our land if you want. We always told Ada that, too, but she never did. I don't know why."

Dulcie knew why. Never burden, never borrow, never beg. That was Ada's philosophy, and she'd lived it until the day she'd died. Didn't matter that she'd freely give maple syrup to every neighbor within a five-mile radius. It didn't matter that Travis's offer might have been the one thing that could save the business—even from here, Dulcie could see the sugar maples across the property line, just waiting to be tapped—her grandma would have said no.

"That's really sweet," she said. "But I don't think I can."

"Well, if you change your mind," he said. "Or I could give you a hand with the boiling when you're ready. I forced Ada to let me help her the last couple years."

Dulcie swallowed down the bit of guilt that was rising in her. Those last few years, when Ada had been falling sick. Sure, she'd never let on to Dulcie how sick she'd been, but Dulcie hadn't come back to check, either. Not until it was almost too late. Never burden, never borrow, never beg.

"Thanks," she said. "But I have to do this on my own."

It wasn't until she saw his face change that she realized she'd said the same words when she'd left him to go to Syracuse. Why had she gone anyway? Sometimes it seemed she couldn't remember. She'd wanted to be independent, to prove that she could make it outside the small world of her grandma's syrup farm and the tiny town where she'd been raised.

She started to say something—sorry or how she hadn't meant it, not now, not then—but Travis had already tucked his hands into his coat pockets and was turning away. The wind picked up, blew a fresh round of snow off the trees between them. "See you around, then," he said. "C'mon Agate, time to go."

The dog gave Dulcie's boots one last lick and then bounded off after Travis. She watched them go, Travis with his long strides and Agate with his short, quick ones, and she couldn't shake the feeling that, once again, she'd managed to screw up something important.

For the next week, Dulcie hit that stand of trees three, four times a day in the hopes of seeing Travis again. Once, she thought she'd heard Agate bark; it was only a little yip though, and she couldn't be sure.

She hadn't seen Travis again, not once, not even a footprint. She hated to admit how much that had bummed her out. She told herself it was about his trees, that she did want to tap them; she'd worked out a plan, to offer whatever he could use—deadfall for firewood, syrup, her grandmother's canned peaches—in exchange for the trees. She knew it was more than that, though. It was his smile, the way he'd choked up about her grandma, the way he'd called Agate in for comfort. But most of all, the way her body had felt, standing in front of him in the woods, and the way that it felt after she'd turned him down.

She couldn't bring herself to go to his house, stand on his porch steps and tell him that she was sorry, that she wanted him in her life. Besides, what if he had a wife, a family?

So she wrote a note. Simple. "I'd love your help with the syrup, but only if you let me pay you back somehow," and she slipped it into a Baggie and tacked it to the maple tree. Every time she went back, the note was still there, in its plastic bag. Every time, she took it down. And every time, she put it back up.

She'd gathered more than enough sap to do her first batch of syrup days ago but hadn't been able to bring herself to start the process until this morning. Doing a batch meant spending the next two days in the kettle shed, boiling and stirring the sap into syrup. It meant no possibility of running into Travis in the woods.

But it had to be done. If she waited any longer, the sap would spoil, and she'd waste the best sap of the season. She'd spent the morning stacking wood beneath the huge kettle in her grandma's syrup shack. Dulcie loved this syrup shack, this small shed where she'd spent so much time as a child. Nothing in it but the huge black kettle, a blue-flowered love seat that had to be a hundred years old, and the bodice rippers her grandma had read while she'd boiled the sap. She'd kept bags of them out there that she bought up from garage sales and then traded back and forth with her friends.

Dulcie lit the edges of the kindling beneath the kettle and fanned her fire to life. The fire had to stay at a steady temperature: too cold and it would die, too hot and it would burn itself out.

The first fire licked at the bottom of the kettle and went out.

"Damn it." She got down on her hands and knees to rearrange the wood. Was she going to fuck everything up her whole life? Some days it felt like it. She'd come home too late to be any real comfort to her grandma, not arriving until she was having more bad days than good. She was fine as a teacher, she'd guessed, but her life in the city felt like she was acting poorly in a bad play. Pulling on skirts and stockings and keeping herself in the prim style of teacher hood. And, now here she was, back in her childhood home, potentially flubbing not only the business her grandmother had taken years to build, but also a friendship—a friendship was all she'd allow herself to imagine—with a man who'd been her best friend from the time she was eight until she'd gone away.

Finally, she managed to get a fire going that stayed. Inside the big black kettle, the sap heated and began to boil. Dulcie stood, stirring it with one hand, reading one of her grandma's old bodice rippers with the other. Dulcie used to laugh at the descriptions—all the euphemisms and clichés—but, now when she read it, she kept imagining Travis. She kept thinking there were parts of the story that didn't seem so bad.

The shed smelled of sweet water and woodsmoke, and the air shimmered with heat. After all the time she'd been spending in the snowy woods, Dulcie had to admit that it was nice to be inside, surrounded by warmth. It wasn't long before she was sweating over the fire, though. Every time she turned a page of the book, her fingers were so sweaty they smudged the ink. The big wooden stirring paddle was making her hand sweat. Was she supposed to stir it constantly? She couldn't remember, so she did, just in case. But standing over the fire was killing her.

"Jesus, Grandma," she said. "How did you do this every day?" Dulcie layered off her jacket and sweatshirt. Her boots and socks went next; it felt incredibly good to keep her bare feet on the cool floor. As the sap boiled, she felt herself sweating through the fabric of her shirt.

She could take her shirt off—her grandma had often worked in her bra. One of those big white ones that Dulcie always thought made her breasts look like big eggs. But Dulcie's bra was a purple lacy thing, what she'd worn under her teacher's outfit when she wanted to feel sexy. She couldn't make syrup in purple lace, could she?

It only took another few degrees to convince her that she could. Who was going to see anyway? She was in a syrup shack in the middle of nowhere. She stripped her shirt off and sighed. Better.

It felt odd to lean over the kettle half naked, but who cared? The sap was boiling away happily, the fire had stayed lit. Maybe she was getting the hang of this, after all.

Dulcie was halfway through a book set in the moors of some foreign country when she heard the jingle of a dog tag. And then his voice: "Hello? Dulcie?"

Her body reacted to his voice, to the way he still called her Dulcie. "Yeah, in here," she hollered before she even had time to think. The jingle came closer, and then she could hear the crunch of boots on snow.

"Oh shit," she whispered. She dropped the book into its bag with all the others and tried to hide the bag behind the rocking chair. "Crap, crap." Dulcie grabbed her T-shirt and slid it over her head just as she heard Travis outside the door.

She wiped the sheen of sweat off her face with her sweatshirt and brushed her short, wet hair back off her face.

"Dulcie?"

She opened the door just a little, feeling the surprise rush of cold air against her face. Travis, dressed in just jeans and a blue T-shirt, stood outside. His arms were crossed over his flat belly. She wondered how he wasn't freezing; the temperature difference was making her shiver. Agate rolled in the snow behind him, ears flopping.

"Hi," she said, suddenly shy.

"Thought you could use a little help, maybe." He must have gotten her note then. Something hammered in her heart. Suddenly she didn't want to let him in to see her messy workplace, her fingers blackened from moving scorched wood and reading her grandma's books.

"*Um*, I think I've got it now," she said. "Maybe next time?"

He looked around her, into the shed. "Then how come you're boiling over and you've got your shirt on backward?"

Dulcie looked down at her shirt. It wasn't just backward, it was inside out. And her lace-wrapped nipples were obviously cold. Or something. She crossed her arms over her chest. "Shit," she said. So much for a good second impression. And what had he said about boiling over? She turned, and realized that the syrup wasn't boiling over yet, but it was so close to the edge that it was going to at any second.

"Ok," she said. "Maybe I could use a bit of help."

He didn't wait for her to answer, just pushed past her. "Swing that door shut, will you?" he said. "Keep the heat in."

"Agate?" she said. The dog stopped snuffing the snow and looked up at the sound of his name.

"He's a big boy, he'll keep himself entertained."

Dulcie shut the door behind her, and felt the heat cover her again. She hoped Travis wouldn't stay around long enough to see her sweat through her shirt. On the other hand, she didn't want to him to go, either.

Travis went straight for the grocery bags filled with books.

Dulcie's face flushed. Now he was going to know that she'd screwed up the syrup and that she'd been reading about sex while she did it. "Wait," she said. "What are you . . . ?"

He unfolded the top of one of the bags and lifted out a pair of heavy work gloves and a bottle of vegetable oil. "Your grandma taught you how to read dirty books, but not how to use vegetable oil?" He had that grin again, those dimples that made Dulcie's insides feel like all that sap in the kettle, boiling and threatening to spill over.

Dulcie watched as he spread the vegetable oil around the rim of the kettle with the gloves. "You're supposed to do this when it's cool," he said. "But I'm guessing this will work. Butter works, too. Keep it all from boiling over."

"How?" She wanted to know, but she was distracted, too, by

his arms, the bulge of his biceps and the crisscross of muscles along his forearms.

"Don't know," he said. "Just does."

As he pulled off the gloves, Dulcie realized he was right. The sap was no longer threatening to boil over. It just rumbled away beneath the oil line.

"What else don't I know?" Dulcie asked.

"Oh, well, being a big city girl and a teacher, to boot, I would guess you know just about everything," he said.

Had Ada told him about her being a teacher? Had he asked about her?

She put her hands again on the wooden paddle and started stirring. It gave her something to do so she didn't have to look at him, to see him looking back at her. Was it pity that brought him here, she wondered? A promise to Ada? She didn't dare ask.

"I feel like I don't know shit," she said.

"Well, let me show you a stirring trick." He put his hands over hers on the wooden paddle. His hands were sweaty from the gloves. Calluses on his palm scratched her skin. She could smell him again, his scent mixed with the sweet sap. It made her head feel light.

"The trick," he said, "is to alternate. Clockwise, counter clockwise, across the middle." He trained her hands in the strokes, slow and smooth through the liquid. His hip met hers as they moved. "Got it?" he asked, and his voice, his lips, were right at her ear. She shivered as she felt his hip press harder.

"Yes," she said, more breath than voice.

"Keep going," he said, as though she had a choice. He let go with one hand and came around the back of her, so that his arms were on either side of her waist. They stirred the sap, clockwise, counter-, straight across, their bodies moving together, in constant motion.

"Okay?" he asked. And she knew he was asking about it all. Not just if the sap was okay, but also the way that he was helping her. The fact that he was here now, touching her hands, holding her, pressing himself against her.

"Yes," she said again. It seemed she'd lost the ability to say anything else.

He put his lips to her neck, right at the bottom of her short hair. They were soft and just a little wet, and she could feel their touch all the way down her spine. He slid his tongue out, touched her with his lips and tongue together. Soft and warm and wet. Somehow cool against her overheated skin.

"You taste like sugar," he said.

"Oh," she said.

"Stir," he said.

She kept stirring, his hands guiding her, even as he sucked the lobe of her ear. Even as he grew hard against her. She leaned back against him, let herself fall into the rhythm of moving hips and his lips on her neck and the spoon through the sap.

"You got it?" he asked, as he took his hands away.

She couldn't answer, so she just kept stirring. His lips touched back down on her neck and soon she felt his fingers at her hairline, lifting her hair so he could kiss higher. He pressed against her, pushing her closer to the heat of the kettle. Her body was melting. She kept herself upright by stirring, stirring.

He put his hands on her shoulders, slid them down over her

inside-out shirt until he reached her nipples. They were still hard, despite the heat, and she shivered as he ran his fingers over them.

"God," he said. "You're still so beautiful."

"You've hardly even seen me," she said. It was a protest, but it sounded weak, even to her.

"Oh, believe me, I have," he said. "In my head. And now, here, in real life."

He slipped his hands under her shirt. Sliding them up her belly strong enough that they didn't tickle her, he pushed the fabric up as he went. When he reached her breasts, he wrapped his hands around them, over the lace, still rubbing his thumbs over her nipples.

"You're not stirring," he said.

"I am so." But she wasn't doing more than moving the spoon in something that sort of resembled a very small circle.

He played with her nipples, rubbing and pinching them through the lace of her bra until she felt ready to pass out. She was leaning on the spoon more than she was stirring.

When he reached the button on her jeans and undid them, she wanted to put the spoon down, to reach around and touch him.

Travis seemed to know what she was thinking. He reached out and put her hands back on the spoon. "Stir," he said. And then he slid her jeans off her hips and down to her thighs, kissing her along the way. Normally she would have been embarrassed standing there in nothing but a T-shirt and underwear—thank God she was wearing decent underwear—but his murmurs, his kisses, and the way he trailed his tongue along the backs of her knees didn't leave any room to think, much less to be embarrassed.

He had her step from foot to foot so he could take her jeans off. "Is this like patting my belly and rubbing my head?" she asked.

"Yes," he said. "Although I think it's the other way."

And then when her jeans were off, he folded them and draped them over the arm of the rocking chair. She knew it wasn't possible, but the air behind her, where he'd left, felt chilly.

When he moved back against her, his erection was harder. It pressed against the soft skin of her ass: rough blue jeans and his cock underneath. She'd never seen his cock; they'd been that young, that innocent, when she'd left, and now she couldn't help but imagine it. The way it felt, the length of it, the taste.

He got on his knees behind her and slid her legs apart. "Don't try this at home," he said. "This is the work of a trained expert." She had only a moment to feel jealous, to wonder who'd been training him, and then his tongue was against her, lapping at her so gently that she didn't know if she imagined it. The sensation of it from behind was something she'd never felt before. She'd had guys go down on her, but always while she was lying down.

And then he used his tongue harder, just the tip, so that she wanted to press herself against him. He spread her wide with his fingers, slid his tongue inside. She was so wet already. Usually it took her so long, or she had to get herself started. But the way he used his tongue and fingers together, she could barely stand. The heat from the fire licked her face and her belly.

She looked down and saw his hands there, so close to the

heat and the fire. The sight of it, him on his knees behind her, leaning between her legs to lick and touch her, was more than she could stand. She felt like she, not the sap, was in danger of boiling over and getting scorched.

"Travis . . . ," she said.

He stopped licking her, looked up at her with his big brown eyes. She would have been embarrassed if he wasn't doing that thing with his fingers . . . she leaned on the wooden spoon, glad it was so sturdy and long.

And then her grinned at her. That goddamn grin. "If you don't stir, it's going to crystallize and you're going to waste all that sap," he said.

She was trying. She was. But the things he was doing to her made it impossible.

"I can't," she said. "I can't."

And then she was, somehow, stirring and coming, and they were the same motion. She felt the orgasm slide up her body with the smooth sweetness of liquid heating up, coming to a boil. The paddle and her legs wouldn't hold her anymore, and she was afraid she was going to fall into the kettle, but Travis stood up and held her from behind, letting her lean back against him until she could breathe again.

"Sit," he said, after.

He was still behind her, holding her up. She'd dropped any pretense of moving the spoon. "What about the——?"

He pushed her carefully toward the love seat. "You ever see Ada stir like that?" he asked.

She sat, putting her sweatshirt on and pulling it around her.

Her skin felt shiny and soft, her body liquid. "No," she said. She never had. "What was that? What did you?"

Travis pointed at the full sap pails that Dulcie had piled in the corner. "These next?"

Dulcie nodded. She stirred, watching him as he bent and lifted the pail full of sap. He poured the fresh sap into the kettle, replacing what had boiled away. His erection still bulged his jeans out, and she wondered how he could work like that. She hadn't known if he was still interested in her like that; now she knew for sure. She had every intention of helping him with that bulge, but not just yet.

"You didn't answer my question," she said.

"The 'what was that?' one, or the 'what did you?' one."

"Yes," she said.

The fire crackled as he filled the kettle back to the top with new syrup and then sat next to her on the love seat. "It seemed like a good way to keep you busy," he said. He swallowed, looked away. "I was afraid, coming here, because I knew if you turned me away again, it would be the last time. I wouldn't be able to ask again. I thought if you were stirring . . ."

"Afraid?" She touched his face, where he was still shiny from her. "Didn't you get my note?"

"What note?"

Dulcie moved forward and touched his lips with hers. "Not important," she said, against his lips. Their first kiss, all those years ago, in the heat of the summer and the cool sweet of ice pops. And now, their second. In the cold of the winter and the heat of her grandma's syrup shed. She liked his lips, liked how he opened them for her and touched her top lip with the point of his tongue. He tasted like her, kind of salty and sweet. She was humming, not just the way her body felt, but literally making noise.

He kissed her full-on, tongue and lips, making her ache. They came apart and she touched the top of his eyebrow, the shiny scar that cut through it. He sat perfectly still and let her explore. More wrinkles now around his eyes than when she'd last touched his skin here. And this time, she wasn't crying and he wasn't bleeding.

She looked over at the fire. "So you're saying that this batch of sap can just boil away and it doesn't need to be stirred at all?"

"Well, you have to stir it a bit."

She leaned over him, letting her sweatshirt fall open. She leaned down until her mouth met his hard-on through his jeans. "But not right now," she said.

"No, not right . . . now."

"Good." She worked the button of his jeans with her teeth, prying it open. She couldn't get the zipper down fast enough that way, so she used her hands, sliding it down until she could grip his cock through his underwear. He lurched against her fingers.

"Off," she said. She was surprised when he did as she said, standing and facing away from her. He stripped off his pants and underwear in one quick movement. He had dimples in his ass that matched the ones in his face, only bigger.

She giggled.

"What?" he said. He turned to face her. She was going to tell him about the dimples, but his cock was in front of her and she couldn't say anything. Usually she thought cocks looked kind of funny, the way they stuck out. But on him, it seemed perfect. It wasn't long, but it was thick, with a perfectly shaped head. The skin was a beautiful golden red, darker than the rest of his body. A drop of come shone at the tip.

She scooted forward on the couch and gave one small lick at the end of him. He tasted like clean and salt and musk. God, she wanted him in her mouth, wanted to suck him to the back of her throat until he was so deep she couldn't breathe. Instead, she forced herself to go slow, to keep licking around the smooth skin of the head, to savor the taste and smell of him. His breathing quickened and he moaned, low and deep, a sound that Dulcie thought she could listen to forever.

Outside, Agate whined, too, echoing them. "Poor guy," Travis laughed. "Doesn't even know what he's missing."

He put his hands in her hair. Not moving her head, but twisting his fingers in the strands. She loved the ridges of him, the way he seemed to stretch even as he was in her mouth. With one hand, she cupped his balls. With the other, she made a firm circle around the base of him. Holding him like that, she could lick him from base to tip. She watched his face as she did so, waiting until his brown eyes opened and met hers.

"Wait, wait," he said. He moved back from the reach of her lips. "I want to . . . I don't want to come just yet."

"I don't have a condom or anything," she said.

"Cold shower it is," he said.

"Let's just go outside," she said. "I'm frying up anyway."

"You're also naked," he said.

"So are you."

"Well, okay then."

She felt suddenly, belatedly shy again. "You first," she said.

"Fine, I see how it is." He got up and walked toward the door, flexing his butt muscles so that Dulcie had to laugh.

"Show off," she said.

And then he was out the door. She followed, prepared for the blast of cold from outside, but it still rocked her back, started her body shivering.

"Holy shit," she said. Agate ran up to her at the sound of her voice and licked her leg. She knelt, rubbed his soft ears. "Where's your daddy?" she asked. "Off peeing, likely."

The snowball caught her right in the side of the hip, spread snow over her and Agate. "*Ouch!*" she said. "Jerk, that had ice in it."

Travis was still hiding, but she could hear his laugh from behind the syrup shed. "You're so dead," she said. She bent down and started her own snowball. She packed it hard in her bare hands. Travis might have had the advantage of surprise, but she'd always had better aim. She'd sworn up and down the pitchfork bit was an accident, but the truth was, she'd caught him looking at that cute girl down the road, and the pitchfork was the first thing her hand had come into contact with. She hadn't meant to hit him that hard, just to poke him, but he'd moved toward her at the same time. Her grandma had teased her forever. "All strength and no finesse," she'd said.

Dulcie came round the shed fast and ran smack into the face full of snow that he was holding. This time, he hadn't packed it at all. Powder went up her nose and into her eyes. She could feel it melting along her eyelashes. "Goddamn," she said. She chucked her carefully made snowball at him, but he was already pulling her into him and she was too close to do any damage.

He tightened his arms around her until she couldn't move and then licked the snow from her face.

"I learned that from Agate," he said.

"*Um, ew?*"

"Well, you weren't saying that when I was doing that other trick with my tongue," he said. "Agate taught me that, too."

"That's a serious *ew*," she said. She tried to smack him, but he still had hold of her too tight.

"So, what did the note say?" he asked.

"Oh, you know, the usual. Something about how I never wanted to see you again."

"Really?" His mouth thinned out, and he still held her, but not as tightly.

"I'm sorry, that was stupid," she said. "That's not what it said at all. It wasn't anything."

He just looked at her.

"Fine," she said. "I said that I'd love your help with the syrup. That I'd gladly trade you whatever you wanted if you'd be willing to help me. I thought that's why you'd shown up today."

He let her go. For the first time, she felt how cold the snow was beneath her feet. The wind made her shiver and cross her arms around herself.

"Is that why you let me . . . do that? So I'd help out? In return?"

She could only stare at him. "What? No."

"Never borrow, never burden, never beg, right?" He must have seen the surprise on her face. "Yeah, I know. Ada's philosophy.

Passed it on to you, right? You thought that's what I'd want in return for helping you out? That that's what I'd ask for?"

Travis turned away, started walking back toward the shed.

"Wait, Travis, it isn't like that."

He was already inside the shed. Dulcie shivered in the snow. Maybe she hadn't realized how much she'd hurt him, going away the first time. They'd just been kids, though. It wasn't fair to hold it against her. She had to think, had to figure this out. Even Agate was no help this time—he just sat in the snow, looking at her, his tongue hanging out.

Travis came out of the shed half dressed, pulling his T-shirt on.

"What the hell, Travis?" she asked, and then instantly regretted it. "What are you doing?"

"The syrup's finished," he said. "It'll be good. And I helped you and you, well, you *helped* me. Now we're even."

He whistled for Agate and then looked at her again. "Put some clothes on before you freeze," he said. And there was so much softness in his voice that it nearly broke her heart. She could fix this, then, she thought. She could make it okay. And then he said, "Be seeing you. Sara."

Dulcie spent three days swearing at him. Swearing at herself, and then at him again. She unpinned the note from the tree and bottled the syrup, which, Travis was right, was good. It was almost as good as her grandma's. The weather had changed enough that the sap flow was going strong. She should have been happy. But even as she thought that, even as she set up a new fire for the second batch of syrup, she kept running it over in her mind. The way Travis had reacted. She wasn't sure it was rational; was there something she didn't know? Something that had happened while she was gone, or something between him and Ada?

She was down on her knees, ready to light the next batch, when she stopped. This time, she was going to deliver him a note that made sense, that made it clear exactly how she felt. She wrote it quick before she could change her mind, on the back flap of one of the books, and then grabbed a quart container of the syrup. Never borrow, burden, beg be damned. Dulcie loved her grandma, and she'd do her best to keep the syrup business from going under, but that other bit, she didn't think she could live with anymore.

His house was quiet and just as she remembered it. He'd lived there with his parents when they were kids, of course, but Ada told her they'd moved to Florida a few years back.

She slipped onto the porch and set the jug of syrup on the rug with the note tucked under it. As she turned, she saw Agate watching her through the window from his perch on the back of the couch, his tail going a mile a minute.

"Shhh," she said.

Of course, as soon as she did that, Agate let out a series of quick, short barks. Not "I see a raccoon" barks, either, but the ones that suggested he really, really wanted to come and play.

"Shhh!" she said again and then laughed, because it had obviously worked so well the first time. She turned and slipped back off the porch.

"You're lucky," he said. "If you were any earlier, I would have met you with my shotgun. As it is, I've got pretty good aim with one of these kindling sticks. Not as good as you, of course. Your shots tend to hit home, don't they?"

He was standing at the edge of the house, his arms loaded with firewood, and she realized he'd been outside the whole time, watching her. His tone was light, but his face was closed, his mouth set into a thin line. Agate barked again, once, and then was quiet.

"I was just, *uh . . .*" God, how could her face get so hot when it was so cold out? "Listen, I just wanted to bring you some syrup. To say thanks."

He moved past her without touching her, dumped the load of firewood into a box on the porch. "Does that mean I owe you now?" he asked. He folded his arms across his chest and looked at her.

She wanted to kiss him, and she wanted to punch him. Why was he being so stubborn?

"Travis, I know I hurt you when I left. Or, well, I don't know that, but I think that. And honestly, I wouldn't take it back. I learned a lot while I was gone, namely how and who I didn't want to be."

She thought he'd tell her to breathe, like he'd done before, but he didn't. Just stood there. She inhaled on her own and realized her hands were shaking.

"I loved Ada. She raised me, but I had to leave her—and here—to become who I am. I'm not her. And I'm not the me that I was when I left, either. And, neither are you. I'm okay with that. Can you be?"

Dulcie waited to see what he'd do, if he'd react, but he didn't. Only his scar gave him away, the way it grew whiter. She waited until the snow wet the shoulders of her shirt, and then she turned in the snow and left, determined not to look back.

For once, she heard him coming before he arrived. She was gathering sap near his property line. It was running strong, and she'd filled her two buckets almost as full as she could and still carry them home. She was nearly done with the season—soon, it would be too warm, and the sap wouldn't run. There was no way she was going to make all the sales she needed, but she was close, and she'd talked the bank into giving her a business loan.

Everything should have been good. Except that she couldn't stop thinking about Travis, about how he'd stood there, just watching her, arms crossed.

And, now here were his footsteps and the jingle of Agate's dog tags coming toward her. Her instincts were telling her to turn and run. She'd left her note, she'd offered as much as she could, and he hadn't come to her. Running into him in the woods was the last thing she wanted. But she couldn't leave the buckets here and she couldn't run with them, so she kept pouring, pretending that she couldn't hear him at all.

"Did you mean it?" he asked.

"What?" she said. She didn't turn, not even when Agate came up and sat beside her.

"In the note? Did you mean it?"

She bent down and rubbed the fat of Agate's back. He wiggled beneath her fingers, his whole hind end going when his tail did. When she stood, he scampered off into the woods, nose buried in the snow.

"What note?" she asked.

He moved to her fast, pulled her by the shoulders, and pressed her back against the bark of the tree. "Do not fuck with me, Dulcie," he said. His dark eyes seemed dangerous and far away, as though there were things in there he was trying not to let out.

It wasn't very cold, but his touch made her shiver. He took her chin in his hand and kissed her, so hard the bark dug into the back of her head. He parted her lips with his tongue, not waiting, not asking. After a second, she met the hard-thrust tongue, drinking in the taste of him. He bit her lip before he let her go. Not hard, but enough to make her wince in surprise.

"Now," he said. "Did you mean it?"

"Yes."

"Tell me." His fingers worked her jacket zipper as he spoke, and she moved forward to help him get access. He pulled her jacket open, and slid his hands beneath her T-shirt. His hands were cool, but not cold.

"I . . ." His fingers were at her nipples now, not soft like they'd been the first time, but pulling, twisting. She couldn't focus, couldn't remember how to make her tongue move. When he let go of her nipples, they burned, a low dull ache that went right to her belly.

"Tell me," he said again, his fingers at the buttons of her jeans. "I want to hear you say it. No more notes. No more written words, promising to come back."

Had she promised to come back? Not in words, no, but she remembered then: a note sent her first week from Syracuse. A note that did promise she wasn't going forever, that once she made it on her own she'd come back to him. How could she have forgotten that? How could she have changed so much, and so little, all at once? No wonder he'd put on his armor, had tried to keep her at arm's length.

"No more notes," she said.

He slid her jeans and panties down, only to her calves, not bothering with her socks or boots. He pressed her legs as far apart as they would go and trailed his hand between her. She shivered, again, something she felt in her whole body. Part cold, but mostly desire. Mostly fear at what she wanted, what she needed.

"Say it then," he said.

"I'd borrow, burden . . . ," she said. "For you."

"No," he said. He knelt before her and stuck two fingers in the snow at his feet. He scooped up a handful of it. When he entered her this time, his fingers were frozen, wet. They burned her insides with cold and movement. She slid closer to him, wanted more. But he pulled out.

He opened his jeans, slid them down just enough so she could see his cock, already rising and shiny and beautiful.

"No," he said again, as he nudged against her. She tried to open herself, to slide over his cock, but he moved away.

"I want to hear the rest," he said.

Dulcie's face burned. Her body ached. "I would . . ." She couldn't get the word out. "I'd beg for you."

"Do it," he said. His fingers moved inside her, the way her body opened around him. He circled his thumb on her clit, the same motion he'd made when he'd showed her how to stir.

"Please," she said. "Please Travis. God."

"That's a start," he said. He kissed her again, pressing her back against the tree with his fingers and his tongue, nearly lifting her from the ground. With his free hand, he worked her nipples through her shirt. "What else? What else do you want from me, Dulcie?"

"Please," she said, into his neck. "Please I want you to fuck me."

He pulled away from her. "That's all?" he asked. His grin was all teeth and dimples. "Why didn't you say so sooner?"

"You're a fucker," she said. Her breath came in gasps, her body already felt wrung out, scraped raw.

"I hope to be," he said. He pulled a condom from his pocket, held it up for her like a question.

"Yes," she said.

When he nudged against her this time, she opened her legs as far as she could. He held her back against the tree, didn't let her move as he slid into her slowly, slowly. So slow that she thought she would split apart from wanting. "Please," she whispered, and she heard him grunt low in his throat. The scar at his eyebrow was bone-white, and a small vein stuck out on his forehead. She knew he was trying to go slow for her, but she wanted him inside her, wanted him to crush her and fill her.

"Pleasepleaseplease," she said, like a mantra, like she couldn't stop the flow of her desire, and the sound made him enter her all the way, made him push her up and back with each thrust of his hips. He bent his head to kiss her, his tongue thrusting as he did, everything matching the rhythm of their bodies and bending them.

"I can't," he said. "I can't last."

"Good," she said. She grabbed his ass, pulled him into her,

bringing him to that final place, so that he growled against her mouth and scraped her back against the bark even through her jacket.

"Oh God," he said, as he came and she could only lean her head back against the tree and feel her own desire coursing through her, emptying out of her, even as he filled her.

They stood that way after, him softening inside her. "I don't want to leave," he said.

"Me neither," she said. And from the way he kissed her, she knew that he understood what she was saying.

He slipped out of her and she was glad the tree was holding her up. She wasn't sure she could have stood otherwise. When he bent down to help her slide her pants back up, she could only grin down at him.

"What?" he asked.

"Oh, I was just thinking I could get used to you down there," she said.

"As long as you don't bean me with a pitchfork, we'll be okay."

He leaned in to kiss her again, his breath warm against the cold. "Your syrup tastes amazing," he said. "I had it on apple pancakes this morning. I couldn't get you out of my mind."

It made her smile, hearing that. How some things changed, and others—the important things like emotions and apple pancakes—didn't.

He whistled the way he did, and Agate came running, ears flopping through the snow.

"Want some help carrying those back to the syrup shack?" he asked.

"Will I have to borrow or beg for it?"

"I'm sure we can arrange something."

"Maple syrup poured on my fingers?"

He kissed her fingers, then, his tongue warm against her cold skin. "Or somewhere else."

"You've got yourself a deal," she said.

He reached down and grabbed both pails. She could only follow him and Agate as they made way their way back to the sugar shack. Around them, the trees bowed and whispered, promising an early spring.

 SHANNA GERMAIN grew up in upstate New York with a pitchfork in her hand, maple syrup on her tongue, and more first loves than she can count. Her poems, short stories, and novellas have appeared in places like *Best American Erotica 2007*; *Best Bondage Erotica 2*; *Best Lesbian Erotica 2008*; *Best Gay Romance 2008*; *He's on Top*; *Dirty Girls*; and *Yes, Sir*. Visit her online at www.shannagermain.com.

Rachel Kramer Bussel

RACHEL KRAMER BUSSEL (www.rachel
kramerbussel.com) has edited over twenty
erotic anthologies, including *Spanked;
Yes, Sir; Yes, Ma'am; He's on Top; She's
on Top; Rubber Sex; Caught Looking;
Hide and Seek; Sex and Candy; Spanked:
Red-Cheeked Erotica; Naughty Spanking
Stories from A to Z 1* and *2*; and *Best Sex
Writing 2008*. Her work has been published
in over a hundred anthologies, including
Best American Erotica 2004 and *2006*;
Zane's *Chocolate Flava 2*; and *Purple
Panties, Everything You Know About Sex
Is Wrong* and *Desire: Women Write About
Wanting*. She hosts In the Flesh Erotic
Reading Series, wrote the popular Lusty
Lady column for *The Village Voice*, and has
contributed to *AVN, Bust, Cosmopolitan,
Diva*, Fresh Yarn, Gothamist, Huffing-
ton Post, Mediabistro, *Newsday, New
York Post, San Francisco Chronicle, Time
Out New York*, and *Zink*. In her spare
time, she likes to blog about cupcakes at
cupcakestakethecake.blogspot.com.